Shades of Truth

Books by Denise Grover Swank

Carly Moore
A Cry in the Dark
Her Scream in the Silence
One Foot in the Grave
Buried in Secrets
The Lies She Told
Shades of Truth

Maddie Baker
Maddie Baker and the Cockamamie Killer

Rose Gardner Investigations
Family Jewels
For the Birds
Hell in a Handbasket
Up Shute Creek
Come Rain or Shine
When the Bough Breaks
It All Falls Down

Neely Kate Mystery
Trailer Trash
In High Cotton
Dirty Money

Rose Gardner Mysteries

Magnolia Steele Mystery
Center Stage
Act Two
Call Back
Curtain Call

Darling Investigations
Deadly Summer
Blazing Summer

Discover Denise's other books at
denisegroverswank.com

Shades of Truth

Carly Moore Book Six

New York Times Bestselling Author
Denise Grover Swank

This book is a work of fiction. References to real people, events, establishments, organizations, or locations are intended only to provide a sense of authenticity, and are used fictitiously. All other characters, and all incidents and dialogue, are drawn from the author's imagination and are not to be construed as real.

Copyright 2021 by Denise Grover Swank

Cover art and design: Bookfly Cover Design
Developmental Editor: Angela Polidoro
All rights reserved

Chapter One

This was likely a terrible idea.

Then again, people found fault in a lot of my decisions. They weren't necessarily wrong, but I'd spent five days on a sofa, recovering from injuries from a car accident, and I was sick to death of searching the internet for ammunition against Bart Drummond and my father.

It was time to actually *do* something.

Like meet Lula Baker Bingham for lunch at Watson's Café.

I sat in my car, parked on the street a couple of businesses down from the café, trying to convince myself this was a good move.

I'd had plenty of experience with being watched over the past year, and I would have preferred to meet Lula in private, but her husband Todd Bingham wouldn't let me set foot on their property. He was pissed at me for a perceived wrong. With any other man, it might not be a big deal, but Bingham was the town's drug lord.

So I'd had to enlist our mutual friend Greta to set up a meeting. Acting as our go-between, she'd told me it was "out of the question" for Lula to visit me at Marco's house. Her suggestion had been for us to meet at Watson's during one of her lunch shifts.

While I would have preferred some privacy, beggars couldn't be choosers. Still, the stakes of this meeting made me nervous. Lula might have evidence that could put Bart Drummond away for good, thereby resolving one of my problems. I couldn't screw this up.

Taking a deep breath, I got out of the car and headed into the café.

The restaurant was pretty full, but Greta saw me walk in and motioned for me to head to an empty booth at the back. Which meant Lula wasn't there yet.

"How are you doin'?" she asked, looking me up and down. Greta was young—early twenties—blond, and pretty. Pretty enough to pull off wearing the 1950s' diner uniforms her boss insisted on.

"The bruised ribs are healing pretty quickly, and the rest is just aches and pains and a few bruises that makeup can cover," I said with a warm smile. Honestly, I was feeling better than I'd expected nearly a week after the accident. Marco's SUV had tumbled down a steep embankment after being run off the road. We were lucky to have survived.

Especially since the guy who'd run us off the road had hoped to kill us.

She gave me a grin. "I hear Marco is playing up the bodyguard role to the hilt." She glanced behind me. "I'm surprised he's not here with you now."

"He had to go into the sheriff's office to catch up on some paperwork before he goes back to work tomorrow." I knew he would have preferred playing bodyguard with my lunch too, but we'd both decided that I'd be perfectly safe in town. Still, he'd made it quite clear he wanted me to check in as soon as our lunch was over.

I slid into the booth seat facing the door. A paper scrawled with the word *Reserved* sat in the middle of the table. I gave Greta a wistful smile. "I wish we'd planned this on your day off so you could join us."

"Me too," she said, "especially since things have been goin' to shit around here. Mr. Watson's crankier and crankier as Drummond's resort gets closer to bein' done. If he's not complainin' about losin' future business, he's worried we'll run off and apply to work there. But lord knows he's drivin' us off to it."

"Sorry, Greta."

"But enough about me," she said, plastering a bright smile on her face. "I plan on comin' by y'all often enough to take part in your conversation."

I loved Greta to death, but I hoped she didn't come by *that* often. I planned on bringing up some sensitive topics with Lula, and I was hoping she might actually answer my questions.

She tipped her head toward the front. "Here she is now."

Sure enough, Lula was walking through the front door with an infant car seat held to her hip.

Greta rushed forward and took the carrier, unabashed love filling her eyes as she peeked into the baby seat.

Lula gave her a hug, then released her and turned her attention to me.

She hesitated for long enough to make me wonder if she'd changed her mind, but then she took the car seat from Greta and slipped it onto the booth seat, between the table and the cushioned back. Once Beatrice was situated, Lula sat across from me.

"Can I get you ladies a drink?" Greta asked.

"Just water," I said, my gaze landing on the precious baby. She was sleeping, and Lula had dressed her in a sweet dress—white eyelet with tiny pink flowers. She wore a pair of white socks, and some of her hair had been gathered into a tiny pink bow.

"Lemonade," Lula said, her gaze still on me.

"Comin' right up," Greta said, then headed to the back.

"Thanks for meeting me," I said, needing to address the fact that she'd only done so reluctantly.

"Todd doesn't know I'm here. He's not gonna be happy when he finds out, so I hope it's worth it." Lula usually sounded sweet and a bit naïve, but today she just sounded weary. The hint of dark circles under her eyes added to the effect.

I gasped. "Are you in trouble?"

"From Todd?" she asked in disbelief. "Of course not."

But it wasn't an *of course not* as far as I was concerned. Todd Bingham had committed multiple murders since my arrival in Drum, Tennessee seven months ago, and the night I'd met Lula, she'd told me to steer clear of him. That he made people disappear. Add in the fact that Bingham's father had killed his first two wives…let's just say I knew apples usually didn't fall from the tree.

In all fairness, I supposed the same could be assumed of me. My father was a partner in an international drug cartel. While Randall Blakely wasn't my biological father, I still had the misfortune of belonging on his family tree. I'd recently discovered that his brother William had added his DNA contribution to my genetic makeup. When Randall found out, he'd had my mother killed in a convenient car accident. His brother had been exiled to Maine.

If you asked me, they were both vile men, and I'd prefer not to be compared with either of them. While my biological father might not have murdered anyone, he likely knew his brother had killed my mother, and he'd left me with a monster.

So maybe it wasn't fair to compare Todd Bingham to his father, but Todd had committed plenty of heinous acts of his own. A fact I shouldn't ignore as I poked at his secrets.

Lula was watching me now, waiting for me to say something since I was the one who'd insisted we meet.

"Have you heard from your mother?" I asked with a soft smile.

"No." Her gaze darted to the note on the table. "Todd blocked her number on my phone."

That sounded controlling to me, but I reminded myself that it was the kind of thing a man might do to protect the woman he loved. Louise Baker was a conniving opportunist who would use anyone and anything to her advantage, including her daughter. With Todd Bingham, I suspected it was a little of both.

"Marco said he gave you the safe deposit box key. Was it for a vault at the Drum Bank?"

She narrowed her eyes, but it wasn't a menacing look. More of a cautious one. "Todd said you'd want to know."

"I only care about what was in that box if it had something to bring Bart Drummond down. Everything else is your personal business to keep to yourself."

"Why do you care so much about Bart Drummond? Todd says we should live and let live."

I gave her a pointed look. "And you believe that?"

She considered it for a moment, then said, "Are you askin' me if I think it's a good way to live or if I believe Todd truly means it?"

Her question caught me by surprise. Lula usually missed the subtlety in things, and it was uncharacteristic for her to get straight to the point. Was this a rare moment of clarity, or had she been letting everyone think she was dumber than she actually was?

"Todd," I said, resting my forearms on the table and leaning closer. "He told me himself that he wants to take Bart down. So either there was nothing helpful in the box, or he intends to use it himself."

Marco and I had danced around this point multiple times over the past few days. What was in the box, and what did Bingham intend to do with it? Marco argued that if Bingham and Bart Drummond got into a duel to the death, the better for everyone. And while I agreed in principle, I argued that we didn't know if Bingham had anything to act on. Besides, I wasn't so sure we could count on him not to create collateral damage.

She placed her hands on the table and clasped them tightly together. "Honestly? Todd and I went to the bank to open the box, but then he scooped it all out, put it in a bag, and we took it home. I haven't seen it since."

"That's not right, Lula," I said, trying to smother my outrage. "That was your property."

She gave me a weak smile. "He says it was my mother's property and she stole it. Which means it goes to the person who snatches it."

"And he snatched it from *you*, Lula."

Looking down at her hands, she shrugged. "He said I wouldn't know what to do with it anyway. Better to leave it to him."

"He didn't even tell you what it was?"

She shook her head.

Greta approached the table with two glasses in her hands, then set them on the table in front of us. "Y'all ready to order?"

Neither one of us had looked at the menu, but I'd been here enough times to know what I wanted. "A Strawberry Fields salad," I said, "with the strawberry vinaigrette dressing."

"Good choice," Greta said, writing it down on her order pad. "That one's about to come off the menu." She turned to Lula. "Lu?"

Lula looked up at her and forced a smile. "I'll take a chicken club sandwich."

Greta studied her for a long moment, then wrote down her order and headed to the back again.

Lula swung her gaze to me. "Todd says he's tryin' to protect me."

"Is he protecting you or hiding things from you?"

She released a sigh as tears filled her eyes. "Maybe both."

I nodded, not wanting to push her too hard, but I needed answers. We'd come so close before the accident, and I didn't want to be shuttled back to square one. "Lula, I think your mother might have had proof that Bart killed another child before he tried to drown you. Louise said she had proof about something that happened fifteen years ago."

Her brow furrowed. "She told you that?"

"No. She told her accomplice, Derek. Jerry recorded them talking." I held her gaze. "Lula, your mother played a part in his death."

Her face paled, and she sat back in the seat.

"The day Louise got back, she went to see Bart. Jerry was out on the Drummond property. He figured she was up to no good, so he filmed her with his phone."

She shook her head in disbelief. "Jerry didn't have a phone."

"Bart gave it to him. Jerry recorded her going into the house to see Bart *and* coming out. Derek Carpenter drove her to see Bart, and she said some incriminating things to him on the video." I paused. "Derek was the one who actually ran Jerry off the road, but Louise was planning on getting information out of him."

She remained silent, picking at a flap of skin on her thumb.

"Your mom was looking for Hank's buried money. She stole it the week before your father died. Two people helped her—Derek and Bruce Abernathy, who worked for Hank. Bruce got himself arrested, but he buried the money first and left the location in that toolbox on your property. He killed himself in jail, so the toolbox was the only record of the location. That's why Louise was so desperate to find it."

Lula glanced down at her sleeping daughter. "Did my mother try to kill you? Is that how you got hurt?"

"Derek ran us off the road. He knew we'd found Jerry's phone and the key to the safe deposit box." I paused. "Lula, Jerry was the one who took the toolbox from your house. He saw it in your loft when he fixed your roof a few years back, so when he overheard Louise telling Derek about it, he knew exactly what she meant. He left a video for me, telling me where I could find the safe deposit key."

"And the location of Hank's gold."

"That too," I admitted. "But you can't tell Todd about Hank getting his gold back, Lula. Who knows what he'll do with that. It could start a war."

A guilty look filled her eyes. "Todd doesn't like it when I keep secrets. Besides, he already suspects. Everyone does."

"But suspecting and knowing are two different things."

She lifted her shoulders into a slight shrug, and I just knew she was going to tell him. I was pretty sure I'd screwed up.

"I know you say you don't know what was in the box," I said, "but did you at least get a glimpse of it? Was it papers? A video tape?" When she gave me a blank look, I added, "She told Derek there was information about the murder of a child in that box, Lula. Don't you think that child deserves justice?"

She sat up straighter. "My mother is a liar. She lied to you about havin' proof that Bart Drummond killed Jerry. You just said some guy named Derek Carpenter did it."

"That's true, but I don't think she was lying about the murder. And if it's true, Todd is letting him get away with murder. *Of a child.*"

"You already said that," she said in a grumpy tone as she pinched the bridge of her nose.

"Have you asked Todd what he plans do with the information?"

"No," she said with sharp shake of her head. "He refuses to tell me anything about it."

I had plenty to say on that topic, but now didn't seem like the right time to discuss equality and women's rights. "Does he seem different?" I asked. "Is he anxious? Is there a lot more activity with his men than usual?"

She shook her head. "No more than usual."

Greta walked out with a pair of plates and set them in front of us, then glanced between me and Lula, frowning. "Everything okay?" she asked with a worried look.

Lula offered her a worn-out smile. "Yep. Peachy."

"Hopefully Bee will sleep so you can enjoy your lunch in peace," Greta said.

Lula put her hand on the baby's stomach and hesitated before turning to face her friend. "Actually, Bee's had a bit of an upset tummy, so I'd appreciate a to-go box. I think I'll take her home."

My stomach dropped to my feet. Not only had I blown my chance to get information, but I'd handed some over to Bingham via Lula.

"No," I said, as I dug into my purse. I pulled out a twenty and a five and put them on the table to cover both of our meals. "I'm sorry, Lula. You stay. I'll leave."

I started for the door and Greta called after me, "Carly! Don't you want to get this to go?"

"No." I'd suddenly lost my appetite.

Chapter Two

I wasn't ready to go back to Marco's house yet and stare at the same walls I'd been looking at for days. Sure, it had been exciting to be locked up with Marco and bask in his adoration for five glorious days, but he wasn't there. Besides, both Marco and I were doers, and there was a lot to be done.

So I headed to Max's Tavern, figuring I could call Marco and give him an update from there. I wasn't cleared to go back to work yet, but I could at least say hi to everyone...and maybe feel out Ruth. Ruth was one of my best friends here in Drum, most likely because we saw each other nearly every day. I'd done a lot of thinking about our friendship the past five days I'd spent sitting in Marco's house, and I wasn't so sure we'd be friends if we'd met outside the tavern. But that didn't matter. What mattered was that we *were* friends, or at least I thought so.

Marco and I had found her boyfriend, Franklin Tate—Tater to his friends—sneaking onto the construction site of Bart Drummond's new resort and meeting someone. I suspected his secret meeting had been with Bart himself.

If Ruth was working, I hoped to find out what she knew. And if she wasn't? Well, I might as well make use of my time and ask Max about his brother Wyatt. I hadn't spoken to the man since he'd admitted to working with Derek. He'd claimed there were extenuating circumstances, but in typical Wyatt fashion, he'd refused to share them. He'd promised to work with me in exchange for keeping his association from the sheriff's department, but I hadn't pushed him to follow through yet. In all honesty, I wasn't sure I should.

When I walked through the door, Max was at his usual perch behind the bar. His eyes widened at the sight of me. A quick glance at the dining room revealed that both Trixie and Ginger were present, which meant there was a slim chance Ruth was working. We didn't usually have three waitresses for the lunch crowd.

Ginger looked up from taking an order and noticed me lingering at the doorway. She shoved her order pad in her apron pocket and rushed over. Grabbing my arm, she started leading me to a table. "Hank says you're needin' your rest. What are you doin' here?"

Ginger was still cleaning Hank's house a couple of times a week…paid for by Wyatt, an arrangement that was sure to change since Hank had recovered his gold. And since Wyatt had proven himself to be a traitor. Sure, he'd supposedly agreed to help me, but that didn't change the facts. He'd been wrapped up with Louise and Derek, and if he'd reported them to the police, Jerry might still be alive.

"I'm going stir crazy," I said. "It was either take up knitting or come into town, and let's just say the last time I tried to knit, I nearly poked my eye out with the knitting needle, so here I am." I tugged slightly against her grip, motioning to the bar. "I'm just gonna sit at the bar and talk to Max."

"Okay." But she looked me over before letting me go, as though making sure I wasn't about to pass out and fall off a barstool.

A customer—one of the construction crew from Bart's resort who came in every day—waved. "Hey, Carly! How're you feelin'? We sure do miss you around here."

Trixie shot him a dark glare behind his back.

"Better," I said with a warm smile, ignoring her. "I'll be back to work next week."

"I need a refill," one of the construction workers called out, lifting his empty glass, and Ginger gave me an apologetic grimace.

"Go on," I said, giving her a slight shove on the arm. "I'm fine."

She gave me a gentle hug, careful not to squeeze too tight. "It's good to see you're in one piece." She pointed a finger at me and gave me a stern look. "No more car accidents."

I released a chuckle, but anxiety brewed in my gut. "I'll try my best." Especially since my father had a thing for arranging car accidents. Now that his high-profile drug cartel, Hardshaw Group, was toast, I'd probably become number one on his unfinished business list. For one thing, he was the kind of man who held a grudge, and for another, he probably suspected I knew more than was good for him.

Needless to say, I was being extra vigilant about my car.

Several of the other customers flagged me down, and I made the rounds, reassuring them I would be right as rain before they knew it, before grabbing a seat at the bar. Across from me, Max was filling a couple of glasses at the soft-drink dispenser.

"To what do we owe the pleasure of your company?" he asked with his shit-eating grin.

"I'm bored."

He gave me a stern look as he set the glasses on a tray. "You're not comin' back to work. Not yet. Doctor's orders."

I gave him a saucy look. "You don't know my doctor."

"No, but Marco does, and he'll have both our hides if you try to come back." He glanced over his shoulder and down at his butt. "And I'm partial to my hide, so no work for you."

"Lucky for us both, I'm not here to work. I need to call Marco."

"Your phone not working up at your lovers' nest?" he teased.

Rolling my eyes, I said, "Marco's catching up on his paperwork in Ewing, and I needed to get out." I didn't want to admit to my failed lunch with Lula. "I promised to check in, and I figured I could use your phone and maybe have a chat with Ruth. But I guess I got her schedule wrong." I leaned closer and lowered my voice. "Have you talked to her?"

His eyes darkened. "About Franklin? No." He filled a draft beer and set it on the tray. "But it's not like I can just ask her, now is it?"

"No." I knew this was going to be tricky. Ruth had come by Marco's house with a small bouquet of wildflowers after my release from the hospital. We'd chatted for a bit, and although I'd been dying to ask her about Franklin, Max was right. It wasn't something you could bring up out of the blue. Especially since part of me worried she knew what he was up to and condoned it.

"But she's been actin' strange the last few nights."

I narrowed my eyes. "How so?"

"Really quiet. Watchin' the door more than usual. Tater came in for dinner last night, and I caught them huddling together, lookin' serious."

"Do you think this has anything to do with Franklin going out to the Drummond resort site?"

He rubbed his neck. "Good question. After Tater left, I asked Ruth if she was okay, and she got pissed and told me everything was fine."

"Maybe I should drop by and see her."

He made a face. "Quiz her at your own risk. You know how she gets."

I leaned closer and lowered my voice. "Have you found out anything from Wyatt?"

His mouth pressed into a thin line. "He's not talkin' to me."

My jaw dropped. "Because you took my side?"

"Bingo."

The day of our accident, I'd seen Wyatt talking to Derek. He'd later confirmed that he was working with the man. According to him, he'd had no involvement with Jerry's death. He'd also claimed he had a good reason for being tied up with Derek, but he'd never seen fit to share it. In fact, he'd tried to steal Jerry's phone from me in Max's apartment, a situation that had ended with Max holding him at gunpoint so I could get away.

I supposed your brother pointing a 22-gauge shotgun at you would make you bitter.

"I'm sorry," I said. "I never meant for you to have to choose between us. Especially since you two had finally started talking again."

He snorted. "Please. Sure, I held a gun on him to help you get away, but the moment I found out he was wrapped up with the man who killed Jerry..." His eyes turned glassy, and his voice tightened. He glanced down at the bar, then looked up at me. "Jerry was good people. He deserved better than that."

I covered his hand with my own, his face blurry through my unshed tears. "I know."

"So now that we got that out of the way," Max said sarcastically, "how about some lunch? Tiny's got his pork cutlets as the special."

My stomach growled, reminding me that I'd walked away from my untouched salad. "With fried potatoes?" I asked hopefully.

He laughed. "For someone who likes to eat healthy, you lose your mind over his cutlet and potatoes."

"We all have our weaknesses," I said, then thought about Hank. "But can you make that to go? And give me two of them?"

"You meetin' Marco for lunch?"

"No. I'm going to take one to Hank."

His brow shot up. "Did you get a concussion in that accident? Because I know for a fact you've whipped that old man into eating sprouts and tofu."

"Oh brother," I scoffed. "He's eating chicken and broccoli. And his blood sugars are better than they've been in years."

"Exactly, so what's with the greasy food? You plannin' on killin' him and takin' his gold?"

"That man's too ornery to kill off with a cutlet," I said. "And I want no part of his money."

"Because it's from drugs?"

"No, because it's his, and he's more of a father to me than I've ever had." Although, admittedly, I'd struggled a bit with the source of his money. But I'd told myself that Marco and I had merely given Hank the location of the buried gold. How he'd acquired it was no concern of mine.

Max glanced around, then asked in an undertone, "How are you feeling about your biological father?"

My mouth parted in surprise. I was still getting used to the idea that Max knew all of my secrets now.

"I don't know," I said honestly.

"I can't presume to know what you're goin' through, but I know it has to be a mess in your head. Maybe you should take a few days to sort through all that before you jump back into all this feet first."

My back stiffened. "By *all this* do you mean bringing down your father?"

He'd promised to help me with that, and I'd believed him. Had another Drummond brother made a fool of me?

Leaning his face close to mine, he said, "Believe me, Carly. I want to bring my father down as badly as you want to topple yours. But you're no good in all of this if you're still dealing with your crap. I've had years to deal with mine."

Trixie walked over and grabbed the tray of drinks off the counter. "You're lookin' good, girl. Not as beat up as I was expectin'."

"Thanks. I should be back to work in a few days."

"Don't you worry about hurryin' back," she said, popping a hip out. "I've been coverin' your shifts for ya. Not a problem at all."

Something about the way she said it, added to her previous glare, made me think she was after my job. "I appreciate it," I said. "But the doctor said I'll be good to go next Monday."

She flashed me a smile before she took her drinks away.

"I'm gonna go give Tiny my order," I said to Max as I slid off the stool. "If you're all right with it, I'll make my call in your office while I'm waiting."

"Sounds good," Max said. "And the order's on the house, so don't be worryin' about settlin' up."

"Thanks."

Tiny was so happy to see me he emerged from the kitchen—a rarity during working hours—and gave me a gentle hug. "Things aren't the same without you," he said, casting a glance at the dining room.

"I'd ask what that means, but I'm not sure I want to know," I said with a nervous chuckle.

"Let's just say that some people are gettin' too big for their britches."

I made a face. "How is that goin' over with Ruth?"

"How do you think?" he snorted.

"I should be back soon, but it will only be part time," I said. "Marco's taking the doctor's orders very seriously."

"We'll take you back any way we can get you."

My chest warmed. It was nice to be wanted. "I'm going to hang out in Max's office and make a couple of phone calls while I wait for my order," I said. "I'll stop by and pick it up when I'm done."

He waved his acknowledgment and headed back in to the fryers.

Max's office was unlocked as usual. When I reached for the phone, I accidentally jarred the mouse, and his computer booted up. A spreadsheet was open—a list of supplies that had been ordered—and I took a glance as I picked up the receiver to punch in Marco's cell number.

Max ordered a lot more food than we seemed to go through. Was he sending food to a homeless shelter?

"This is Marco," Marco said when he answered. He probably thought Max or Ruth was calling him.

"It's me," I said, smiling at the sound of his voice.

"Your lunch is already done?" he asked in surprise.

"It didn't last long," I said with a sigh as I sat back in the office chair. "I pretty much blew it in every conceivable way."

"Ah, Carly. I'm sorry."

"I handled it all wrong. I jumped into it feet first, skipping the small talk. And then I kept pushing." Tears stung my eyes. "I really screwed up, Marco."

"Hey," he said warmly, "it's okay."

"It's *not* okay," I said. "We need to know what was in that box. We've got nothing without it."

"So we go to plan B."

Plan B was what used to be Plan A—find evidence Bart had coerced people to kill for him in repayment for favors. Following up on Louise's claim that she had evidence of a murder Bart had personally committed had become our new priority. It would be a lot easier to prove he'd murdered someone than that he'd coerced someone into murdering for him. The only problem was that I'd done extensive research online and Marco had gone through the sheriff's database, and neither one of us had found any mentions of a missing or murdered child from fifteen years ago. Not in Drum or all of Hensen County. The only thing we had to back up Louise's statement was whatever she'd put in that box.

"Honestly," Marco said, "I doubt she had anything. She's a known liar, Carly. She was probably lying about it."

"But why would she have lied to Derek?" I protested. "What did she have to gain?"

"Some people are compulsive liars. They just can't seem to help themselves. Or maybe she thought she'd look tough. Who knows? Lula wouldn't even give you a hint about what was in it?"

"She doesn't know herself," I said. "Bingham dumped it in a bag and told her she didn't need to worry about it."

"Damn."

"He even deleted Louise's number from her phone. To 'protect her.'"

"Huh."

"He's using her, Marco. He's manipulative."

"I know you're worried about Lula, but there's nothing we can do unless she wants help. Did you get the impression she wants help?"

"No," I admitted sullenly.

"Then there's nothing we can do for now."

I closed my eyes and sank my back into the chair. "We're back to square one."

"Don't let this get you down."

"I asked Max about Ruth, and he said she's been acting strange. Like she's anxious. I'm thinking about dropping by her house to see how she's doing. She seemed fine when she came by last week."

"Good idea," Then he added, "One more thing, Care. I talked to the deputy who took the report about Franklin's accident. In addition to the lack of evidence that another truck was involved, Franklin hasn't called once to ask if they have leads on the supposed suspect."

"Would he?" I asked in surprise. Franklin had wrecked his truck the night before Marco and I were run off the road. Only the evidence didn't match his claim that he'd been hit by another vehicle.

"Seems like he'd want the other guy's insurance to pay for the damages. The deputy said he only had liability insurance, which means he won't get anything."

I squinted at the desk. "That makes no sense. Ruth said he'd almost paid off the loan. He would have had to have full coverage."

"Dave checked his insurance card. It's on the report."

I wasn't sure what to make of that. "When do you think you'll be home?"

Shades of Truth

"That's a good question. I'm hoping by five or six. What do you plan to do for the rest of the afternoon besides talk to Ruth?"

"I didn't get a chance to eat my lunch with Lula, so I'm picking up today's special and taking some to Hank."

"When did Tiny start serving baked chicken and brown rice?" he asked with a laugh.

"Very funny. You and Max certainly share a sense of humor, because he made the same joke. Tiny's making pork cutlets and fried potatoes."

"And you're takin' some to *Hank*?"

"Hey, his sugars have been really good lately. He can have a cheat day every now and then."

"I'm teasin' you, Care. You take good care of him. He's lucky to have you."

I felt like the lucky one, to have found both Hank and Marco, but I didn't comment. Marco already knew that.

"Well, have a good afternoon but don't be doin' any of his housework. You're still on your medical leave."

I snorted. "Like he'd let me. He's nearly as protective as you are."

"He cares about you. Almost as much as I do," he teased. "But don't be tryin' to do anything behind his back. Just have a nice visit."

"Okay."

"I love you," he said insistently. "And I need you healthy and alive."

I laughed. "I like me that way too. I'll be careful."

"Good. See you later."

Chapter Three

Months ago, Ruth had told me that she and her boyfriend were planning to buy a house, but they still lived in the same mobile home that I'd briefly stayed in with them when I first came to town. It was a short bit down the road past Hank, but I was anxious enough to talk to her that I decided to stop there first. The food would keep.

Her tank of a car was parked out front, but my gaze caught on Franklin's smashed truck parked in the side yard.

I pulled in behind Ruth and got out of the car, surveying the yard as I walked to the front door. Ruth had planted flowers, but they were in desperate need of watering.

I knocked on the front door, and she opened it a few seconds later, surprise covering her face. She was wearing a pair of jeans shorts and a pink T-shirt, and her shoulder-length blond hair was pulled back with a stretchy headband.

"Carly. What are you doin' here?"

"I wanted to drop by and pay you a visit. Are you busy?"

She took a step back, opening the door wider. "Just folding laundry. Come on in."

I followed her inside and saw a pile of towels on the coffee table.

"I thought you still had a few days to hole up with Marco," she said as she headed into the kitchen and opened her refrigerator.

"Marco had to go in and do some paperwork, and I didn't want to be cooped up in the house."

"So you decided you might as well be slummin' it with me?" she teased, but I could see she partially meant it.

"Of course not. I miss you," I said, trying to stuff down my guilt. I *did* miss her, even if I was here for another reason. "I stopped by the tavern, and I got the impression that Trixie's hoping to take over my job."

She pulled a pitcher of tea out of the fridge. "Over my dead body. Max is gonna have to let that girl go. It's not your job she's after—she's angling for mine. She's been actin' all kinds of weird around me. I have to wonder if she's wantin' to get me fired."

My brow shot up. "You're kidding." Ruth wasn't the easiest person to work with, but she was a hard worker and super dependable. "What does Max say?" And, more importantly, why hadn't he told me?

"Typical Max bullshit," she said in a sneer as she pulled two glasses out of the cabinet. "He just tried to smooth things over."

"Are you really going to ask him to fire her?"

"You just admitted that she's after your job too. I don't know what she plans to do with *both* of our jobs," she said with a derisive laugh. "She can barely handle the one she has."

Ruth had a point. "When I come back next week, how about we approach Max as a united front? I'm pretty sure Ginger's tired of her antics too. But what happened? I thought you two were friends. That's why you wanted to hire her in the first place."

She filled the glasses with ice and then poured the tea. "Yeah, well…things change. We'll need to replace her. Got any ideas who we could hire?"

"Honestly? I can't help thinking that Greta might be interested in working with us."

"Greta from Watson's?" she asked in disbelief as she handed one of the glasses to me. "The one Max screwed and dumped?"

I cringed. "We both know there's only one Greta who I'd be talking about, and I suspect there's a whole lot more to *that* story. Even though they're both on again, off again."

"And you think it's a good idea to have her workin' there right under Max's nose?"

She had a point, but we needed someone good, and Greta wasn't happy at her current job. "Maybe I'll feel her out and see if she's open to the idea."

Ruth made a face that said *your funeral* and headed back into the living room. I followed her and sat in a chair next to her spot on the sofa. She took a sip from her glass, then set it down on the end table before grabbing a towel and starting to fold it.

"How's Franklin?" I asked. "I saw his truck out front."

She drew in a deep breath and placed her hand on her chest. "That man liked to have given me a heart attack with that crash."

"Has he gotten a new truck yet?"

"Not yet," she said, continuing to fold her towel. "Most days, he's been catchin' a ride with Tinker, but the days I go in late, he takes my car. He'd already have a new truck if he'd sell his busted up one to Bingham for scrap, but the stubborn fool refuses."

"Why?" I asked in surprise. "I didn't think he and Bingham had a beef."

"Neither did I, and when I try to press him on it, he gets pissed and tells me he's takin' care of it." She set the folded towel on top of the stack of already folded linens.

Was there something going on with Franklin and Bingham? I hesitated before I asked, "Ruth, are things okay with you and Franklin?"

Her brow shot up. "What?" Then she rolled her eyes. "Why? Because we're havin' a disagreement about sellin' his truck to Bingham? He's just bein' a stubborn fool."

"Has he said anything else about his accident?"

"Nope."

"Has his insurance said how much they're going to pay him for it?"

She narrowed her eyes. "No. Why are you askin'?"

Did she really not know that Franklin only had liability insurance?

I leaned closer. "Ruth, you know if you're ever in trouble, you can come to me, right?"

She studied me for several seconds before shaking her head. "That's very generous of you, Carly, but I'm not takin' your money." Then she grinned. "Takin' some of your shifts has been good enough. So thanks for gettin' into an accident of your own." But she quickly turned serious. "Just don't do it again. You nearly gave me a heart attack too."

Max said she'd been acting anxious. Maybe it really was about money. I wanted to believe she was clueless about what Franklin was up to. Or maybe she knew something was up but not what.

Should I press her?

"Has Franklin taken any side jobs lately?"

Her nose scrunched in confusion. "You mean since the accident?"

"Or before."

Her eyes narrowed. "Why are you askin' that?"

What did I tell her? That I thought Franklin was working for Bart Drummond? And what would I do if she said I was right? It would be foolhardy to admit that Marco and I had seen the two of them meeting late at night. "I thought I'd heard he was doing something with the resort."

She looked even more confused. "Where on earth did you hear that? He's only workin' for the county, although if that insurance doesn't come through, he really will have to get a second or third job."

"Maybe you could take over Trixie's shifts," I teased.

Releasing a groan, she said, "Maybe I'll have Tater do it."

I laughed, then said, "I thought you two had saved up money for a house."

She shook her head. "We're not touchin' that."

I decided to let the topic go. While I was disappointed that I couldn't get anything out of her, I suspected she had no idea about Franklin's business with Bart. That meant she couldn't help me, but her ignorance also came as a massive relief. I didn't want to believe Ruth would have anything to do with Bart's machinations.

She grabbed another towel and started to fold it. "Looks like things are getting' serious with you and Marco."

"Yeah," I admitted.

"Does that mean you're stayin'?"

"What?"

She offered me a knowing look. "Come on, Carly. I've known you've had one foot in Drum and one foot out since the moment you walked into the tavern."

"Where did you think I planned to go?"

Shades of Truth

"Not that cockamamie story you tried to tell me about going to Wilmington." She pursed her lips, staring down at the partially folded towel in her lap, then she looked up with determination in her eyes. "Before Franklin's accident and then yours, you told me that Bart Drummond was blackmailin' you. What's that all about?"

Part of me wanted to tell her to go ask Franklin since he seemed so cozy with Bart, but obviously I couldn't do that. I genuinely believed she didn't know what Franklin was up to, and I didn't want to throw her in harm's way. People who messed with the Drummonds got hurt, and she was a smart woman. I suspected it wouldn't take much for her to start putting things together.

"Does it have anything to do with the real reason you're in Drum?" she asked, watching me carefully.

I should deny it, but I could tell her something without giving away everything. "I really did end up in Drum because my car broke down."

"Where were you goin'?"

"Honestly? I had no idea. I was just running."

"From the police? Now that I think about it, you seemed pretty nervous around the sheriff deputies before you started dating one."

I could see why she'd think so, and I could let her think that, but I was tired of lying. I figured I could keep it vague enough that she wouldn't be able to piece things together. "No, my father."

Her eyes flew wide. "Why?"

"In the beginning, for reasons I don't want to get into, because he wants me dead."

She gasped. "Why?"

I shrugged. "Because he thinks I know too much."

She was quiet for a few seconds. "No wonder Bingham doesn't scare you. You're used to dealing with someone dangerous."

I almost corrected her but decided to let it stand. "Maybe. I can't help thinking I'm an idiot for not seeing Bingham as more of a threat."

"No," she said, uncertainty filling her eyes. "It's good you don't let him run over you. He respects you for it."

"But one of these days I'm probably going to push him too far." After my failed lunch with Lula today, that eventuality would likely come sooner rather than later.

She didn't contradict me, probably because she agreed but didn't want to admit it.

"So is that what Bart's blackmailin' you about? You do as he says or he'll turn you in to your father?"

"Yeah."

Fear filled her eyes. "What's he want you to do?"

"Believe it or not, he told me I couldn't leave town."

"Why?" she asked, leaning toward me a little.

"I have no idea. So he can use me later? He also threatened to hurt Hank."

"So you've stayed."

"Yeah," I said, then started to panic. Max had made it very clear he didn't think I should share my story with her, but I cared about Ruth, and it had hurt to keep so many secrets. But now one more person knew more than they should. "But you can't tell anyone, Ruth. Not even Franklin. If the wrong people found out—"

"Like Bingham?"

"Exactly." I took a breath. "It could be extremely dangerous."

"I won't tell anyone," she said. "Not even Franklin."

"Thanks." I grabbed a towel and started to fold it as an uncomfortable silence settled around us.

Ruth started to fold a new towel as she asked, "Is Carly your real name?"

I looked her square in the eye. "Kind of."

She laughed. "What does that mean?"

"It's not the name on my birth certificate, but it's the name my mother called me."

Her brow furrowed. "I thought you were smarter than that. If your mother called you Carly, then you've made it that much easier for your father to find you."

"I doubt he even remembers," I said with a sigh.

"Did your parents divorce?"

"No," I said, my voice tight with emotion. "He killed her when I was eight."

Ruth gasped loudly. "What?"

"Everyone thought it was an accident, but I recently found out he arranged for it to happen."

"And that's why he's after you?" she asked. "Because he's worried you'll tell the police?"

"One of several reasons."

Her phone rang and she gave me an apologetic look as she got up and answered her wall landline. "Hello?" She was silent for several seconds, then turned her back to me and said in a hushed voice, "I can't talk right now."

I got up. "It's okay, Ruth. I was on my way to take Hank lunch, but I was missing you so I decided to see you first."

She turned around to face me, looking torn as she held the phone to her chest. "I don't want you to go."

I pulled her into a loose hug, feeling better that I'd shared some of my story with her. It was a risk, sure, but it was one I'd taken with the other people I cared about. Besides, the situation with my father was escalating. What did it matter if one more person knew? "It's all right. I'll talk to you soon, okay?"

A small smile lifted the corners of her lips, but she looked tired as she said, "Okay."

Still holding the phone to her chest, she watched me walk out the door, and I heard the deadbolt lock behind me.

Chapter Four

Hank was inside when I pulled up to his house. It was June in Tennessee, and the temperature was rising fast, so I wasn't surprised. He preferred to sit on the deck in the morning, then move into the house to watch daytime TV right before lunch. There was a good chance he'd eaten already, but if so, he could save the food I'd brought him for dinner.

I knocked on the front door before opening it and walking in. "Hank, it's me."

"What are you doin' here?" he asked, turning around in his recliner to see me. His kitten Smoky was sitting on his lap. "And what you got that's smellin' so good?"

My own kitten, Letty, shot out of my old room straight for me. I set my purse on the end table next the sofa and picked her up, stroking her back. "I brought you a cheat meal, but we might need to rewarm it. Have you had lunch yet?"

Smoky jumped off his lap onto the floor.

"Nope," Hank said, pushing himself out of the chair and getting up using his crutch. "But I'd eat another lunch if whatever you brought me tastes as good as it smells."

"Tiny's pork cutlets and fried potatoes."

His brow raised as he gave me a sharp look. "You butterin' me up for something?"

Laughing, I put Letty down and headed into the kitchen. "No. I miss you and thought I'd bring you food. But maybe we should check your blood sugar first."

He scowled as he followed me. "I already did a bit ago. It's fine."

I washed my hands, then grabbed two plates to reheat the food while he took out silverware and sat down.

"Where's all your gold?" I asked.

He snort-laughed. "I love you like a daughter, Carly-girl, but I ain't gonna tell you that."

After I transferred the food onto the plates, I started one of them heating and pulled two glasses from the cabinet. "I don't need to know the location, I just want to make sure it's somewhere safe. You didn't bury it somewhere again, did you?"

"Don't you be worryin' about it," he grumped. "No one's gonna get my gold again."

"I heard you were gone a few days. Did you take care of it then?" I asked, filling the glasses with ice.

"People sure do like to talk in this town," he grumbled.

"Rumors are flying that you found your money. Of course they're gonna talk." I poured water from the filtered pitcher into the glasses and set them down on the table. The microwave dinged, so I put the first plate in front of Hank, but he pushed it over to my side and motioned for me to hand him the unheated one.

"I don't need it piping hot." I set it in front of him, and a look of pure joy filled his eyes. "I can't remember the last time I had one of Tiny's pork cutlets."

Shades of Truth

"You've been good. You deserve a cheat day every so often." I sat down, my stomach growling in anticipation of the food in front of me. Letty rubbed her side along my leg, purring.

He picked up his fork and knife. "So that's why you brought me lunch?"

"I told you. I miss you."

He glanced up at me. "I miss you too, girlie. Whatcha been up to?"

"Marco has made me follow the doctor's orders to a T—which meant staying locked up in his house for days. But he got me a laptop," I said with a grin. "And he just got satellite internet, so I can do my research at his place."

"I told you that boy's good for you."

"I know." And I did, but I'd been nervous about staying with him. We'd only professed our love to each other a couple of weeks ago. Living with Marco this soon felt like I'd just strapped myself into a supersonic jet. Still, I loved it, and it felt exactly right. I'd needed the push.

"You find out much?"

I gave him a wry grin. "I've long since discovered that a town with limited access to the internet doesn't have a big footprint on the internet."

He laughed. "I coulda told you that. You need to talk to people." He pointed his index and middle fingers at his face. "Look 'em in the eye."

"Agreed. But Marco doesn't want me doing it alone, and he's back to work. He also thinks people won't talk to me if a sheriff deputy is hanging out at my side."

"The boy has a point." He sawed off a piece of cutlet. "I'll go with you."

My eyebrows shot up my forehead. "What?"

He shrugged, keeping his eyes on his food. "I'll go with you. I know a lot of the people in Drum, and they might be more willin' to talk if I'm there offerin' encouragement."

I narrowed my eyes. "When you say offering encouragement...?"

"I don't plan on threatenin' anyone if that's what you're worried about. But my presence will be seen as me givin' my blessin'."

"Why haven't you ever offered to do this before?"

He hesitated. "I believe in you, girl, and after watchin' you before the accident, well…" He looked up and gave me a soft smile. "If anyone can take down that man, it's you."

My chest tightened. This man's respect and adoration meant more to me than he likely knew, but he'd always discouraged me from digging deeper in this town. Why was he suddenly so eager to pick up a shovel? "Why are you *really* helpin' me?"

He held my gaze with a fire in his eyes. "Because you're determined to do this, and it's a dangerous game." Then he tilted his head to the side. "Besides, I meant what I said, girlie. You've got a shot at this. Maybe I can tip the balance."

"Thanks, Hank."

He gave a sharp nod, then turned his attention back to his food. "So what's your plan?"

"Find information that can tie him to something illegal and have him arrested. Same as always. I just need to find that missing piece."

"It'd be faster and easier just to have him killed, you know."

My fork dropped out of my hand, clanging on the Formica tabletop. "Hank!"

He shrugged nonchalantly. "I'm just statin' the obvious."

"No one's killing anyone!"

He looked up at me again. "Just seein' where your boundaries are, because you're gonna need to know before you slog into the muck."

"I've been slogging through muck for months, Hank," I said with plenty of attitude.

Releasing a bitter laugh, he said, "Oh, girlie. You've barely dipped your toe in. If I help you, we're gonna be bathin' in it."

I didn't laugh with him because I suspected he was right.

"Bart Drummond's not gonna go down without a fight. I suspect there will be bloodshed before this is all said and done."

The few bites of food in my stomach began to churn. "I know. There already has been."

"So you got a place to start?"

"I've spent the past six months lookin' into his favors, but Louise claimed to have evidence that Bart killed a kid fifteen years ago." I looked him in the eye. "One of his own children."

His brow lifted. "A bastard?"

"People don't call children born out of wedlock bastards anymore, Hank," I said with a scowl.

He shrugged. "Callin' it by some other name don't change the circumstances."

He had a point, but still…

"So where is this supposed evidence?" he asked.

"One of the things Jerry found was a key to a safe deposit box in Lula's name," I said, scooping up a bite of potatoes. "The evidence was supposed to be in there. Louise blackmailed Bart about it, saying she would share it with the world if he didn't pay up. So he asked her why she'd risked telling him about Lula if she knew what had happened to this other child. She said it had seemed worth the risk, but he refused to pay her a dime."

"How do you know any of this really happened?" he asked, shaking his head. "She's a known liar."

"I saw it all on video. Louise went to Bart the night she got back to town. Jerry was working on the Drummond property and knew she was up to no good, so he snuck in the back door and recorded it. He saved the recording for me to see."

He was quiet for a moment, chewing his food as he stared at the wall with an unfocused look. "Have you talked to Lula?"

"Yeah, but she has no idea what was in it. Bingham took it all away and didn't tell her what any of it was."

"At least that's what she told you," he said pointedly.

I frowned as I cut a piece of pork. "Why would she lie?"

"Or you could ask yourself why she'd tell you the truth. That girl don't owe you nothin'."

"But she knows I'm tryin' to bring Bart down."

"And she just found out he's her daddy. That's bound to complicate things."

He had a point, but I couldn't see Lula defending Bart. "Anyway, I pissed her off, and Marco and I can't find anything about a child being murdered fifteen years ago, so it's a moot point."

"So you stick to the original plan. You go after the favors."

"Easier said than done. I only know of one person who's admitted to being asked for a favor by Bart, and Louise Baker isn't exactly reliable."

He leaned back in his chair and crossed his arms over his chest, his fork still in his hand. "Why are you so determined to get a favor seeker to admit to it? It would be easier to go after Drummond for something else. The bribes he paid county and state officials while he was running his lumber mill. The sheriff deputies he paid off to ignore his moonshine operation, which was no small endeavor. Seems to me we'd get a lot further that way."

"But those things wouldn't bring him down for long," I said. "He'd get a slap on the wrist. A few years in prison."

"The man's in his seventies. Even a few years behind bars is gonna be a blow." He leaned closer, his gaze piercing mine. "So why go after him for the favors?"

I thought about it for a moment. "I suppose an arrest for anything makes him pay, but he took advantage of desperate people. He could have helped them out of the kindness of his heart, and instead he profited off their misery. It takes a despicable person to do something like that, and do it repeatedly. Especially when he asked them to do things that ultimately ruined their lives as well as the lives of the people around them. If I can't get him for outright murder, then I want him to pay for *that*."

He drew in a breath and dropped his arms, then stabbed a forkful of potatoes. "It could be argued that time served is time served. Look at Wyatt."

"I don't want to talk about Wyatt. He was workin' with Derek Carpenter," I said, my voice breaking at the thought of his betrayal. "He may not have driven Jerry off the road, but as far as I'm concerned, he's guilty by association."

"You can't pin that responsibility on him," Hank said grumpily. "Just like you can't pin your father's sins on you."

"Those are two entirely different things, Hank," I said in exasperation. "And I'm not holding Wyatt accountable for having a crappy father. I'm holding him accountable for the people he *chooses* to associate with." Then, getting even more worked up, I added, "Not only did Derek kill Jerry, but he broke into Marco's house and threatened me." I leaned closer, grasping the edge of the table. "Wyatt's been desperate for me to leave town. It's not too far of a leap to guess he was behind that threat."

He took a bite of his pork and thought a moment. "Have you discussed this with Marco?"

"I mentioned the possibility. Marco's so pissed at Wyatt he says he'd arrest him if he had enough evidence to tie him to Derek's break-in."

"Just because Wyatt knew the guy doesn't mean he condoned what Carpenter did."

"You really believe he didn't know?" I asked in disbelief.

Scowling, he took another bite of his cutlet.

I took another bite too, tired of just talking about all of this and not *doing* anything. I cast Hank a sideways glance. "Are you free this afternoon?"

"Where do you plan to start?" he asked, stabbing his fork into some potatoes.

"I've found a couple of people who might have done favors for Bart. I'd like to talk to them, but Marco and I decided it wasn't a good idea for me to do it alone. You can go with me."

He nodded sharply. "I ain't ever played bodyguard before, but it might be a fun side gig."

"You looking for some part-time work, Hank?" I asked with a laugh.

Shrugging, he said, "I'm startin' to get tired of starin' at these four walls."

His answer caught me by surprise, but in a good way. I'd only recently asked Wyatt to hook up Hank's car so he could drive it without his amputated right leg. Maybe a bit of freedom had given him a taste for more.

"I'll grab my notebook," I said. "You can see who I want to check out."

He nodded his approval as I headed to the living room. I got my notebook out of my purse and headed back to the kitchen, already opening the cover as I sat down.

"I've already ruled out a lot of the people I'd suspected," I said with a sigh. "Like I thought this guy"—I pointed to a photo clipped into the book—"might be the victim of a favor, but it turned out to be just an accident. And with the remaining cases, most of the people involved are either dead or in prison."

"That makes sense," he said. "Drummond wouldn't want witnesses. Which means we'll need to talk to the families."

"In some cases, the families are dead too. But last week, I did find this." I turned to the last pages of the book. "Clarence Braswell killed the owner of a convenience store during a robbery and was sentenced to fifteen years for manslaughter."

His brow furrowed. "I remember this one. What makes you think it has ties to Drummond's favors?"

"For one thing, Clarence wasn't there to rob the place. The police report says he walked in, got a fountain drink and a bag of chips, then lollygagged around for a bit looking nervous before finally approaching the counter when no one else was around. Instead of paying, he pulled out a gun, said something to the owner, then shot him. Left his drink and chips behind."

He gave me a sly look. "You know all that from the police report?"

I shrugged. "Marco pulled it."

Tapping his fork on the edge of his plate, he said, "If no one else was around, how do they know that's what happened?"

"Security cameras."

"And they don't know what he said?"

"No. There wasn't any audio, and the footage was too grainy for them to read his lips."

He frowned. "Huh."

"You want to hear something even stranger?"

He grunted.

"This wasn't the first act of random violence involving someone from that convenience store."

"Robbery that time?"

"No. A clerk from the store killed a mailman named Dudley Franken and then killed himself. But he didn't do it in the store. He shot the mailman while he was in his truck."

"What makes you think that one had anything to do with a favor?"

"For one thing, Roger Pierce—the convenience store employee—used to work for Drummond Lumber. For another, they could find absolutely no connection to the postal worker. It was like Roger Pierce killed him completely at random."

"Who's to say he didn't?" Hank asked.

"I suppose it's possible," I admitted. "I mean, I was sure Pam Crimshaw had killed that insurance agent in Ewing for a favor, but it turned out she had her reasons. But Thelma Tureen says Roger had a gambling problem. He made good money working as a foreman at the mill, but he was in so much debt he was about to lose his house. Then one day his money troubles were magically solved."

Hank cocked a brow. "You think he got money from Drummond?"

"He'd definitely be in close enough proximity to Bart to ask him for a loan."

"Maybe, maybe not," he said. "Drummond wasn't always at the mill." He made a face. "But he *was* known to glad hand his employees."

"I guess Pierce couldn't kick his gambling addiction," I continued, "because he was in debt again at the time of his death, and this time he lost his job and his family. Miss Thelma said his wife and kids moved to Nashville. He held several other jobs after he was fired from the mill, but his last one was at the convenience store."

"How long ago did this happen?"

"Twenty years ago."

"So you suspect Roger Pierce's favor was that Drummond loaned him money. What was Dudley Franken's favor?"

"I have no idea. Miss Thelma didn't mention anything about him."

He pursed his lips and looked lost in thought for a few seconds. "Which case are you wantin' to look into first?"

"Clarence Braswell. He just got out of prison last fall, which means we can talk to him."

"What about that Dudley fella?"

"Well, for one thing, he was murdered twenty years ago, Hank. Braswell's case is newer."

"But barely," Hank said. "If he was sent away for fifteen years and just got out, then he shot that man at least sixteen years ago. Twenty years, sixteen years. Don't see much difference."

"But at least he's alive and we can actually talk to him," I countered.

He laughed. "You think we're gonna drive up to Braswell's house and he's gonna spill his guts to ya?"

My back stiffened. "Of course not. I didn't think it would be *that* easy."

"Start wide and work your way in, girlie," he said, pointing his finger down at the table and moving in a spiral, his circles growing smaller and smaller.

Something I already knew, but I bit back a retort.

"Just trust me on this, girlie. We need to start with Franken. I feel like we'll get more information. I know you're hoping for something more current," he said. "But since Bingham's gained power and Drummond is losing it, rumor has it the favors have been much less prevalent the past five or six years." He gave me a wry look. "Beggars can't be choosers. You got any info on the mailman's family?"

"No."

"Then let's go get some."

Chapter Five

Since we didn't have any information on Dudley Franken's family, we decided to head back to Marco's place and use my new laptop and his mediocre speed internet to do some research.

Hank was mostly quiet on the way to Marco's, staring out the window, seemingly deep in thought.

"You really never paid much attention to Bart's favors?" I asked, my dubiousness leaking through. "A shrewd businessman such as yourself wasn't paying attention to your competition?"

"Drummond wasn't my competition," he grunted, his gaze still out the window. "He ran moonshine and the lumber industry. I ran recreational enhancements."

I shot him a look. "*Please.*"

"What exactly are you disagreein' with?" he asked, turning to face me.

"Well, first of all, *recreational enhancements* is something I'd never expected to hear come out of your mouth, and second, you must think I'm a damn fool if you believe for one minute that I believe you didn't see him as competition.

You've admitted as much to me in the past. I know there's no love lost between the two of you. You were watching him, Hank. Just admit it."

He was silent for several seconds before he grudgingly said, "Drummond was good at keepin' his secrets. They were like rats, everyone knew they were there, but no one actually saw 'em scurryin' about."

"It's hard to believe so many people kept their mouths shut," I said. "The first rule of secrets is the more people who know, the more likely it is to get blabbed."

"He definitely turned people down for that reason," Hank said. "I've heard of people who went to him and were turned away."

My brows shot up. "Do you remember who any of them were? We could ask them what Bart said."

He snorted. "Girlie, you think he went and told those fools something like 'I ain't grantin' you a favor cause you're a blabbermouth'?" he scoffed. "He would have lied and said he had no idea what they were talkin' about."

I tapped the steering wheel with my thumb. "Really? Why wouldn't he have just told them that the rumors were wrong? Even if he never granted a favor in his life, he had to know about the rumors."

Hank shrugged. "Semantics, girlie. Who cares how he said it? The fact remains that he turned them down."

Maybe so, but I couldn't help thinking that semantics mattered very much to men like Bart Drummond. I knew they mattered to my father.

I turned onto the road that led to Marco's house. "Have you ever been here?"

"Nope. Haven't been much of anywhere the past couple of years."

"Good thing we're changing that."

I turned onto the drive to Marco's house, and the familiar feeling of home filled my chest, surprising me with its warmth and intensity. Pulling up in the driveway, I turned off the engine.

"He's got a front porch," Hank said, reaching for his door handle.

"He uses it too," I said. "Just like you. It's one of our favorite spots when I come here after work."

He got out, studying the one-story house for a few seconds before he headed to the front door. I unlocked the door and turned off the security system, and he nodded in approval as he followed me in.

"We can sit at the dining room table," I said. He got settled in at the table, and I grabbed my laptop and joined him, pulling up the article I'd found about Dudley Franken's murder. It didn't offer up any information beyond what I'd told him.

Next, I looked up Dudley's obituary, taking note of the survivors listed as well as the address. A wife, two daughters, and two sons. His mother had still been alive, but his father had predeceased him.

"Dudley was forty-two," Hank said. "Which means his widow is likely in her early sixties or possibly younger."

"She's likely still alive." I did a search for Rhonda Franken and found out she'd gotten an honorable mention at the county fair three years ago for quilting.

"This confirms she's still alive and in the area," I said. "And she hasn't gotten remarried."

"As of three years ago," Hank said.

I gave him the side-eye. "If she stayed single that long, I highly doubt she's gotten married since."

He shot me a scowl.

"What? It's a thing. Older women are purposely choosing to stay single. They're tired of taking care of people and want to be free."

I continued to search for Rhonda but came up with little else.

"Look into the kids too," Hank said. "They might not know anything, but then again, one of 'em might."

Biting my tongue to keep from telling him that had been my next plan of action, I started a search for the sons. I wasn't used to the armchair directing. "The daughters might be married, so it could be harder to track them down, especially since y'all don't seem to care for wedding or engagement announcements here."

"You can find out anything in this town," Hank said. "You just need to know who to ask. I say the first thing we do is pay a visit to Rhonda Franken."

***

The last address we had for Rhonda was listed in the obituary, so we headed there first. Hank told me addresses used to be published in the obits so people would know where to take food. Seemed like a great way for robbers to case out the newly deceased's house while everyone was at the funeral, but maybe that didn't happen around here. There seemed to be a different code of ethics in Drum.

We pulled up to a run-down ranch house that had a couple of older model cars parked in the yard. Several hanging plants hung from hooks, suggesting that a woman lived here. It might not be Rhonda, but I was going to take it as a good sign.

"Is there a chance Mrs. Franken might know who you are?" I asked.

"To the best of my knowledge, I've never met the woman, but she might know me."

Shades of Truth

"So you need to wait in the car."

I thought he might argue, but he just reached into the backseat and grabbed his shotgun.

"Just in case," he said.

"Well, if it's Mrs. Franken at the door, keep it hidden. No need to scare her."

"And if it's someone else?" he asked.

"Then use your own discretion." People around here weren't known for their kindness to drop-in guests.

The curtains in the window fluttered as I got out and walked up to the front door. After I knocked, I could hear movement inside. A few seconds later, the solid wood front door cracked open.

"Can I help you?" a woman asked in a wary tone, one of her eyes appearing in the crack. She was shorter than me, and I could see her salt-and-pepper hair.

"Hi," I said in my friendliest voice. "Is Rhonda Franken here?"

"Who wants to know?" she asked.

"I'm Carly Moore," I said. "I work at Max's Tavern in town."

"I've heard of you," she said, still sounding wary. "Whatcha want?"

From the way she said it, I wasn't sure whether the fact that she'd heard of me would work in my favor. "I want to talk to you about Dudley, Mrs. Franken."

There was a moment's pause before she opened the door all the way, and I stood face to face with a woman who appeared to be in her late fifties or early sixties. The years hadn't been kind to her. Her skin was sallow, and the dark circles under her eyes looked like bruises. "And who's that out in your car?"

"That's my landlord," I said, giving him a wave, but he didn't wave back. "We're on our way to Ewing to pick up his medicine but we decided to stop here first."

"Whatcha wanna know about Dudley?" she asked, keeping her eye on Hank.

"I wanted to ask some questions about his murder."

Her eyes narrowed. "That was twenty years ago. Why're you askin' about it now?"

"I'm doing a study on the high homicide rate here in Drum," I said. "I'm trying to see if there's a pattern."

"There's a pattern, all right," she grumped. "They're all dead."

I gave her a kind smile. "I understand this is coming out of the blue, Mrs. Franken, but believe me when I say I have an important reason for asking, and there might be a chance I can get justice for your husband."

"How can you get justice?" she asked, starting to get angry. "When Roger Pierce took the easy way out and killed himself."

I folded my hands together. "Mrs. Franken, I realize you'll never get *true* justice, but I'm sure you have questions, like why Roger Pierce killed your husband. Did you ever find out?"

She closed her eyes for a moment and leaned against the door before she opened them. "No. They said Dudley had never met the bastard. Claimed it was random, but why would a man living in Ewing come find my Dudley on a rural postal route? Seems pretty intentional to me."

"I agree. I'm trying to find the connection."

"Are you with one of them true-crime podcasters?" she asked. "The ones who talk about cold cases?"

"No. I'm just trying to get answers for people in Drum."

Her eyes narrowed. "Even if they aren't askin' any questions?"

"You're telling me you haven't asked?"

"Oh, I've asked plenty," she grumbled. "I just never got a *satisfactory* answer. The sheriff's department told me that I'd have to live with not knowin'."

"I'd like to find a connection between your husband and Roger Pierce," I said. "I'm not sure how deep the sheriff's department dug, but I'd like to go even deeper." When she hesitated, I said, "We can start with a few questions, and if you feel comfortable, then I'll ask more."

Her mouth twisted to the side. "You gonna leave your landlord sittin' out in the car while you come in for our chat?"

"I suppose that's up to you," I said. "If you feel more comfortable with him waiting outside, then he's more than happy to do so."

She squinted up at me. "You really ain't from around here, are ya? *Happy to do so,*" she mimicked, then laughed.

I wasn't sure how to answer that, so I said nothing.

"Go get your landlord and come on in. I'll get us some refreshments." She left the door open and disappeared inside.

Jogging down the steps, I hurried over to Hank's rolled-down window.

"She wants me to come inside, huh?" he asked, squinting at the front door. "She probably wants to keep me in her sights so I can't case the property while you have her busy."

"What?" But then I realized it was likely a legitimate fear. "Yeah. I guess. But she doesn't seem to know who you are. I told her that you're my landlord and we're on the way to Ewing to pick up your medication."

"Good cover story. How'd you get her to let you in?"

"I told her the truth—or at least the partial truth. That I was hoping to find out why her husband was murdered."

He gave me a soft smile. Then he opened the door, shoved his gun under the front seat, and grabbed his crutches. "I suppose that's why you're successful at this sleuthin' stuff. You still pretty much tell the truth."

I hadn't been so successful with Lula, and his words were a sharp reminder. I'd probably been a little too truthful. "Not always, but it makes it easier to keep track of what I tell people."

"Smart girl."

Hank hobbled up the porch stairs, and Mrs. Franken yelled out "Come on in," as we approached the front door.

Her living room was furnished in clean but decades-old furniture. "Would you like some tea? Or maybe coffee?" her voice called out from the kitchen.

"Nothing for me," I said, and Hank echoed my response.

She walked out holding a coffee mug, her eyes on Hank as she motioned to the sofa. "Have a seat."

We both sat on the sofa, and Mrs. Franken lowered into a worn, faux-leather recliner across from us. Hank leaned his crutch against the arm of the sofa next to him.

"I'm still not sure how you're gonna find a connection when the sheriff's department couldn't, but I'm game to try," Mrs. Franken said before she took a sip from her mug.

I pulled my notebook out of my purse. "Why don't you tell me about Dudley's activities. His friends."

She shook her head with a look of disgust. "The sheriff's department already did that."

"Why don't you tell us anyway," Hank grumped, sitting back on the sofa.

I shot Hank a warning look, but Mrs. Franken was already regarding him with an assessing gaze.

"I know who you are," she said. "And my Dudley wasn't part of your drug organization."

Shades of Truth

I froze for a moment. "That's not why he's here, Mrs. Franken."

"Then why's the former drug lord of eastern Tennessee sittin' in my livin' room?"

Hank leaned forward, resting his left forearm on his thigh. "You seem like an intelligent woman, Mrs. Franken—"

"Call me Rhonda," she said, holding his gaze with a no-nonsense look.

"Okay, Rhonda," he said. "We could waste the next hour beatin' around the bush and shootin' the shit, but you seem like the kind of woman who would appreciate gettin' right to the point."

She leaned back in her recliner, a smug look filling her eyes. "Go on."

"Did your husband have anything to do with Bart Drummond?"

"He never worked for the man," she said. There wasn't an ounce of defensiveness in her, but her answer sounded like a challenge. It wasn't a no.

"Did your husband ever approach Drummond for a favor?" he asked.

"I don't have proof of any such thing."

Still not a denial.

"But you think that he did," I said.

Her gaze shifted to me. "As I said, I have no proof, but I've always suspected."

I gave her a reassuring smile. "What did he ask for?"

Her head dipped, and she stared into her coffee mug. "If he asked that man for a favor, it wasn't for himself. It was for his father."

"What would he have asked for?" I said.

"His daddy was lookin' at ten years in prison. Then, the next thing I knew, the charges were dropped. I'd told Dudley that he best not be thinkin' about asking that rat bastard Drummond for a favor, but I suspect he did. The DA had a solid case. There was no reason for those charges to be dropped."

"So if Dudley asked for a favor, that means Bart likely asked him to do one in return. Do you have any idea what it might have been?"

She shook her head. "Nope. The mess with his daddy was five years before, and honestly, I'd plum forgotten about it. Until Dudley wound up dead, that is."

"Did Dudley seem off before his murder?" I asked. "Was he worried about anything?"

"Yeah. The week before he was killed, he was pretty quiet, which was unusual for him. He could talk your ear off. I asked him what was wrong, but he wouldn't tell me. Said things weren't goin' well at work." She took a sip from her mug. "But I think he knew it was comin'. After he died, I found all his information in his bedroom drawer." When I gave her a blank look, she clarified, "His life insurance policy, the bank information, information about the loan on his truck. It was like he'd gotten it all ready."

"Did you tell the sheriff's office?" I asked.

"Yeah, but they didn't think much of it," she said with a scowl. "Just told me it was his job as a husband and father to make sure his family would be taken care of if anything happened to him."

I shot Hank a look, then turned back to Rhonda. "Did he have all that information together before?"

"I know for a fact he didn't. I put his clean underwear in that drawer at least once a week. It hadn't been there the week before."

"And you told the sheriff's deputy?"

"Of course I did," she said, getting irritated. "Not that they gave a shit."

I wrote what she'd said in my notebook as I asked, "Do you happen to remember who you gave your statement to?"

"Sure do," she said, setting her mug on the table next to her. "Deputy Eric Barnes. He bowled in the same league as Dudley."

I wrote his name down. "Was he your contact throughout the entire investigation?"

"There weren't much of an investigation," she said bitterly. "They talked to a few people and then called it closed."

"Did you mention the favors to Deputy Barnes?"

She shook her head. "People have died for this shit." Tapping her fingers on the arm of her chair, she added, "Or at least that's what people say. I have four kids. If Dudley was killed over a favor, I considered myself lucky the kids and I were left alone."

"Why would people go to Bart and ask for a favor if they suspected he killed people for not following through?" I'd asked my friend Thelma similar questions in the past, but it still baffled me.

"People are desperate," she said, her voice breaking. "A lot of people here are dirt poor, and they get themselves into a bad place. Drummond seemed like their only hope…until he wasn't."

"So, hypothetically speaking, let's say someone approached Dudley and told him it was time to pay back his favor, do you have any idea what he might have been asked to do?"

Her face paled. "Something bad. My Dudley wouldn't have hurt no one. And if he refused…well, he had to be made an example. To make sure other people followed through."

Chapter Six

Rhonda didn't have much to say after that. When I asked permission to talk to her children, she shook her head. "They don't know nothin' about any of it, and I aim to keep it from them."

I gave her a reassuring smile. "Then I won't talk to them. But if you think Dudley might have gotten a favor for his father, what about talking to Dudley's siblings?"

"His sister's dead, but his brother's still around. Simon Franken. He's retired and livin' in Ewing. I'll give you his address if you want."

"That would be great."

Rhonda recited it without consulting anything, and I wrote it down. When Hank and I got up to leave, she got up too and gave me a hopeful look. "Do you think you'll get us some answers?"

"I can't promise that I will, but I'll try. And if I get some, I promise to let you know what I find."

She took one of my hands in both of hers. "I know it don't really mean much, not after all this time, but I'd still like to know."

I held her gaze. "My own mother was killed a little over twenty years ago. There are still a lot of questions, and I want answers too. It won't bring her back, but maybe it will help me make sense of it all."

"Is there any sense in a murder motivated by revenge?" she asked with tears in her eyes.

I gave her a wobbly smile. I knew she was talking about her own husband, but her words pertained to my situation too. "No, but I still want to know."

She nodded her head with a teary bob.

Hank and I walked out to the car. We were quiet for a minute before he said gruffly, "You shouldn't have told her about your mother."

"Why not?" I asked. "She doesn't know anything about Charlene Moore's history."

"You're playing a dangerous game, girlie."

"I'm walkin' on two razors' edges, Hank. It's all dangerous at this point."

He was quiet for a moment, then said, "You wanna go pay Simon Franken a visit?"

"Feel like takin' a trip to Ewing?"

He turned to me and winked. "We were headed that way to pick up my medication, now weren't we?"

I laughed at his acknowledgment of my fake story. "Touché. Once we get cell service, I'll send Marco a text with Simon Franken's address. That way if we get into trouble, he'll know where to find us."

I plugged Simon's address into my GPS, which would kick in after we got in the range of cell service, then headed to Ewing.

***

Simon's house was in an older neighborhood with narrow streets. While some of the houses had been well maintained, others had become neglected. Simon's fell into the latter category. I pulled up to the curb in front of the pale blue house that looked like it needed a paint job and sent Marco a text.

Hank and I are dropping by Simon Franken's house, Dudley Franken's brother, to find out if he knows anything useful. We talked to Dudley's wife earlier. If you don't hear from us within the next thirty minutes, come look for us here:

Then I sent Simon's address.

He replied immediately.

You were supposed to have a nice quiet chat with Hank. Not start questioning people.

I couldn't tell from the text if he was mad, but if I got something out of this meeting, I was sure he'd understand.

Love you too, I sent, then stuffed the phone in my pocket. "Okay. Let's go."

We opened the car doors and got out. Rather than leave his weapon in the car, Hank slung it over his shoulder and used his crutch to move toward the driveway. I had to admit I was happy he was armed, but I wasn't sure what good it would do us if we were ambushed. Not to mention he looked like a threat. Then again, I suspected half the town had concealed weapons, so maybe Simon wouldn't think much of it.

We started up the crumbled concrete driveway toward the house, Hank slowing down to pick his way over the uneven surface. We were almost to the house when we heard a man call out, "I'm in the back. Come through the gate."

I shot Hank a look. He nodded, but his jaw was tight. "I'll go first," he said quietly, but in a tone that dared me to contradict him.

I wanted to, but I also suspected Hank didn't plan on sashaying into a trap. Sure enough, when he reached the gate, he pushed it open a few inches and peered around the edge. "Simon Franken?"

"I ain't lookin' for no trouble, Chalmers," the man grunted.

"Good, 'cause I ain't lookin' for any either," Hank said. "But I came prepared if you planned on sneakin' around the corner."

"You mean like you're doin' now?" the man asked.

Hank walked through the gate and moved out of the way so I could follow.

An older man was sitting on a lawn chair next to a wooden shed, working on the engine of a motorcycle standing next to him. His long, mostly gray hair was pulled into a low ponytail at the base of his neck. He glanced up at me and bobbed his chin. "I thought I'd be talkin' to just the girl."

I decided to ignore the "girl" statement. "If you got the head's up that I was coming," I said, "then you knew I wasn't alone."

He turned his attention to the sprocket wrench in his hand and gave something on the engine a crank. His non-response was answer enough.

As Hank and I headed over to join him, I took in the overgrown shrubbery next to the house as well as the bare patches of grass. The exterior of the house wasn't the only part that could do with some work. Hank leaned against the wooden fence while I moved to Simon's other side, presuming he *was* Simon. He still hadn't introduced himself.

"I'm Carly," I said, "although you must know that already."

"Sure do," he said without looking at me. "Know that you brought Hank Chalmers too, and no, I didn't know he was comin'."

That was interesting. Rhonda hadn't told him about Hank. "You must know why I'm here."

"Yep, and I might have been more willing to talk if Chalmers hadn't shown up with his .22."

"What game are you playin', Franken?" Hank asked. "I've got no beef with you."

"I don't know what you're talkin' about," he said, keeping his gaze on the engine. "I'm tryin' to work on this bike."

"*Bullshit*," Hank ground out.

This was getting us nowhere, so I waved my hands, gesturing for Hank to put his gun away. "Mr. Franken," I said, squatting down on the other side of the bike so we were eye level even if he wasn't looking at me. "I suspect we're delving into some dangerous waters, and Hank is a bit overprotective of me. He was worried we were walking into an ambush. Rhonda really didn't tell you that he was with me?"

"Nope. Probably because she knew I wouldn't agree to see you if I knew he'd be comin'."

"Hank's just here to make sure I don't get hurt," I said with a warm smile. "This is *my* investigation."

He gave me an incredulous look. "You expect me to believe that *Hank Chalmers* is acting as your *bodyguard*?"

It was understandable why he saw it that way, but I really needed him to talk. "Hank, go wait in the car."

"The hell I will," he barked.

"I'll be okay. Simon and I are just going to have a nice chat."

Hank hesitated, but to my surprise, and probably Simon's, he hobbled to the back gate. "I'll be standing in the driveway."

I waited until the gate's latch closed, but before I could say anything, Simon stood up and wiped his forehead with a rag from his pocket. "It's a hot one. I'm goin' inside. Feel free to follow me or not."

I cast a glance at the gate. Hank wouldn't be happy if I went inside the house, but we were here, and I wanted to hear what Simon had to say.

I headed for the back door.

Chapter Seven

The door led to a cluttered, stuffy kitchen. The counters were covered with dirty dishes, and it smelled of rotting fruit. The window over the sink was open as well as a window next to the small kitchen table, which meant the house either didn't have air conditioning or it was broken. Or maybe Simon was just too cheap to turn it on.

Opening the refrigerator, he asked, "Want some iced tea?"

"No thanks," I said. "I'm good."

He gestured for me to sit down at the table, covered with newspapers and mail, and I selected a seat in front of the least cluttered space and pulled my notebook out of my purse.

"You know the sheriff didn't find out jack shit about why my brother was murdered," he grunted as he pulled out a plastic pitcher.

"Rhonda said they wrote it off as a random incident, but she believes it might have had something to do with your father."

He poured tea into a plastic cup, then set the pitcher on the counter. "The old bastard got himself into big trouble, and

Dudley was dead set on gettin' him out of it. I'm not sure why. Our father spent most of his life drunk as shit. Couldn't hold a job, and we went to bed hungry as kids because what little money he had was spent on booze. But for some reason Dudley always took the Fourth Commandment to heart. I told him that our worthless father didn't deserve our respect, but the stupid shit never listened." While his last words were harsh, his voice broke.

"What did your father do that sent Dudley to Bart Drummond?"

A slow smile lifted the corners of his mouth. "Rhonda said you've figured that part out." He lowered himself into the chair next to mine. "He got arrested for a DUI. His fifth offense. He was facing jail time."

Interesting how she hadn't told me that part. "Rhonda said she didn't know for sure that your brother had gone to Drummond. Was she lying?"

His grin spread, but it didn't reach his eyes. "No."

I studied him closely. "But *you* know."

He was silent for a moment. "When my brother told me he was gonna approach Drummond, I told him he was a damn fool to put himself on the line for that bastard we called our father. But he said he *had* to do it for our momma." He took a long drink of tea, then lowered the glass to the table, setting it on top of a newspaper. "Dudley never confirmed that he'd gone to Drummond, but lo and behold, a week later, all charges were dismissed. Our daddy was a free man."

I had real problems with a man getting his father out of his fifth drunk driving arrest. Maybe prison would have been the best place for him. But I wasn't here to judge. "Dudley never admitted to asking for the favor?"

"No. I never asked, and he never told me. But a week before Dudley's murder, he told me it was time to pay the piper."

"Bart Drummond had come to collect his favor?"

"Dudley didn't say so directly, but I knew. I asked him what he needed to do, and he said it was bad. It was a kid."

I sucked in a breath. "What do you mean?"

"That's all he said. 'It's a kid.'"

"Do you think he wanted Dudley to hurt a child?" I asked, needing confirmation.

"I'm sure of it," he said, his hand tightening on the glass, "just as I'm sure Dudley would never do such a thing. So Drummond had him killed for it." He gave his head a little shake. "That bastard's evil. Hell, he could have me killed just for tellin' you this, which is why I ain't never told a soul up until now. Not even my wife, God rest her soul."

"So why tell me?" I asked in bafflement. "I'm a complete stranger."

"Because nobody's asked before, and Rhonda seems convinced you'll get answers. Maybe I'm tired of lettin' that bastard get away with whatever he wants." He took another sip. "I'm sure as shit tired of keepin' it a secret."

"How did your father react when his charges were dropped? Did he have any idea that Dudley went to Drummond?"

Simon shook his head. "No. The bastard thought he was just lucky." Bitterness drenched his words. "He weren't so lucky when his car hit a tree about three months later and killed him." His gaze pinned mine. "That's the worst part of all. Dudley sold his soul for nothing."

"What about your father's attorney? Would he be willing to talk to me? Maybe tell me what happened with your father's case? I'd likely need you to give him permission to talk to me."

He was already shaking his head again before I finished speaking. "His lawyer died of a heart attack over a decade ago, and so did the DA. Anyone who was directly involved is dead."

Which meant I couldn't prove a thing. I was one step closer to tying a favor to Bart Drummond, yet "close" wouldn't do me any good. "You never found out anything about the kid?" I asked.

"Nope. Never heard of a kid gettin' hurt or killed around that time either. And trust me, I had my ears open."

"Is there anything else you think could help me?"

He sat back in his chair. "Nothing."

I closed my notebook and stuffed it back into my purse. "I appreciate you taking the chance to talk to me at all."

"Well...it's not like it did much good now, did it? It's all whispers and hearsay. It's not like it's gonna put him away." His jaw hardened. "That man's been milkin' the poor folk of Drum for decades, charmin' with his smile all while his hands were in their pockets...or up their dresses."

"Wait. What?"

He looked taken aback. "If you're out to get the man, surely you know he's been takin' advantage of the people he claims to protect."

"Well, yeah, but no one's told me specifics. Do you know any?"

"Bart Drummond has had his little schemes for decades. They often involve bringin' in an outside resource, all in the name of helpin' the citizens of his namesake town, only everyone ends up forkin' out some kind of money that makes him even richer."

"Like the cell phone carrier."

He blinked, looking surprised. "Yeah. Exactly. He got a company no one's ever heard of to put a tower on his property, then got the people to use the carrier. Course they couldn't use it in places like Greeneville. People weren't so likely to jump into his schemes by the time the cell tower came up, though. They might not publicly berate him, but they've grown weary of his plans to make the town better."

"Like his new resort."

"Exactly. People are hopin' it will give them jobs and the town new life, but most people no longer see Bart Drummond as the answer to their prayers. And Drummond…" Disgust filled his eyes. "He don't like not being needed."

"You mean worshipped," I said dryly.

He pointed a finger at me. "Bingo."

I tilted my head. "You said he had his hand up women's dresses. Has he sexually assaulted any women?"

"You mean raped them?"

I cringed. "Yes."

"I know for a fact he liked to sleep with the women around town. Many of them wanted attention from him, but I heard of a few that didn't care for it. But it wasn't like they could turn him in for it. The sheriff's department was in his pocket."

"Did you ever hear rumors of Bart having any illegitimate children?"

"Nah," he said, sitting back in his chair. "But I have heard that he had a few pregnancies taken care of." He waggled his eyebrows. "If you know what I mean."

"Abortion?"

He nodded.

"Do you know anyone who aborted a baby fathered by Bart?"

"Not personally," he said, "but I think one of Dudley's girls was friends with one."

"Can you tell me which daughter?"

"Tammy. She lives up in Knoxville now, but I bet her mother can get you her number."

I wrote the information down. "Okay. Did she get married? What's her name now?"

"Married a guy named Bob Chester. Got a couple of kids."

I let this new information soak in for a couple of seconds, then closed my notebook. "Thank you for being so forthcoming, Mr. Franken."

"It's Simon. And like I said, I'm tired of hidin' from the truth about that man. He may have everyone else fooled into not talkin', but I ain't under his control no more."

"You were under his control before?" I asked in surprise.

"Everyone who lived in Drum was in one way or the other," he said. "But his power's slippin', and he's a desperate man. Especially since his oldest son turned his back on him."

Wyatt. "Do you happen to know anything about that situation?" I asked. "Why they became estranged?"

"Them two had a big fight over something, and Daddy Drummond used it to teach his boy a lesson."

"And what lesson was that?"

"That Drummond controlled everything. Including his son's freedom, or lack thereof."

"So he was trying to teach the people in town a lesson as much as his son?"

One of his brows lifted slightly. "I guess you can say it was. Fat lot of good it did him. Drummond's still on his way out, and Todd Bingham's on his way in."

I tilted my head. "How much do you know about Bingham?"

"We go back a ways."

Had Simon worked for Bingham? Was that why Hank had walked up with a gun? I knew there'd been bad blood between the two men, even if they seemed to have some sort of agreement in place.

His eyes narrowed. "Is Chalmers plannin' a comeback to the drug world? Are you scoopin' up information for him?"

"No," I said with a warm smile. "I live with Hank…or used to." When his eyes widened, I quickly added, "It wasn't like that. I rented a room in exchange for helping him after he got out of the hospital. He's like a father to me. He's just here to protect me while I ask questions."

"You expect me to believe that Hank Chalmers is playin' bodyguard a week or so after he got his millions back?" He released a bitter laugh in response to my surprised look. "Yeah, I know about that. Everyone from Drum does."

I leaned forward, resting my elbow on my thigh. "So you think he's out to do what? Get his drug empire back?"

"Knock Drummond off his throne," he said with a wave of his hand. "This game is all about the money, and that makes Chalmers king. He just ain't made his grab for the crown yet." He stood in a slow, unsteady movement. "My back ain't what it used to be, that's for damn sure. Chalmers may be like a father to you, but he's always put himself and his operation before any of his kin. You'd best remember that." Then he walked out the back door, letting the storm door slam behind him.

I took a second to process his words. Although I knew plenty about Hank's past, including that he had a lot of regrets, there was a lot I didn't know. I'd do best to stay on my toes.

Chapter Eight

Hank already looked pissed when I walked out Simon's front door. "What were you thinkin', goin' inside?"

I shot him a scowl as I moved past him toward the car. "I was talkin' to him, just like I've talked to dozens of people since last November."

"I'm supposed to be here to protect you," he grumbled as he hobbled to the passenger door.

"And you did," I said over the top of the car, then got inside.

He tossed his gun and crutch into the backseat before he got in too. "What's got you all riled up?" he asked as he shut the door. "What'd Franken say?"

I wasn't about to admit that Simon's words had gotten under my skin. Hank cared about me, there was no doubting that, but his new interest in helping me *was* very sudden. Could it actually be for his own benefit? I needed to discuss it with Marco.

After I turned on the engine, I pulled out my phone and saw he'd responded to my text.

I've got several meetings this afternoon so I won't be able to see you before you leave Ewing, but let me know how the interview with Franken goes.

I smiled to myself. That was code for *let me know you're safe.* I sent back: *Meeting went as well as could be expected. We're probably headed back to Drum now. I'll see you tonight.*

"Well?" Hank said, scanning my face. "What'd he say?"

"Not as much as I'd hoped, but more than I was expecting."

"Which was?"

I put the car into gear and pulled away from the house. "Dudley's father had been arrested for a DUI—his fifth—and was facing jail time."

"So that's what he'd been arrested for," Hank muttered to himself.

"Dudley decided he couldn't let dear old dad go to prison. He never admitted to going to Bart, but Simon's sure he did because the charges were dropped within a week."

"Well, if Simon is sure of it, let's just head to the sheriff's office right now and make this a done deal," he said sarcastically. "I bet Drummond will be behind bars by supper time."

I shot him a dark look. "What did you expect? We never went to meet him expecting actual proof. We're just digging deeper and deeper until we strike gold." His brow lifted, and I added, "No pun intended. Why are you so cranky?"

He scowled. "We're no better off than we were before you talked to him."

"Not true. You didn't let me finish. A week before his murder, Dudley told Simon it was time to pay the piper. When Simon pressed, Dudley said it was a kid and he didn't think he could do it."

Hank's eyes narrowed. "Do what?"

Shades of Truth

"Nothing good. After Dudley was murdered, Simon said he watched for the news for something involving a kid, but he never saw anything."

"Like I said," Hank said, sitting back in his seat. "We got a whole lotta nothing."

"No," I said drawing out the word. "We just need to look for something tragic that happened to a kid twenty years ago."

"You mean like the kid from fifteen years ago that Louise Baker claims to have evidence on. The one that you can't even find?" Hank snipped. "You really wanna waste your time lookin' for another shot in the dark?"

I cast him a questioning look. Where the hell was his attitude coming from? He'd wanted to help, hadn't he? "This isn't that far-fetched, Hank. Sure, I haven't found any leads about the kid Louise mentioned, but we know for a fact that Bart nearly killed Lula. You witnessed it yourself. We also know that Bart couldn't keep it in his pants. In fact, Simon said he used to sometimes force himself on women and also that he orchestrated a few abortions, so it's not too crazy to think he has other kids out there."

"So you're suggesting he went around killing all his illegitimate kids?"

"Of course not," I said, starting to get pissed. "Only the ones whose mothers were making trouble." I cast another quick glance in his direction. "Like Lula. Come on. Bart's got a lot of money, and Simon said he took advantage of young, poor girls. But when they couldn't put food in their baby's mouth, what do you think they did?"

"Applied for welfare."

"Or went to their rich baby daddy and asked for money. Maybe even blackmailed him like we know Louise probably did. I can't see Bart tolerating that."

He was quiet for a moment. "So what are you proposing? That we search for Bart Drummond's bastards?"

"I don't know," I said in frustration. "It's not a plan really. I guess I'm thinking out loud."

We rode in silence for a minute or so before I decided to make a leap from what Simon had told me and what I suspected. "You knew Simon Franken worked for Bingham. That's why you showed up in his backyard with a shotgun."

"Nearly everyone in this area has worked for Drummond, Bingham, or me in the past. That don't mean much."

Meaning Simon Franken *had* worked for Bingham. "So I take it there's some bad blood between you and Simon?"

"Contrary to what you might think," he said, sounding exhausted, "I don't have it out for every man who's been employed by either one of the Binghams."

"The other Bingham being Todd's father, Floyd?"

"That's right. People gotta eat."

"You're trying to convince me you're okay with people who helped the man who tried to take over your drug empire?"

He turned to me, his face expressionless. "Either you believe me or you don't."

He was right, and although I'd heard plenty of stories from his past, I only knew the man sitting next to me right now. "I believe you."

He reached over and patted my hand on the steering wheel. "You'd be a fool not to ask. Never be afraid to ask questions, but also know the right time to ask 'em."

"Why did you leave the drug business?"

"I already told you," he said, keeping his eyes on the road. "Mary was hounding me to get out of it."

"But she wanted you to leave before you did. She wanted to move to Florida, right?"

He shifted in his seat. "Let's just say I was a different man back then." He released a sigh. "I thought we had all the time in the world. I was a fool." Melancholy drenched his words.

I reached over and snagged him, squeezing tight. "I'm really sorry, Hank. For everything." Mostly I was sorry for questioning his loyalty to me, especially after everything he'd done for me.

He squeezed back. "Don't you be worried about me, girlie," he said with a soft smile. "I made my bed. I can live with the consequences."

We were riding in silence, heading back to Drum, when Hank asked, "So what do you want to do right now?"

"I don't know," I admitted. "I guess we just go home. I'm tired. I think maybe I've overdone it." It wasn't completely a lie. I was suddenly exhausted of this entire thing.

When I dropped Hank off at his house, he gave me a long look. "Sorry I got cranky. It's just..." But he didn't finish his thought. Instead, he got out of the car and hobbled up the steps and into his house.

I studied his front door for a few seconds, wondering what he'd tried to tell me. When I came up with nothing, I headed back to Marco's. I really was tired, and it was still early enough that I could get a nap in before Marco came home for dinner.

I was thinking about Marco's fluffy pillows when I pulled into his driveway, but I hit the brakes as soon as I saw a car I didn't recognize parked in front of the house.

I was about to back up and head to Hank's, but then I saw a woman sitting in one of the wicker chairs on the porch.

Her gaze locked on me as she stood, and I gasped when I realized who she was.

Emily Drummond had come to pay me a visit.

Part of me still wanted to drive away, because her showing up here could mean nothing but trouble, yet I was curious to see what had driven Emily to lower herself by coming to me.

She was in a long-sleeved dress, which I found odd with the heat, heels, and her very short hair was immaculately styled. She looked stronger than the first time I'd seen her, at Hank's grandson's funeral last November. Back then, she'd seemed like a woman with no fight in her, but now her arms were crossed over her chest, her index finger tapping impatiently against her bicep, and she exuded determination. As I parked the car next to hers and got out, I found myself thinking that our roles seemed to have reversed. I'd been the only one full of fire and fight back then, but she looked like she was spoiling for a fight now.

"Have you made any progress on the lead I gave you?" she asked, her brow raised with a look of disdain.

"By lead, do you mean your vague instruction to talk to Bingham about the supposed evidence he has that could incriminate your husband?" I said as I walked toward the porch. "I already told you he won't talk to me. You're going to have to be more specific if you want me to actually do something."

She waited for me to climb the steps to the porch. "I thought you were more resourceful than this, Carly Moore. I thought you had a fire in your soul for justice."

I climbed the last step and stared her in the eyes. "Maybe I did before I was run off the road last week and nearly killed. Or the previous times I've nearly been killed in this town.

How many times have you nearly been killed, *Emily*?" I asked bitterly.

"A time or two, but I confess it usually doesn't go that far," she said, her eyes blazing. Then she pulled back her sleeve to reveal four oval-shaped bruises on her forearm.

I looked up at her in surprise, but it lasted all of a second. Why wouldn't Bart Drummond physically abuse his wife? I was about to ask her why she didn't go to the sheriff, but the answer was obvious. Her husband had a hand in the department. It would come back to bite her in the ass.

"You're going to have to find a way to get Bingham to talk to you," she said, tugging down her sleeve. "You have to finish the job."

I held her gaze. "When you say finish the job, you mean put your husband away in prison, correct?"

"I know you're not stupid, Caroline."

We both knew she was aware of my real identity, so she was obviously trying to wield her knowledge over me to get me to do her bidding. While I did feel sorry for her—she was clearly in an abusive relationship and she'd confessed last spring that she was trapped in her marriage due to her husband's reach and influence—that didn't grant her the privilege of treating me like a hired servant. Not that I trusted her. I was beginning to suspect she ran her own shadow world, and she was trying to rope me into it.

"Let me get something perfectly straight," I said. "I don't work for you. I owe you absolutely nothing."

"I'm sorry," she said mockingly, "for some reason I thought you wanted my husband out of the way."

"If you have information on your husband, then use it against him yourself. Or find some other sucker to fall into your trap. I'm tired of being everyone's lackey." I walked past her and inserted my key in the deadbolt on Marco's front door, eager to get away.

"Why do you think this is a trap?" she asked, sounding surprised.

I released a sarcastic laugh. "You've got to be kidding me. Everything in this town is a trap of one kind or the other. *Especially* anything to do with the Drummonds."

"You don't seem to think Max is dangerous."

"That's because Max is actually my friend," I snapped.

"Is he?" she asked in a tone that suggested I was a fool.

I turned to look at her as I removed the key from the door. "Do you know something I don't?"

Her face softened. "I'm not here to fight with you, Caroline."

"My name is Carly, and you sure could have fooled me."

She walked closer and lifted a hand to my face, cupping my cheek. I stiffened at the contact, but if she noticed, she didn't let on. "You look exhausted. Why don't we go in, and I'll make you a cup of tea. Then we can discuss why I'm really here."

I wasn't falling for her motherly act for one second, but I was curious enough that I opened the door and walked inside, leaving Emily to follow.

Chapter Nine

I headed straight to the kitchen and Emily walked into the house, shutting the door behind her. She stopped at the entrance and took in the living room, dining room, and kitchen. "You've domesticated Marco." There was an unexpected fondness in her voice.

"Hardly. I only moved in a couple of weeks ago. It was like this the first time I came to see him." Then, for good measure, I added, "When I came to check on him after he came home from the hospital after he was shot."

She had the grace to grimace. "Point taken. I didn't come visit my son's best friend, but I *did* send a few meals."

"That's something."

A frown creased her forehead. "You have to keep in my mind that the man who ran Max's father's land for decades was the one who tried to kill Marco. I wasn't sure I was someone he'd want to see."

"I'm sure he appreciated the casseroles."

"I can hear the judgment in your voice," she said as she walked into the living room. I moved to the edge of the kitchen so I could watch her as she trailed a hand across the top of the sofa. "But I did what I thought was right." She peered out the window into the trees next to his house. "He's built a lovely home. He's put down roots. Marco is as much a part of Drum as my sons are."

The hair on the back of my neck stood on end. "What does that mean?"

She turned around and faced me with a look of pity. "What's your story, Caroline Blakely? I know your car supposedly broke down here and then you ended up staying with Hank Chalmers. But you're still here, long after you broke my son's heart and snagged Marco's. So what's your end game?"

I lifted a brow in surprise at her bluntness. "I could ask the same of you."

"I've made no secret of that," she said, moving around the end of the sofa and stepping into the kitchen. She passed me and started opening upper cabinets until she found the mugs and pulled out two. "Tea bags?"

She'd claimed she was going to make me a cup of tea, but I hadn't expected her to actually do it. I turned to face her, leaning my other hip into the counter. "Don't you have people to do that for you?"

Laughing, she opened another cabinet and found the tins of tea Marco kept for me. "I do, but I'm perfectly capable of making tea. And you didn't answer my question. How do you hope to see this all resolved?"

I crossed my arms over my chest. "You know that we seem to have cross purposes."

"Right," she said as she opened a tin and sniffed it. She glanced over at me. "The chemo's messed with my sense of smell. Which one is your favorite?"

"Uh…the hibiscus."

She nodded her approval and put two tea bags into the mugs. "You say you're intent on avenging Seth, yet I can't help wondering why you're still here. Why aren't you trying to go after your own father?" She gave me a knowing smile that didn't look the least bit friendly. "We both know the reward he's offering for your safe return is a bounty on your head, otherwise, why would you change your name, your hair, and hide out in this backwoods mountain town?"

"I really did break down here," I said, figuring there was no harm in admitting that, but a small sense of panic was brewing in my gut. This was the second time today I'd discussed my past, and it felt a lot closer to catching up with me.

"So why did you stay?" The kettle clicked off, and she poured hot water into each mug.

"Honestly? I had nowhere else to go. Max is a great boss, and I felt like Hank needed me."

"Max is a pushover," she said, moving past me with both mugs. She sat at the head of the table, then placed the other mug in front of the chair next to her. "He lets that Ruth Bristol practically get away with murder." She gave me a tight smile. "Honey?"

Against my better judgment, I grabbed the honey and a couple of spoons, then sat in front of the mug she'd prepared and handed her the second utensil.

"I'll agree that Max isn't as assertive as he could be, but he's a kind man, and he cares about his employees. He calls us family."

Her lips puckered in distaste. "He has a family, yet he still insists on spouting that nonsense." Reaching for the honey bottle, she squeezed some into her mug and stirred. "Do you know the saying blood is thicker than water? That means something in these parts. If push comes to shove, Max will always choose his family over his so-called friends and employees. Always."

I wasn't so certain of that. He'd turned his back on his brother after discovering Wyatt had dealings with the man who'd killed Jerry. But I figured I'd let her keep her delusion.

"Hank Chalmers was with you when you went to see Rhonda Franken."

The blood drained from my face. "You're having me watched?" I asked, outraged.

She released a short laugh. "Don't be stupid. Rhonda called me." She took a sip of her tea.

"What? Why would she call you?"

The smug look on her face irritated me. "Because I reached out to her myself about ten years ago. We both presumed that Bart had granted her husband a favor, but we never could find any proof."

Something about this wasn't ringing true. Emily had previously insinuated she knew many of Bart's secrets, including Wyatt's ex-girlfriend, Heather, blackmailing Bart. I found it difficult to believe she didn't know the details of all or at least most of his favors.

"So you and Rhonda have an arrangement?" I asked. "She tells you if she finds out new information?"

She blew on the surface of her tea. "Something like that."

"Why do I feel like it's not a reciprocal relationship?"

"I told her I'd let her know when I find proof. Obviously I don't have any yet."

Just as I'd suspected. Rhonda disclosed every little detail she learned to Emily, who kept everything to herself. "How did you know she wouldn't run to Bart and let him know you were snooping on him?"

"She's terrified of him. And besides, I approached her a good decade after the actual deed."

"Obviously I didn't learn anything new," I said, lifting the mug to my lips. "I'm sure you know as much or likely more than I found out today."

She cocked an eyebrow. "That's not entirely true. I know you went to see her husband's brother."

"Are you saying you never talked to Simon Franken?" I asked in disbelief.

"He refused to talk to me. He blames the Drummonds for his brother's murder, not that I disagree with him. I suspect he's right." She tilted her head. "Did he share anything noteworthy?"

I wasn't about to tell her that Dudley had probably been asked to hurt a kid. Knowing your husband is a philanderer was one thing. Knowing he had multiple children spread throughout the county, and had possibly arranged for them to be killed, was another. Did she know he forced himself on women, then had them abort accidental pregnancies that popped up? Of course, I had no proof of that. Simon Franken's words were just hearsay. I needed to talk to Tammy. "Do you think he was willing to talk to a stranger?" I asked.

Something flashed in her eyes, as though my inner thoughts had betrayed me, but she said, "That's a pity."

I cocked my head. "I still don't understand why you're here. Because you wanted to find out if I knew something you didn't? You told me at the block party that you have enough information to bring your husband down."

"I'm not in possession of it. Todd Bingham is."

"You keep saying that, but if it's so all-fired important, why has Bingham sat on it all this time?" But even as I said it, my mind blinked back to Louise Baker's safe deposit box. Bingham had said he wanted to get Bart out of the way, so if he had evidence linking Bart to the murder of a child, why hadn't he done anything with it? "Besides," I added for good measure. "I'm not Todd Bingham's favorite person."

"I thought you had more gumption in you," she said. "You're going to let Todd Bingham thwart you?"

"This isn't my fight," I said, wondering yet again if it was time I started acting like I meant that. My father was closing in on me. I'd confessed part of my story to Ruth, and although I'd been pretty vague, it was possible she'd tell Franklin, intentionally or not. The smart thing to do would be to put my resources toward saving my own hide. "Let Bingham sort it out."

"And what do you think he's going to do with the information?" she asked.

"Nothing, just like he's done with it for however long he's had it."

"Wrong. He's collecting information, and he plans to use it."

"Bingham's going to turn it over to the sheriff?"

She released a bitter laugh. "You think Bart doesn't have people embedded in the sheriff's department?"

"But they cleaned out the department a few months ago."

"You poor fool. You think they got rid of everyone?"

No, but I'd hoped. "You know for a fact Bart still has someone in the department?"

"No, but he's not cleaning out our bank account and making plans to move to the Cayman Islands, so he's feeling safe." She arched her brow. "Even if Bingham gathered enough evidence to get Bart arrested, what do you think will happen to the county? Who's gonna run it? And yes, while Bart has had his questionable ways, Bingham's are much rougher and more dire."

"More dire?" I said with a hard laugh. "Your husband had people killing each other for stupid favors. Not to mention he tried to kill his own daughter."

Pain flickered in her eyes, and I realized I'd struck a nerve. Was it the fact that I suggested he'd try to kill his illegitimate daughter or that she actually existed? Or maybe it was the reminder her husband had slept with Louise Baker, of all people. I know I'd be showering in bleach. But I needed to focus on something else.

"So what you're saying," I said carefully, "is you're actually worried about what Bingham plans to *do* with his evidence. Your goal isn't actually to have Bart arrested—you just don't want Bingham to take control."

While I sounded accusatory, I couldn't deny it was a legitimate concern. Still, I didn't believe her. Everything I'd heard from her was concern about herself. I'd never once heard her express concern about the town. Which meant there was plenty she wasn't telling me.

"Do you think Bingham in control would be good for anyone but him?" she asked in disbelief.

"No. Absolutely not, but if you want me to risk my life to find out what he has on Bart, you're going to have to give me more to go on."

Her mouth pursed. "You're just going to have to trust me on this."

Did she honestly think I'd get the evidence and hand it over to her, no questions asked? "Do I look like a delivery person? Tell me what he has and what it leads to. Otherwise, I'm going to forget it even existed."

She watched me for several long seconds and got to her feet. "I thought you were smarter than this. I thought you were more cunning. I thought you had the guts to take on the world." Her mouth twisted in disgust. "Turns out you're just like every other stupid girl in this town. You're going to hide here for the rest of your life, and you're going to rot. So much wasted potential. What a damn pity." Then she shot out the front door.

I stayed in my chair, but I kept my eyes on her through the window. She got in her car and drove away, and for the umpteenth time since I'd decided to stay in Drum, I wondered if perhaps she was right.

Chapter Ten

After she left, her parting words kept rolling around in my head. And when I wasn't thinking about her calling me a coward, I thought about what would happen if Bingham really did bring Bart down. Nature abhors a vacuum. While I wanted to believe Bingham would just let the people of Drum live their lives, I knew he didn't have their best interests in mind. He was ambitious. I'd known that since I first met him. And Emily was right. He was probably just as deadly as Bart, if not more so.

Where did Hank fit into all of this? Had he realized the same thing?

It also occurred to me that I hadn't told Hank about Simon's niece supposedly knowing someone who had been abused by Bart. Had I subconsciously decided to keep it to myself because I didn't fully trust him?

One thing was certain, if Rhonda was sharing information with Emily, I wasn't going to call her and ask for her daughter's phone number.

I noticed the blinking light on the small answering machine. Cringing, I hit play, surprised to hear Simon Franken's voice.

"I got to thinkin' after you left," he said, "and I realized Rhonda's not very likely to give you Tammy's number. In any case, if you still wanna talk to her, her number's—" then he rattled off a number I scrambled to write down on a pad of paper in the junk drawer.

He hung up right after that and I stared at the number, feeling leery that he'd been so forthcoming. Was this some kind of setup or was Simon really sick of it all?

In the end, it didn't matter. I was calling either way. I picked up the phone and dialed the number. A woman answered, and I could hear a commotion behind her.

"Tammy?" I asked. "Tammy Chester? You used to be Franken?"

She hesitated, then said, "You must be the woman Uncle Simon just called me about."

"That's right," I said. "I'm Carly Moore and I—"

"Stop right there," she said in a rush. "Don't tell me any more. I don't want to be any part of this."

My disappointment hit me center mass. If she had something that could help…

"I'm only gonna say this once," she said, lowering her voice. "My friend was pregnant, and the baby's father—a very powerful and dangerous man—strongly pushed her to take care of it, if you know what I mean."

"Yeah," I said gravely. "I do."

"He gave her an address and a contact in Chattanooga to take care of it. Turned out it was a bar, which she thought was weird, but he put so much pressure on her, she went anyway."

"Do you remember the name of the bar or the contact?"

Shades of Truth

"That was ages ago, so not really. But it seemed like the bar had an animal name, and the contact name…" She hesitated. "I can't remember. Sorry."

"I really hate to ask this, but do you think you could ask her?"

"I can't. She killed herself a few years later."

"Did she really kill herself?" I asked. "Or did someone make it look that way?"

"And now you know why you can't say you heard this from me. I'll call you a dirty liar if you try to claim you got this from me." Then she hung up before I could assure her I'd keep her secret.

When Marco came home around six, he found me stirring a pot of chili on the stove. He had a slight limp that had me worried. Although he'd rested his leg for a week, he was still having problems with it. I started to say something, but he pulled me into his arms and gave me a long, soulful kiss. I leaned into him, scared to realize how much I needed him.

He pulled back and studied my face. "What happened today?"

"You're still limping."

He gave me a dark look. "I'm fine. But you're not. You look tired. Tell me what happened today."

"Which part?"

"Everything."

Since he knew about my meeting with Lula, I skipped over my chat with Ruth and went straight to my visits with the Frankens. When I got to what Simon had said about the kid, Marco's eyes widened.

"A kid?" he asked. "How long ago was this?"

I pushed out a sigh. "If you're like me, you're hoping to tie it to Louise's supposed evidence that Bart killed a kid fifteen years ago. But it's off by five years. Dudley was murdered two decades ago."

He pursed his lips. "We don't know for certain the evidence is from fifteen years ago. For all we know, it's older and she just gathered it fifteen years ago."

"But in Jerry's video, Louise said 'remember that kid from fifteen years ago'? I think we're looking at two different incidents."

"Jesus," Marco groaned, rubbing his face. "Two?" The news seemed to devastate him, and I shot him a worried glance.

He looked down at me. "I know you've looked for evidence of a suspicious disappearance or death fifteen years ago, but how about twenty years ago?"

"No, because I had a visitor when I got home."

A hard look filled his eyes. "Should I be concerned?"

"Maybe not. She *did* compliment your decorating taste."

"She?" His brow shot up. "I take it the visitor wasn't Lula or Greta since they've been here before. Was it Ruth?"

"No, but we'll talk about her in a minute. It was Emily Drummond."

He studied me for several long seconds, then cupped my cheek. "Did she threaten you, Carly?"

"No, not really," I said, pulling away to stir the chili.

"What does that mean?"

I glanced up at him. "She wanted to know if I'd gotten whatever piece of information she claims Bingham has about Bart."

"That again? Jesus," he groaned in disgust. "Why the fuck doesn't she just get it herself?"

"That's what I asked her. She didn't answer, of course, and she still refused to tell me what I'm supposed to be looking for."

"She's stringing you along," Marco said. "You need to ignore her."

"She's up to something, but if she's trying to set me up, she's going about it in the strangest way possible. I've told her twice now that Bingham's pissed at me and won't even talk to me, let alone give me something that he can use against Bart. She won't listen."

"Maybe she knows that Bingham had a soft spot for you. He really does treat you differently than everyone else. She was bound to hear about it. She probably thought you could charm him into giving it to you."

"Well, that's definitely not true, and I'm pretty sure I just burned my bridge with Lula too."

"I'm sorry, Care." He pulled me into a hug. "What else did Emily say?"

"That's where it gets confusing. She's always led me to believe that she's wanting to put Bart away. But then she asked me what I thought would happen if Bart were removed from the picture. She said Bingham would fill the void, and that's not necessarily a good thing."

His eyes narrowed. "So you think she's setting Bingham up instead?"

"Honestly, I hadn't even considered it until just now."

He turned the stove burner down to low, took my hand, and led me to the table. After I sat down, he lowered into the chair beside me, turning it to face me. "I'm not gonna lie, Carly. This terrifies me. Think about it, she has no reason to want Bingham in charge. She has plenty of reasons to want to put him away too. You're the expendable chess piece on her chess board."

"A pawn." I gave his suggestion consideration, not liking the conclusion. "You might have a point. She made a big production of it, saying she used to think I was smarter and more cunning than all the 'other girls in this town.' She said if I don't do it, I'm a coward and I'll stay here and rot for the rest of my life."

His jaw tightened. "She said that to you?"

I grimaced. "I confess I spent some time dwelling on it after she left."

"That's Emily's specialty. She has a way of gettin' under people's skin without them even realizing she's done it. She always knew how to give Max epic guilt trips."

"Like the one that made him quit his senior year of college and come back to run a dead-end bar."

"Yeah," he said quietly. "Exactly like that."

"Speaking of guilt, there's something else we should consider." I took Marco's hand, lacing our fingers. "Simon wasn't very happy to see Hank with me. He asked if Hank was playing bodyguard because he wants to take Bart's place. Because he wants to find out everything I know."

"What?" he asked, jutting his head back. "Do you really think Hank would use you? Hell, I thought you pretty much told him everything you know already."

"Yeah, but I can't ignore the fact that he's never shown one ounce of interest in helping me before. I'd like to think it's because he thought he almost lost me, but Simon put that earworm into my head, and after everything with my father…I can't quite let it go."

Marco squeezed my hand. "Carly, Hank loves you. I have no doubt about that."

"I know he loves me, but in the past he always put his business before his family. I sort of asked him about it in the car, and he said he's learned from that. But they say old dogs can't learn new tricks. I can't help wondering if maybe he *is* using me even if it's unconsciously."

He leaned back and stared into my eyes. "Care, I saw how worried he was at the hospital. There's no way he's using you, and you have to know that I'm pretty cynical when it comes to this sort of thing. But for the sake of argument, let's say he's helping you partially so he can gain control." He sat back and ran his hand over his head. "I can't believe I'm saying this, but don't you think he would be more fair and just than Bingham or Bart?"

"Why does *anyone* have to rule?" I asked defensively. "Why can't the people in this town just coexist, for God's sake?"

A weary smile lifted his mouth. "There's always gonna be crime, Care. No matter how hard we try to make the world right, there's always going to be evil people living in it."

"That's pretty fucking depressing, Marco," I said, pulling back. Then I saw the haunted look in his eyes. "I was so busy talking about my day I didn't get a chance to ask you about yours. What happened?"

"That kid I was telling you about," he said, his voice tight. "The one who vandalized the barn, and I was trying so hard to get him out of trouble?" He swallowed. "He got out of foster care a couple of days ago and went home to his mother." His jaw worked, and his Adam's apple bobbed as he swallowed. "His stepfather killed him this morning."

I gasped. "Marco! Why didn't you tell me sooner?" I pulled him into a hug, wrapping my arms tightly around him. "I'm so, so sorry."

"Yeah, me too," he said, his voice gruff. "That poor kid never had a chance in this godforsaken place." He leaned back and looked into my eyes. "I want to leave, Carly. I want to go somewhere far, far away from here."

It looked like Emily was wrong about at least one thing. But it was a fleeting thought as I pulled him back into my arms. We both knew misery existed no matter where we'd go, but Drum sure seemed to have more than its fair share.

I pulled back and cupped his cheeks with both of my hands. Staring deeply into his eyes, I said, "You're a good man, Marco Roland."

He shook his head, tears welling in his eyes. "No. If I were a good man, I would've saved that boy. Instead, I just let it happen."

"That's not true. You did what you could." Marco had poured his heart into helping him. He'd tried to show that kid he could have a better life.

"Maybe I'm goin' about this all wrong," he said with a dazed look in his eyes. "I followed the rules, and look what happened? Some poor kid no one will remember died because of it. Maybe Hank has the right idea. Maybe I should be workin' *outside* the rules. Maybe that's where I can make a real difference."

I stared at him in horror. The man I loved *needed* the rules. He thrived with them. He'd stuck to them despite the rampant corruption in the sheriff's department. He'd bided his time, gathering evidence about internal corruption, and then helped clear out the department. But he'd also been working with me, and every time we worked a case together, he would cross one more ethical line to help me. I'd always feared there'd come a time when he'd reach a line in the sand he wasn't willing to cross, yet he'd do it anyway. For me.

And then, inevitably, he'd resent me for it.

I took his hand and slowly shook my head. "No, Marco. That's not who you are. That's not the man I fell in love with." I placed a tender kiss on his lips, and his body sagged into mine.

"He was just a kid, Carly."

No wonder he'd been so horrified that Bart might have hurt two kids. My news had poked him in a fresh wound. "I know," I whispered, brushing a tear off his cheek with the pad of my thumb. "You're right. Evil is everywhere."

Were we foolish to think we could stop it? Was all this a waste of time?

No, I refused to believe that. Just because evil existed didn't mean we should let it go unchecked.

"You might be right," I said. "Maybe you could do more good outside of the system, but you'd never be happy." When he started to protest, I placed a finger on his lips. "No. You need the rules. And so do I. Without them, this place would be in complete chaos. We're going to change things by taking away corruption and abuse of power. You've already helped with cleaning out the sheriff's department."

"But it's not completely clean."

"I know," I acknowledged. "Emily confirmed that Bart still has influence over the department. She could have been bluffing, but I'm not sure why she would. Finding information to put him away could end up being a complete waste of time if he has help in the right places."

Marco sat up a little. "Unless she never intends for him to go through the wheels of the justice system. Let's not forget that she doesn't want Bingham to take charge."

"That doesn't make sense. She wants hard evidence against him," I protested, then it hit me. "But she never said she's building a case for the DA to press charges. Only that there's evidence to bring him down. Maybe she's wanting to take it to the state police," I said.

He drew in a breath. "That would be a sure sign of her desperation. She's always hated outsiders coming in and thinking they have the right to control Drum. Like with forestry rules and moving the state park entrance."

"We don't have to solve this tonight," I said, placing another kiss on his lips. "And it looks like I'm not the only one who overdid it today."

He scowled. "I'm fine."

I kissed him again, taking my time and savoring his lips.

He slipped an arm around my back, grinning against my mouth. "Why Carly Moore, are you tryin' to seduce me?"

"If you have to ask, then I must not be doing it right."

He laughed.

I started working on the buttons on his uniform shirt.

"I thought we were havin' chili for dinner," he said, nibbling my ear. "Aren't you hungry?"

"I'm hungry, but not for chili."

His hand snaked through my hair, pulling my mouth to his, and we ended up on the sofa, leaving a trail of clothing behind us.

Afterward, he held me close, my cheek resting on his shoulder.

"Do you ever feel like this whole thing is hopeless?" I whispered.

His fingers traced circles on my back. "Honestly? Lately, yes."

"But it's not," I said. "We'll find justice for all the people Bart Drummond used and destroyed. We'll find justice for Drum."

"It won't make things right," he said. "They arrested that piece of shit who killed Adam, and while that might be justice, it won't bring him back."

I turned my head to face him. "I know. But we still have to try."

He nodded. "And that's one of the many reasons I love you, Carly Moore."

"I love you too."

But I loved the people of Drum too, and I was more determined than ever to save them.

Chapter Eleven

We didn't talk about Bart or the boy Marco had been trying to help, but I did tell him about my visit with Ruth. He wasn't happy I'd given her clues about my real identity, but he was slightly mollified that she'd agreed to keep it quiet, even from Franklin.

"She could have been snowing me," I said, "but I got the impression she doesn't know what Franklin's up to. Besides," I added, "she doesn't like Bart Drummond. It's a stretch to imagine her working with him."

"Even for money?" Marco asked. "It seems like they're pretty desperate."

I didn't like how I had to answer. "Maybe. She is desperate, but I can't believe she'd do anything that could get me hurt." I shook my head. "I doubt she'd hurt *anyone*, even if they really annoyed her. She doesn't know."

"And you didn't ask her?"

"I couldn't come right out and admit we'd seen Franklin meeting Bart, now could I?"

He made a face. "I suppose not."

I realized I hadn't told him about my call with Tammy Chester and her information about the bar in Chattanooga, so I did that next. "I guess I can scroll through the bars in Chattanooga and write down which ones have animal names," I finished.

"If it's still in existence," he said. "It might very well be closed."

He had a point.

"But it can wait until tomorrow," he said, holding me close. "Right now, I just want to hold you."

After that, we snuggled on the sofa and watched an episode of *Schitt's Creek* while we ate our chili.

Marco had trouble sleeping, waking up several times because leg cramps and once because of a nightmare. I rubbed his leg and got a wet washrag to wipe his sweaty forehead, then burrowed into him as he held me tight.

When he woke up to his alarm, he had dark circles under his eyes.

"Maybe you should stay home today," I said softly, my fingers caressing his cheek as we lay side by side in bed. "You look exhausted, and no wonder after the night you had."

"I'm on desk duty, Care," he said, rolling over and cupping my face. "I'm not overdoin' it, I promise."

"You're telling me you didn't go out to the crime scene yesterday?" I challenged.

He grimaced. "I stood around. I'm *supposed* to be walkin'."

I raised my brow with a playful grin. "So you're saying desk duty is actually hurting you?"

"You're incorrigible, woman," he growled, rolling me onto my back, and then spent the next twenty minutes showing me how unexhausted he was.

When we finished, he got up to head for the shower but stopped in the doorway to look back at me. "Why don't you invite Hank to dinner?"

"What?"

"Yeah, it's a great idea. We can butter him up with food, then ask him some of the questions you're dying to get answers to."

"I'm not sure that's a good idea."

"That's because it's a *great* idea," he said again. "But don't serve him tofu or cauliflower rice. You're trying to butter him up, not feed him like a prisoner of war."

I threw a pillow at him, which he easily dodged, laughing heartily.

"He happens to like cauliflower rice, thank you very much," I countered. "You're just thinking of yourself."

He laughed again. "Guilty as charged."

We'd woken up late, and he hurried to get out the door so he'd get to work on time. I sent him off with a kiss and his coffee mug, a reversal of our usual pattern, but I realized I could happily get used to waking up with Marco in my bed and falling asleep next to him every night.

I opened my computer and searched for bars in Chattanooga with animal names. It turned out to be harder than I'd expected. The searches brought up things like "the ten best downtown bars" and "dog friendly bars." Frustrated, I didn't have the patience to deal with it at the moment. Instead, I started doing housework, trying to keep my mind off Emily Drummond and Dudley Franken. An hour later, I caved and decided to research the deaths of children twenty years ago that might have been played off as accidents or illness. It wouldn't hurt to look.

Shades of Truth

My search came up with a whole lot of nothing, so I sent Marco an email asking him to look into any suspicious deaths twenty years ago.

He replied in less than a minute, saying he was glad I hadn't given up.

Sure, I had the hint of a name in Chattanooga, but even if I compiled a list, what would I do with it? Drive down there and go from bar to bar, hoping someone would confess to working for Bart Drummond? It felt kind of hopeless.

I hadn't called Hank yet, although I wasn't sure why I was hesitating. Marco's idea had merit.

He barked a hello into the speaker, before I got out, "Hey, Hank, how's your morning going?"

"Hey, girlie," he said lightheartedly. "You ready to go out sleuthin' today?"

"I would, but I don't have any new leads to follow." At least here in Drum. I wasn't ready to make the trek to Chattanooga yet. Not until I had a plan. "I'm calling to see if you want to come over for dinner."

"To Marco's?" he asked in surprise.

I laughed. "Where else would it be? I'm going to make a home-cooked meal. Any requests?"

"You're presumin' I'm comin'," he said.

"Of course you're coming," I said. "Marco gets home about six, so why don't you show up at six thirty?"

"You're steamrollin' me," he said.

"I'm inviting you to dinner," I said good-naturedly. "You like my cooking, or at least you say you do, and you like Marco. What's the problem?"

He was quiet for a moment. "None. And don't make cauliflower rice." Then he hung up before I could ask if he'd been eating it all along to make me happy while he quietly detested it.

I decided to make a new chicken curry recipe, which required a drive into Ewing to visit the grocery store. I'd just finished making up my shopping list when Trixie called, asking if I could cover her lunch shift.

"I know you're not supposed to come back for a couple more days, but I can't get ahold of Ruth and I'm desperate," she said, her tone surprisingly apologetic given the vibe I'd gotten from her yesterday. "I've got the shits like you wouldn't believe. Even if I could make it in, I'd be in the bathroom half the time."

Not to mention spreading her germs to all our customers. Talk about a health code violation nightmare.

"Don't worry about it," I said. "I don't think I was meant to be a lady of leisure. Besides, I'm feeling great, and the lunch shift is only a few hours."

"I'm supposed to stay late today, until Ruth gets in at four."

I'd have to hurry to get into Ewing to shop and get back, but I should still have dinner ready close to six thirty. "Oh. Well, that's not a problem. I can do it."

"You're a life saver, Carly!" She gasped. "Oh shit. Literally. Gotta go." Then she hung up.

I scrunched my nose at the phone before I hung it back in its cradle on the wall. Looked like I was going to get out of the house after all.

***

Max was not pleased to see me when I walked into the dining room about fifteen minutes before the start of my shift.

"Oh, hell no," he groaned, holding up a hand before I could even cross to the bar. "You turn around right now and go on back home."

I rolled my eyes as I continued to approach him. "Please. It's not like I stayed home yesterday. I roamed half the county.

I might as well roam the dining room and get paid." Then I flashed him a bright smile.

"She's got you there, Max," Tiny called from the kitchen.

Max shook his head, grumbling as he picked up a glass and wiped it with a towel. "I take it you're coverin' for someone?"

"Trixie. She's got some intestinal issues. Trust me. I heard enough to know you don't want her here."

He groaned again. "I could have gone without knowing that."

"Count yourself lucky for not getting the details." I leaned against the counter and lowered my voice. "Your mother paid me a visit yesterday."

He froze. "She came out to Marco's?" he asked in surprise.

"She was waiting for me after my trip to Ewing."

"What did she want?"

"Let's just say she wants me to use my investigative skills without actually hiring me."

He frowned and turned to put the shiny glass at the end of a row on the back counter. "Whatever she wants, don't do it."

"Don't you want to know what she asked me to do?" A little voice inside my head, the one that doubted everyone and everything asked, *Or does he already know? Is he still trying to protect his father?*

He picked up another glass and began to wipe. "I figure it's an extension of what she cornered you about a couple of weeks ago. Whatever she's up to, she'll hang you out to dry."

I had no doubt he was right, still…

I leaned in closer and lowered my voice even more. "Do you remember your father having affairs?"

He set the glass on the counter in front of him and slung the towel over his shoulder. "So she's got you lookin' into his past mistresses?"

"Not exactly..." I took a breath. "She still hasn't told me what Bingham supposedly has on your father, but she's very eager for me to get it. Do you think it has to do with any of that?"

He pursed his lips together, defeat filling his eyes. "Wyatt and I tried to find out whether we had other siblings out there, but we never found anything."

"Was it a team effort, or did you each do digging on your own?"

His eyes widened slightly. "The latter."

"So he could have lied to you, and you'd be none the wiser."

He shook his head. "Why would he do that?"

"Why was he working with Derek?"

A dark scowl covered his face. "Obviously he chose not to tell me." He turned serious again. "You take it easy today. No overdoin' it."

I'd been about to tell him that his father allegedly sent women to Chattanooga to take care of his half-siblings, but we were just about to open, and it seemed rude to tell him, *Hey, did you know your dad had enough illegitimate kids that he had a whole abortion system in place?* so instead, I focused on what he'd just said. "You should be givin' that speech to your best friend."

"Is Marco rushin' back to work?"

"Yes, and I'm worried. His leg is bothering him, and he's supposed to be moving it, but they've got him on desk duty, which isn't helping anything."

"What's the long-term prognosis with this?" Max asked with a sigh.

"Honestly? There's a chance he'll get all the way better. But Carson Purdy did a number on the muscle on his thigh when he shot him, and Marco's reinjured it more than once over the last couple of months." I paused then said with a grimace, "It's not looking good."

Max cursed under his breath. "What's Marco gonna do if he can't work for the sheriff's department?"

"You'd be a better judge of that than me," I said. "But he's also torn up about this teenage boy he tried to help. Marco had been talking to him, getting him to redirect his energy away from illegal pursuits like tagging barns..."

Max grinned from ear to ear. "Sounds like something me and Marco might have done back in the day."

"You're kidding."

"Cross my heart and hope to die," he said. "Go on."

I made a face. It seemed abrupt to shift from such a lighthearted memory to the dark outcome, but the truth *was* dark. "He was from a bad family, and long story short, his stepfather killed him yesterday."

Max's face paled. "Oh shit."

"Yeah." I swallowed. "Marco is devastated. And now he's spouting crazy talk about not following the rules anymore, and..." I searched Max's face. "I'm scared for him, Max. He needs the rules, and he needs to be a deputy. What if he loses his job because of his leg?"

He placed a hand over mine. "Now don't go worryin'. Marco wasn't one of those kids whose sole goal in life was to be in law enforcement. He only joined the force to help keep me out of trouble. If he has to get another job, he'll be all right."

Max had a point, but I wasn't so sure he was right. Sure, Marco hadn't set out to join the sheriff's department, but he'd definitely grown into it. He got a huge sense of self-worth from protecting the citizens of the county.

Ginger came in, tying an apron around her waist seconds before it was time to open the front doors. "What in tarnation are you doin' here, Carly Moore? You're still supposed to be restin'."

"Saving you and all of our customers from getting sick." I shot her a grin. When she gave me a confused look, I added, "Trixie has some nasty bug. You're welcome."

"Stubborn fool." She rolled her eyes as she tucked an order pad into her pocket. "What's the special?"

"BLT," Tiny called out.

A crowd of men walked past me as I unlocked and opened the front door. Several of them greeted me warmly and told me how much they'd missed me. I warned the customers in my section I might be slow, but I managed to keep up without wearing myself out. The lunch rush was just about done when Todd Bingham walked through the front door.

I was at the bar, waiting on a couple of soft drink refills, and watched as he headed to the booth we usually sat in during our conversations.

"Well, shit," Max grumbled as he set a glass on the counter. "He's obviously here to see you."

"He's probably pissed I had lunch with Lula yesterday."

"But you got lunch here yesterday," he said in confusion.

"That was after I tried to have lunch with Lula. It didn't go so well, and I left my salad on the table."

His shoulders lifted in a lazy shrug. "You got the better end of the lunch stick with Tiny's cutlets."

"Don't I know it," I said, sneaking a glance at Bingham, whose gaze was pinned on me.

"I suppose you're gonna go talk to him."

I grinned. "It's like you know me."

"I've got your back, but be careful. Rumor has it he's got a short fuse lately."

That was an interesting piece of information I hadn't heard, but then again, I'd been tucked away for over a week. If Bingham had secured enough evidence to bring down Bart, wouldn't he be in a better mood?

I dropped the refills off at the table occupied by an older couple, then headed over to Bingham, who was watching my every step.

"People are going to start thinking you have a thing for me if you keep watching me like that," I said dryly as I slid into the booth.

His hands fisted on the tabletop. "Are you suggestin' I cheat on my wife, Carly Moore?" he growled.

"No. Bad joke."

His scowl deepened.

Great, this was already off to a bad start. "What can I help you with, Bingham?"

His brow lifted. "Funny you should ask."

I didn't respond, deciding to wait him out.

"I hear you tried to coerce Lula into tellin' you what was in the bank box."

I lifted my chin. "You heard correctly."

"You don't seem to know when to keep your nose out of other people's business, do you?"

I leaned forward and lowered my voice. "If you have information that could put Bart Drummond away, then it's everyone's business."

He sat back in his seat and laid his arm along the back of the booth. "Now, now, who says I have something like that in my possession?"

"I noticed you didn't answer the question," I countered.

He kept quiet but made a face that suggested I was on to something.

"So are you here to tell me to mind my own business or are you here to share what you've learned with me?"

A toothy grin cracked his serious façade, but it didn't look friendly. "I'm here to make a proposal."

Chapter Twelve

I hadn't been expecting that. "I'm listening."
He leaned forward so that our faces were only a foot apart. "I need you to find Louise."

I narrowed my eyes. "Why?"

"You don't need to know that part."

"Why don't you just have Lula call her?"

"Because I made Lula delete her number, and now I don't have it."

That had been short-sighted of him, but I wasn't fool enough to say it out loud. "What's in it for me?"

"I'll let you see what I found in the box."

"That's it?"

"You got Lula to defy me so you could find out the contents of that box, so don't pull that disinterested shit with me," he huffed.

"Even if I was tempted to accept your 'offer'"—I grimaced—"I wouldn't know the first place to look for her. It would be like looking for a needle in a haystack."

"You said you wanted to bring Drummond down," he said. "Isn't that worth the effort?"

"And you told me the same thing but based on the probable contents of that box, not to mention whatever Emily Drummond thinks you have, it sounds like you're not in much of a hurry."

"You can't listen to that bitch," he said.

"But I should listen to you?" I countered.

"You shouldn't listen to anyone except for yourself."

A hard-earned lesson, but one I was surprised he was "teaching" me considering he wanted something from me too.

"Okay," I said, relaxing a little. "I'll try to find Louise, although I'm telling you right now, I don't hold out much hope for finding her. But if I agree to try, then I need something from you first."

He released a snort. "It don't work that way."

"I just need you to answer one question. That's it."

He released a short laugh. "Like it's ever that simple with you."

"It doesn't have anything to do with you," I said. "It's about Drum history."

His body froze for half a second, and I knew I'd unintentionally hit a nerve. Carnita, the town librarian, had told me that Bingham and Lula had been looking up their family history, going a century or so back, although she had no idea why.

"Pretty recent compared to the research you and Lula have been up to."

He rubbed the scruff on the side of his jaw. "Heard about that, huh?"

"I need to know if you know anything about the death of a kid about twenty years ago."

He let out a belly laugh. "You're kiddin'."

"I'm serious as a heart attack."

"Just some random kid?" he asked with a grin, but then it wobbled slightly, and the humor left his eyes.

I leaned closer. "No, not just some random kid. I suspect he or she was Bart Drummond's illegitimate child. You know something. I saw it in your eyes."

His humor fell completely away, replaced with a dark look. "What the fuck are you talkin' about?"

"You know that Lula can't have been the only child he sired with another woman," I said. "And it stands to reason he would have done away with them. You *know* something."

"This ain't *Game of Thrones*, Carly Moore. There's no throne to take."

"No, but at one time, there was a considerable inheritance. One that could have been taken away from his sons. As quickly as everything turned to shit after the lumbermill closed, I'm guessing he was cash poor back then. Which meant he couldn't afford to pay them off." I shrugged. "Not to mention, I'm sure some of the mothers tried to cash in with good old-fashioned blackmail. Just like Louise."

He was silent for a second, taking in what I'd said. "Why twenty years ago?"

That was an interesting question. If he wasn't lying to me, the information he had wasn't about the murder of a child twenty years ago. That didn't mean Louise had been lying, however. Maybe she had information about a different child. Either that, or Bart didn't act on Dudley's "assignment" for a few years. "You have your secrets, and I have mine."

He frowned, and I could tell he wanted to threaten me to tell him, but surprisingly, he remained silent.

"So do you know of a child who died under mysterious circumstances within that time frame?"

"No, but I wasn't payin' attention either." His words sounded sure, but there was something in his eyes that told me he was lying.

"I can't find anything suspicious in the records, and there are no sheriff reports to back up my suspicions."

He turned his hand palm up. "I take it you're lookin' in Hensen County."

"Well...yeah."

A smirk lit up his eyes. "Then perhaps you're lookin' in the wrong direction."

Oh. Crap. Why hadn't I thought of that? "And where should I be looking?"

"Bart was known to do business in Knoxville and Chattanooga back in the day. You might try lookin' in those places."

Chattanooga. "What did he do there?"

"A little bit of lumber business. A little bit of moonshine. A whole lot of who knows the fuck what."

"Plenty of time to find and keep a mistress."

"Or a quick screw."

That too.

"Do you know if he had connections to a bar?" I asked.

"As in owned one or frequented?" He shook his head. "No idea."

I wasn't sure I believed him, but I doubted he'd change his story if I pressed. Instead, I pushed out a breath. "Okay. Thanks."

"Now I need *you* to tell *me* something."

"I told you I'd try to find Louise, although I'm not promising anything."

"Not that." He shifted in his seat and leaned forward. "I need you to tell me what Hank plans to do with his gold. Does he plan on makin' a move on my empire?"

"Do you really think I'd tell you if I knew such a thing to be true?"

"Maybe not," he said with a knowing grin. "But your body language would have given you away. You don't know shit."

I laughed. "You think I can't lie to you?"

His gaze darkened again. "You plannin' on tryin', Carly Moore?"

"I plan on doing whatever I need to do to survive."

He paused, then tapped his index finger on the table. "Interestin' choice of words—survive."

My blood ran cold. "Is that a threat, Bingham?"

"You've gotten yourself a few enemies, Carly Moore. You'd best watch your back."

"And are you on that list?" I asked, hoping my voice didn't shake.

"Not at the moment." He held my gaze. "But let's just say you want to stay on my good side. I suspect you're gonna need a few allies." He leveled his gaze, moving closer again. "Find Louise Baker." Then he leaned back, slid out of his seat, and walked out of the tavern.

I sat there for a few moments, trying to process what he'd told me. So Bart used to frequent Knoxville and Chattanooga. Why hadn't Hank shared that information? Because I knew darn well he'd kept tabs on Bart's comings and goings back in the day. Bingham's last comment had bothered me more than I'd wanted to show. The only enemies of mine I knew about were Bart and my father, unless Louise considered me an enemy, which wasn't hard to believe. There was always Wyatt to consider, but I didn't think he saw me as an enemy. More like an annoyance.

But I went back to Bingham's reaction about a kid being murdered twenty years ago. What did he know about the murder of a kid two decades ago that I didn't?

His little brother.

Marco had told me that Todd's little brother was his age, and he'd disappeared when they were eight. That would have been eighteen or nineteen years ago, so it wasn't a perfect fit, but just because Bart asked Dudley Franken to kill a kid twenty years ago didn't mean it had actually happened then. It may have taken him a year or two to find someone else to do it. Besides, people tended to lose track of time and something they remembered happening twenty years ago could actually be twenty-two or seventeen.

Todd's father had told the sheriff deputies his mother had taken him to Hickory, North Carolina, but that seemed unlikely since she'd disappeared shortly before her son did. Marco seemed convinced Floyd Bingham had killed the boy and buried him somewhere on Bingham land, along with Floyd's two wives since the first had mysteriously run off too. The fact that Floyd had been killed in a woodchipper accident only six months after Rodney disappeared seemed to confirm it. Especially since Todd had conveniently been the only witness.

But what if that wasn't true? What if Bart Drummond had killed the boy instead?

Oh. God. Had Bart had an affair with *Floyd Bingham's wife*?

I slid out of the booth and headed to the bar.

"Well?" Max asked when I rested my hands on the counter.

I rubbed my forehead, trying to figure things out. "He wants me to find Louise."

"Couldn't he just have Lula call her?"

Shades of Truth

"I guess he deleted her number."

His brow furrowed. "Why don't I believe that?"

"Maybe because you're a smart man?" I asked with a laugh.

"This isn't funny, Carly."

"No, it's not, especially since he said he'd let me see the contents of the safe deposit box if I find her."

He shook his head in confusion. "What safe deposit box?"

I quickly caught him up to speed about finding the key in the toolbox.

"So let me get this straight," he said, rubbing his jaw. "He wouldn't even show Lula what was in there, but he's suddenly gonna show it to you? Sounds suspicious."

"Agreed."

The front door opened, and Franklin's work crew walked in.

"Kind of late for them to be takin' their lunch break," I said in a hushed tone.

"I know," Max said, his forehead furrowed. "And Tater's not with them."

Sure enough, he wasn't. "What do you make of that?"

"I don't know."

They sat in Ginger's section, so she walked over to take their order.

"What else did Bingham say?" Max asked, giving them a sidelong glance.

"I asked him if he knew about a kid dying under suspicious circumstances twenty years ago. He claimed he didn't but suggested that I look in Knoxville or Chattanooga if I can't find anything in Drum or Hensen County."

Max's face paled.

I leaned closer, standing on my tiptoes to close the distance between us as my heart started to race. "You know something?"

"Just that I remember my father takin' trips to both places when we were kids. I always wanted to go but was scared to ask. I know he took Wyatt a few times." He shook his head. "I don't know why I didn't think of it sooner."

"He took Wyatt?" I asked in surprise. "He might be able to help."

"If he has information, he's not gonna tell me and he's definitely not gonna tell you." He gave me a weak smile.

Wyatt may have agreed to work with me, but he wasn't exactly forthcoming.

"What do you know about Rodney Bingham?"

His eyes flew wide. "Todd Bingham's brother?"

"Yeah."

He drew in a breath, then leaned forward. "Not much. He went to school with me and Marco. He disappeared when were in…" He scratched his chin and got a faraway look. "Third grade, I guess." Then a knowing look filled his eyes. "Oh. Shit."

"It doesn't match twenty years. I'm guessing eighteen or nineteen, but…"

"Everyone suspected Floyd killed him and buried him on his property. His wives too."

"And how convenient for your father if he did it."

"Shit." He looked horrified.

"It's all speculation at this point, and honestly, it seems more likely Floyd got carried away and killed his own son. I mean, he did die in a woodchipper a few months later with Todd as the only witness. It stands to reason that Todd killed him in revenge for his brother."

Max looked troubled, but then he seemed to shake it off and asked, "Did he say anything else?"

"Only that he wanted to know what Hank plans to do with his money. He's worried Hank's going to try to get his empire back. I told him I had no idea what he plans to do." Then I added, "He also said I was accumulating enemies. I know I have your father and mine after me, but is there anyone else? Should I be doing a better job of watching my back?"

He leaned his elbow on the counter. "I might add Bingham to that list, but seeing how he wants you to find Lula's mother, I'd say you're safe for now."

"There's Louise," I said. "She might blame me for what happened to Derek, but I wouldn't have trusted her anyway." Then I dared to ask, "What about *your* mother?"

"My mother's a lot of things, but a murderer isn't one of them." He added, "You're not her enemy."

"But your brother might be after last week," I said with what I tried to make a teasing grin. It fell miserably short.

He stayed somber. "No, Carly. No matter what you do, you'll never be Wyatt's enemy."

A customer called for their bill, and I headed over to take care of them without responding, because, honestly, I had no idea what to do with that.

Chapter Thirteen

I headed over to take care of a table when Billy, one of Franklin's friends, reached out toward me from several tables away. "Hey, Carly. What are you doin' back? Tater said you wouldn't be here until next week."

"Trixie called in sick, so I'm coverin' for her."

"Why didn't she call Ruth?" Billy asked.

I shrugged, walking over to their table. "She said she couldn't reach her."

He scratched his chin. "That's weird. Tater didn't show up for work today, and he didn't even call in sick."

I felt a weird crawling sensation over my skin. Something wasn't right. I could see Ruth not answering her phone. She could have gone out and, like everyone else, she didn't have a cell phone that worked around here. It was Tater's absence that had me worried. He rarely took time off, and I couldn't see him not calling in. Especially since he needed the money to cover that truck.

I shot a glance at the bar and noticed Max was listening to the conversation.

He looked just as worried as I felt, so I headed straight for him.

"What do you make of that?" I asked in a hushed tone.

"Knowing everything else? Honestly, nothin' good."

I started untying my apron. "I'm going out there to check on Ruth."

His jaw tightened. "I'm comin' with you."

I glanced around. Besides Franklin's crew, there was only a handful of customers. "Ginger can handle this crowd by herself, but not if anyone else comes in."

"Then we'll close. You go throw up the closed sign on the door and settle up your tabs while I run upstairs. I'll tell Ginger and Tiny that we're runnin' an errand, and I'll meet you out back."

I discreetly turned the sign and settled with my two tables, then grabbed my purse and started for the back door.

Tiny stopped me short with a question. "Max told me what's happening. Should we be worried about Ruth?"

"Nah," I said, forcing a smile, then lied. "She didn't seem like she was feeling well when I dropped by to see her yesterday, so we're just going to check on her."

"But you're worried enough to close up the tavern?"

I shrugged. "What can I say? Max and I are overreactors." Then I hurried out the back door before he could ask any more questions.

Max was already in his truck, which he'd pulled out of his parking space and parked perpendicular to the door.

I climbed in next to him, and he pulled out of the parking lot without waiting for me to buckle my seatbelt.

"We're just overreacting," I said, repeating what I'd told Tiny on my way out.

"Do you really believe that?" Max cast a glance at me as he turned onto the highway. "Deep in your gut, do you believe that?"

"No," I whispered, feeling like I was going to throw up.

Max drove over the speed limit, only slowing down when he reached curves in the road. He turned up the county road, his engine groaning as we climbed in elevation. We flew past Hank's house, driving on to Ruth's trailer. The back tires skidded as he pulled onto their property and then hit the brakes, sending gravel and dust flying.

"Her car's here," he said, his voice tight.

"Her car was here yesterday," I said, trying to keep it together. "Franklin's been getting a ride to work with one of the guys on the crew."

"But Franklin didn't show today." He'd barely thrown the truck into park before he jumped out and ran for the front door.

"Max! Wait!" I shouted as I pushed my door open and raced around it, right on his heels.

He reached for the doorknob and turned, but it was locked.

"Maybe they really aren't home," I said from the bottom of the steps.

He cast me a glance as though considering my statement, then turned back around and gave the door a vicious kick.

It burst open, bouncing off the inside wall and swinging back toward Max. He lifted his hand to stop it from smacking him in the face and entered, shouting, "*Ruth?*"

Part of me wondered if I should have called Marco before we came out here, but it was too late now. I hurried up the steps after him, calling out, "Ruth!"

He headed through the living room, into the kitchen, and then made his way down the hall. Pushing open doors, he checked the guest room I'd slept in all those months ago, then the bathroom. The master bedroom was at the end, the door shut.

Max pushed it open and started to rush inside but stopped in his tracks.

"What?" I asked in a strangled cry, trying to look around him, but he filled the doorway and wouldn't budge when I pushed him. "Max! Is she here?"

"Ruth." Her name was a guttural sound as he dropped to his knees.

It was then I caught sight of her, slumped on the edge of the bed, on her side. She was wearing shorts and a T-shirt that were covered in blood. The blue comforter was soaked in it.

"Ruth!" I cried out in a panic, trying to get around Max so I could reach her. "Max! Move! We have to see if she's alive."

He grabbed my arm as I tried to slip past him. "She's not alive, Carly," he choked out.

"You don't know that!" I insisted, trying to tug myself loose. "We have to check."

He got to his feet and pulled me to his chest, his arms trapping me in a hug. "We have to check, Max!"

Max began to sob, but I tried to hold it together. One of us had to think straight. But my head was fuzzy from shock, and I could see part of Ruth's face through her tangled hair, her eyes open and unfocused.

"No, Max," I said, starting to cry. "No! No!" I tried to tug free of him, but he held on tight. "Please, God! No!" I collapsed into his chest, sobbing in horror and shock. "No!"

He released me but cupped my face with both of his hands, his eyes red and his cheeks wet with tears. "Carly. She's gone."

"No," I wailed.

"Stop," he said, his voice suddenly firm. "We have to think this through. Someone killed her, and we have to look for clues."

"We need to call Marco," I said. "And 911."

"And we will, but we need to look around first. I have a pair of gloves out in the truck." He released my face and grabbed my hand, tugging me down the hall.

I turned back to look at Ruth, her vacant eyes staring up at me. My peripheral vision began to fade, and I started to fall to the floor.

"Don't you go passin' out on me," Max said, wrapping an arm around my back and holding me up as he continued to walk down the hall.

"We shouldn't be in here," I said, fighting to stay conscious. "We're contaminating the crime scene."

"Which is why we're goin' back out." He led me across the kitchen toward the open front door.

I stumbled down the steps and collapsed in the front yard, sitting up and then tucking my head between my knees. That was when it hit me. "Where's Franklin? I didn't see him."

"Maybe he's on the floor on the other side of the bed," Max said as he headed toward the truck and rummaged around behind the seat. "He definitely wasn't on the bed."

The blackness had cleared from my head, even if the horror hadn't. "What are you doing?"

He got out of the truck, barely giving me a glance. "I told you. I'm lookin' for clues." But first he opened her car, did a quick glance in the back and under the seats, then he went inside.

What was that about?

I didn't want to stay out by the truck by myself. Part of me was terrified Ruth's killer was lurking around, waiting to kill me next, even though the rational part of my brain knew it was highly unlikely. The rest of me wanted to go inside to see what Max was up to.

I got up, giving myself a second to make sure I wasn't going to pass out, then crossed the yard to go inside.

Max was donning a pair of work gloves and opening the drawers on the end tables beside the couch, rifling through the contents.

"What are you looking for?"

"You should wait outside, Carly," he said, his voice strained.

"No," I said. "I'm in this with you, but what are you looking for? Don't you dare tell me nothing, because you look like a man with a purpose."

"Paperwork," he said.

"What kind of paperwork?"

"Don't you worry about that. Why don't you grab a towel or something so you don't leave fingerprints and get ready to call 911."

"Get *ready* to call?" I asked with a start. "Max, Ruth is lying in her own blood, *dead*." My voice broke as the truth sank in.

He moved to the kitchen and began to search the drawers in there. "Which is why you should go back outside and wait. I'll be done in a few minutes, and then we can call. Five minutes won't matter at this point."

This was crazy. What on earth could he be looking for that was more important than reporting her murder? What was Max mixed up in? Was he in league with his father? But all I could think about was how Max was so willing to help me after Seth's murder, and how he was ready to find my gun by Seth's body, no questions asked. He'd barely known me then. Now we were closer friends. I had to stand by him. I owed him this.

"Tell me what you're looking for and I'll help. The sooner we find it, the sooner we can call the sheriff's department."

He turned around to face me, his face grim. "A file folder full of spreadsheets."

I had so many questions, but now didn't seem to be the time to ask them. "And you're sure she has it?"

He spun back around to continue searching. "She took 'em home last night. We can't let the sheriff department get their hands on it or…"

"Or what?"

"Just help me find the papers."

I opened a drawer where I knew Ruth kept towels.

"What the fuck are you doin'?" he shouted. "You can't touch anything!"

"I was just here yesterday," I said, pulling out a kitchen towel. "I helped Ruth fold towels. I can tell them I put some away." My voice broke again. I'd seen her a little over twenty-four hours ago. She'd been alive. Talking. And now she was dead. "Where the fuck is Franklin?"

"I don't know," he said, moving to the hallway.

I followed him, if for no other reason than I had to see if Franklin was in there with her. Max went into the bathroom, but I headed down to the end of the hall, stopping in the doorway to the master bedroom.

"Carly," Max called out. "What are you doin'?"

"I'm lookin' to see if Franklin's dead too."

"Don't be passin' out in there!" he grunted. "You do that, you really will contaminate the crime scene."

"Thanks," I said sarcastically under my breath and hugged the wall inside the room with my backside, easing around the dresser to get a look at the other side of the bed. I tried my best to keep my eyes off Ruth, but it was hard to block her out completely. Tears stung my eyes, making my vision blurry, but I blinked to get a clear view of the floor. There was no sign of Franklin.

"He's not here," I shouted. But if he wasn't here, where was he? Had *he* killed Ruth? From everything I had seen, Franklin had really loved her. I couldn't make it fit. But what if Bart had had her killed and the murderer had dragged Franklin off? Or what if it was Bingham? Ruth had mentioned that they didn't get along.

Max appeared in the doorway, his gaze firmly attached to the bed. "Fuck," he said, his voice cracking. "Who did this to you, Ruth?"

"Did you find it?" I asked, turning my back to the bed and opening a dresser drawer with my towel.

"No." He opened a drawer at the opposite end and started rifling through a pile of underwear while I sorted through shorts and T-shirts.

"Franklin's not here," I said, shutting the drawer and tugging open the one below it. "Do you think he killed her?"

Max answered immediately. "No. He loved her too much."

"I thought so too, but you have to wonder if you ever really know someone."

"He wouldn't have done it," Max said, "besides, his busted-up truck's out front with Ruth's car. If he killed her, how'd he get away?"

"How'd he leave period? Walk? Ruth said he'd been borrowing her car."

"Which means it's more likely someone showed up, killed Ruth, then took Franklin with them," he said, confirming my thoughts.

"So they killed her because of Franklin?" I asked, tearing up again.

"Maybe. Or they could have been after that file." He slammed a drawer in frustration, then moved on to the closet.

Killed her for the file? What in God's name had Max gotten mixed up in that could have gotten Ruth killed?

The sound of a car engine outside filled the silence, and Max looked at me with wide eyes.

"Someone's here," I whispered, as though they could hear me.

"Go out to the kitchen and call 911, try to keep them out of this room by telling them they'll disturb the crime scene. Tell them I'm back here, but I'm sitting with Ruth."

My chin trembled as I stared at him.

"Go on," he encouraged with a weak smile.

I nodded and headed to the kitchen, using the towel to pick up the receiver. It was impossible to use on the buttons so I used my index finger to gingerly touch the keys. Once the call went through, I took advantage of the long cord and moved to the open front door, not surprised to see a truck carrying Franklin's crew pulling to a stop. It wouldn't have been that hard to figure out where Max and I had gone in such a hurry.

"911, what's your emergency?" a female operator asked.

"There's been a murder," I said, my voice tight. "My friend has been murdered." Tears flowed down my cheeks.

"Are you sure the victim's dead? Did you check for a pulse?"

"She's dead."

The truck doors opened, and Billy, Tinker, and Pete got out. I had to keep them out of the house. Sure, I needed to protect the crime scene, but I would have been lying if I didn't admit to buying Max more time.

"What's your location, ma'am?"

I quickly gave her the address, then said, "But hurry. Someone just pulled up, and I'm worried they're about to contaminate the crime scene."

After I hung up the receiver, I wiped my cheeks with my hands, then walked back to the open door and stood on the porch, looking down at the men.

Tinker cast a glance at Ruth's car, then back at me. "Did you find 'em? Are they here?"

I took a long, slow breath to keep it together. "Ruth's here, but Franklin's not."

Billy took off his ballcap with one hand and rubbed the back of his neck with the other. "Did Ruth say where he was?"

"Ruth's dead."

All three men stare at me in shock. "What?"

"Ruth is dead. Murdered." My voice broke and I looked up at the sky, taking a breath before I leveled my gaze on them again. "She's lying on the bed, but there's no sign of Franklin."

They stared at me for a long moment, until Billy broke loose and started for the porch steps.

I held my hands out at my sides, making it visually clear they weren't getting inside. "I've called 911. They told me to keep everyone out." Or they might have if I hadn't hung up on them. "We can't contaminate the crime scene."

"Are you sure she's dead?" Pete asked. He was young and had only joined their work crew a few months ago, and right now he looked like a lost little boy.

I nodded. "Trust me." My chin trembled, and I took a breath, trying to hold it together. "I wouldn't be out here right now if I wasn't sure."

"What happened?" Billy asked, propping his hands on his hips.

"I don't know," I said. "All I know is there's lots of blood."

Tinker squinted his eyes and looked around. "Where's Max?"

This was where things could get dicey. "He's back with—"

"I'm here," Max said in a weary voice behind me. "I was sittin' with Ruth. It didn't feel right leavin' her alone, but then I realized I was possibly contaminating the scene." He walked past me, down the steps and toward the truck. He was no longer wearing the gloves, and I had no idea where they were.

He got into his truck through the still open driver's door. He rested his hands on top of the steering wheels, then broke into sobs.

I started to follow him but stopped, wondering if I should put more effort into keeping Franklin's crew out of the house, but I didn't have any fight left in me at the moment. It was like I was having an out of body experience as the reality of this nightmare finally started to sink in.

Ruth was dead, and there was every likelihood that Max was somehow involved.

Chapter Fourteen

Sirens sounded in the distance. Franklin's friends peppered me with questions, but I didn't respond, falling deeper and deeper into myself. Their voices blended together, blurring with Max's wails and the sirens.

One of the men led me over toward a tree and tried to get me to sit down, but I couldn't. I had to stay on my feet, although I had no idea why. My mind kept replaying the vision of Ruth's lifeless body on the bed, covered with blood. How had she been killed? Had she been shot? Stabbed? What had made her bleed that much? How much pain and terror had she endured before the end?

I began to sob. One of the men tried to wrap an arm around me to comfort me, but I shrugged him off and took several steps away from him. I needed space. The only person I wanted touching me was Marco, but I couldn't call him on my cell phone, and going back into the house was out of the question. All I knew was that I needed him, and the only way to get him was to call him. With that in mind, I headed for the road, planning to walk the half mile to Hank's house. I wasn't thinking about practicalities, such as the police needing to talk to me. I was only thinking about getting to him.

"Carly," Pete said, sounding confused. "Where you goin'?"

"I have to call Marco," I said, feeling dead inside while simultaneously feeling like I'd been torn open, my heart ripped out.

Billy stepped in front of me, worry on his face. He lifted his hands to stop me but made sure to not touch. "I've got a CB radio in my truck. I'll contact the sheriff station and get someone to contact Marco, okay?"

I considered it for a couple of seconds and decided that would work. "Okay."

"You come up here and sit in the shade, okay?" he asked softly. "Pete's gonna get you a cold bottle of water out of the cooler in the back of the truck."

I nodded and headed back toward the house. All three men fussed over me as they helped me find a good place to sit, and then one of them broke off to fetch the water.

The sirens were closer, and Max's sobs had grown quieter. My mind wandered, trying to consider the possibility that Max had killed her, but I quickly dismissed it. Even though I'd told him you never knew about a person, I knew Max well enough to know he wasn't capable of such a thing. Besides, he was even more torn apart by this than I was. Still, while he might not have killed her, he probably had some idea of who had. *Or they could have been after that file*, he'd said.

But what could be in a file full of spreadsheets? Something to do with his father?

A deputy's patrol car pulled into the drive, its lights flashing, but the siren had been turned off. A younger deputy got out, and Pete wandered over and shook his hand. The two of them conversed for several seconds, their voices too faint for me to hear, but I got the impression they knew each other.

The deputy's gaze shifted from me to Max, who was slumped over his steering wheel, spent, then he sauntered over to me. "Ms. Moore?"

I got to my feet, still holding the bottle. "Yes."

"I take it you're the one who made the 911 call?"

"Yes," I said, my tongue feeling heavy in my mouth. I took a sip of the water, my hand shaking. Water dribbled down my chin, and I used the back of my free hand to wipe it off.

"What did you find when you entered the home of the deceased?" He had kind eyes, and I focused on them.

"She's in the back bedroom," I said, pointing to the rear of the trailer. "On her bed."

"Was there anyone else inside?"

I shook my head, then furrowed my brow. "Wait. Are you asking if I found anyone else inside or if anyone went with me?"

"Both, I guess."

"Uh... Max went in with me. He busted down the door and I followed. We searched the trailer until we found her." My voice broke, and I took another sip of water. "Franklin wasn't in there."

"Franklin?"

"Franklin Tate. Her boyfriend. He lives here too."

The deputy nodded, shooting a glance at the door, but made no move toward it.

"Don't you need to go in there?" I asked, fresh tears filling my eyes. "Shouldn't someone be in there with her?" I couldn't stand the thought of Ruth being alone, even if I didn't want to be the one with her.

"I'm waiting for backup, ma'am."

I nodded.

"You're Marco Roland's girlfriend?" he asked softly.

I nodded again, then swallowed. "Yeah."

"He radioed me as I was pulling in. He said to tell you he'd be here in about ten minutes."

"Thank you."

Turned out that Marco beat the backup deputy. He bolted out of his car and took off in a run for me, only to start limping.

I headed toward him, worried. "Marco. Stop."

He pulled me into a massive bear hug, whispering in my ear, "Are you okay?"

I nodded, my cheek rubbing against his uniform. "Physically, I'm fine. But Max and I were the ones who found her. I think she's been dead for a few hours."

He grabbed my biceps and pulled me slightly away. "What makes you say that?"

"Obviously, I'm no expert, but the vacant look in her eyes." I shuddered at the memory. "It wasn't her anymore. There was nothing in there that made her Ruth."

"The coroner's on his way, so we'll know soon enough." He looked into my eyes. "What made you and Max come out here to check on her?"

"Franklin didn't show up at work, and Ruth wasn't answering the phone. I don't know…" I rubbed my forehead with the back of my free hand. "Something just didn't feel right. Franklin never misses work, and the fact that he didn't call in? It seemed suspicious. And we were right."

Marco rubbed my back. "I'm gonna go inside with Deputy Higgins. You good out here by yourself?"

"I'm not by myself," I said with a weak smile. "I've got Franklin's guys and Max. I'd rather you go inside and help find out who did this than stay out here with me."

He searched my face, probably looking for evidence I was telling the truth, then nodded. "Okay, but holler if you need me."

I nodded. "I will."

"One more thing," he said, lowering his voice. "Who went inside?"

"Me and Max," I said. "Max kicked in the door. It was locked when we got here."

His brow lifted. "Good to know." Then he turned and called Deputy Higgins to follow him inside.

I watched them walk in, Marco in the lead, and after a few seconds I went over to Max, who was still sitting in the truck, the door hanging open.

The devastation on his face nearly undid me again. I wrapped my arms around his shoulders, and he turned to face me, his legs hanging out the side. He hugged me back, and we held each other for several seconds before he said in a whisper, "I can't believe she's gone."

"I know. Me either." I hesitated, then said in a hushed tone so we couldn't be overheard, "Do you know who did this, Max?"

He pulled back a bit and looked into my face. Wariness filled his eyes.

I dropped my arms and took a half step back. "Did you find the file you were looking for?"

"No."

"Do you think whoever killed Ruth took it?"

"Maybe."

"It's that important?" I whispered. "What on earth is in that file, and don't you be telling me it's just spreadsheets?"

He rubbed a hand over his face, then looked down in his lap.

"Something that could get you into trouble?"

He nodded again.

Which meant he wasn't going to tell the sheriff's department. They'd be conducting their investigation blind.

Shit.

I turned away and ran my hand over the top of my head. I could rat Max out, but he'd stuck by me and risked himself countless times. I couldn't believe Max was capable of anything truly bad. I suspected he'd just been caught up in something that had spiraled out of control.

I turned back to face him. "I'm not going to say anything about the file to Marco or anyone else. This is between you and me. At least for now." Until I could figure out what she'd had and *then* make a determination.

The relief on his face was palpable.

Part of me still wanted to tell Marco, but my loyalty to Max was stronger in this situation.

"But I'm not letting it go, Max," I said still in a hushed tone, but my words were sharp. "You have to help me find out who killed her."

His eyes widened, but then something settled in him. "You really plan on keepin' this from Marco?"

God, I hated that part. "If that's what it takes to find out who did that to her, yes."

He got out of the truck and pulled me into another hug, resting his cheek on top of my head. "Thank you."

"Don't thank me yet," I said. "We have to find her murderer."

Marco came out of the house, his face pale. He limped down the stairs and moved toward us.

"Shit, his limp is bad," Max said under his breath.

"I know," I said. "They'll probably put him on desk duty. Which actually is where he's supposed to be."

Marco stopped in front of us and looked us over. "How are you two holdin' up?"

"Not great," Max said. "Ruth was like a sister to me."

"I know," Marco said. "And you can be sure we're gonna find out who did this to her. Got any ideas?"

Max shook his head. "None. Ruth may have rubbed people the wrong way, but not enough for anyone to kill her."

"And no sign of Tater?" Marco asked.

"No," I said.

"What made you bust down the door?" Marco asked.

"I just knew in my gut that something was wrong," Max said, tearing up again. "I knew I needed to get to her as soon as possible." His voice broke. "But it wasn't soon enough." He took a breath. "Do you know how they killed her? We didn't touch her."

"That was good thinkin' in what had to be a mind-numbing experience," Marco said. "We've got a forensics team on their way, along with the coroner. We should have a better idea once the coroner gets a look, but until we get some photographs, we're not touchin' her."

I nodded.

Marco turned and squatted until we were eye level, then ran his hand up and down my bare arm. "How are *you* doin'?"

"Better now," I said. "Admittedly, I didn't do so well after we found her."

"That's to be expected." He stood upright and glanced back at the trailer. "If you two want to go home, or somewhere together, we can take your statements later. *I* won't be able to take them, but I'll try to get Detective White," he said. "Carly, I figure you'll be comfortable with her since you've dealt with her on some previous cases."

"Okay," I said, looking at the trailer. It didn't feel right to leave Ruth, but I didn't really want to stay either.

"We'll go," Max said. "I don't think it will do either of us any good to stick around."

"Will you keep an eye on her?" Marco asked. "For all we know, someone's targeting your waitresses."

"That seems like a stretch," I said.

Marco's jaw tightened. "Maybe so. But I'd rather err on the side of caution. I don't want anything to happen to you. Your father is enough of a threat. I'd prefer for you not to be alone."

I remembered part of my talk with Ruth the day before, and my heart skipped a beat.

"I'll take her home with me," Max said. "I'll shut down the tavern indefinitely."

I stared up at Marco, and fear filled his eyes when he saw the look on my face. "What?"

"I told Ruth a little bit about who I am. Not my last name or many details. But I admitted I was running from my father, who was capable of bad things. What if someone killed her to get that information?"

Marco ran his hands up and down my arms. "Okay, let's look at this logically. If someone was looking for information about you, they'd be far more likely to go after me or Max or Hank. I highly doubt that's the reason why she was killed. Especially since Franklin's missing too."

But was he just trying to make me feel better? Would Bart Drummond have had Ruth killed for knowing more than he'd like?

"I agree," Max said. "I think that's a stretch. I'll bet this is related to whatever Franklin's mixed up in, but you still shouldn't be alone. We'll head back to town and hang out in my apartment."

Marco studied his friend. "Thank you, Max. And I'm truly sorry about Ruth."

Max's face crumpled. "Me too."

Chapter Fifteen

Max and I were silent most of the drive back to town, but as we approached the town limits, he asked, "What am I going to tell Tiny and Ginger?"

I reached over and clasped his hand. "I'll tell them, if you like."

"No," he said, squeezing my hand and then releasing it. "It needs to be me."

Turned out that neither one of us had to say anything. They already knew. They were sitting at a table close to the kitchen, Ginger quietly sobbing as Tiny tried to comfort her, but his nose and cheeks were red from crying.

"Please tell us it's not true," Ginger said, lifting her face as we walked in.

"I wish I could," Max said, keeping his eyes downcast. "I wish to God I could."

"What are we gonna do?" Ginger asked.

"I don't know," Max said, heading behind the bar. "We'll stay closed for now. I have no idea when we'll re-open." He grabbed a bottle of whiskey and poured two fingers into a glass. "Don't worry about your missin' wages. I'll pay you." He downed the entire amount, then poured another.

So Max planned on getting shit-faced. I couldn't say I blamed him.

"We're not worried about that," Ginger said meekly, but I knew she and Junior lived paycheck to paycheck, so that wasn't exactly true.

"You both are free to go whenever you like," Max said, suddenly sounding exhausted. "Or you can stay if you like. Carly and I are gonna head up to my apartment and wait for the detective to show up and take our statements."

"You really were the ones to find her?" Ginger asked as she got out of her seat.

"Yeah," I said, choking back a sob. I wasn't sure I'd ever get the image of Ruth's lifeless bloody body out of my head.

Ginger rushed over and pulled me into a hug, then moved over to Max. "I'm so sorry," she said. "This shouldn't have happened to her."

Max looked like he was about to fall apart again, so I grabbed his upper arm. "Come on, Max. Let's head on up."

"We'll lock up," Tiny called after us.

Max carried the bottle and his glass up the stairs to his apartment, a loft space that was only partially finished but had lots of windows overlooking Main Street.

"Getting drunk isn't going to solve anything," I said after I shut the door behind me.

He plopped down in the middle of the sofa. "Maybe not, but it will help numb the pain."

I sat on the coffee table in front of him and held his gaze. "How old were you when you started drinking to numb the pain?"

His eyes narrowed. "I'm not an alcoholic."

"I never said you were." I took the bottle from him and sipped. "I was too stupid to realize alcohol would shut down my emotions. I could have been living in blissful numbness a whole lot sooner."

"And when would you have started drinkin'?" he asked, snatching the bottle from me and taking a sip of his own.

"Are you asking when I first experienced the kind of pain that makes a person want to be numb? Because eight seems to be too young to start drinking. Your turn."

He released a scornful laugh, then shook his head. "I don't know. I always remember feeling pain of one kind or another. Either physical or emotional. I started drinkin' at thirteen. Snuck it out of my father's liquor cabinet."

"Did it help?"

"Hell, no. Not in the long run, but at least it helped me feel better for a little while."

I took the bottle back and swigged another drink. "Are *you* feeling better yet? Because I'm sure as hell not."

"We've got a lot more to drink before that happens." He patted the seat next to him, and I moved over to the sofa.

I leaned my head back into the cushions, staring up at the unfinished ceiling. "You're gonna have to tell me what was in that file, Max."

He lifted the bottle to his lips and sipped. "I know. Let me get shit-faced first."

I reached over and snatched the bottle. "That's not gonna help. We can drink enough to help numb the pain, but we have to keep our wits about us. We need to find the person or persons who killed Ruth."

He turned to look at me, his eyes bloodshot and glassy. "What if her murder is my fault?"

"And what if it's mine?" I asked. "I asked her not to tell Franklin what I said about my past, but what if she told him, and he told your father?"

"You didn't tell her enough for her to be killed over it," Max said. "But if my father found out about the file..."

"You think he killed her?" I asked, because the same thought had occurred to me. "Or *had* her killed," I corrected, "because we both know he doesn't like to get his hands dirty."

Max grimaced. "Possibly. Or Bingham could have done it."

I sat up a bit. "Bingham? What the hell is in that folder?"

He snatched the bottle back and took a long chug before resting it on his thigh. "Proof that I've been launderin' money."

I gasped, unsure of what to say. Part of me was shocked, but then it all fell into place. All the free food and drinks he gave away. The numbers on the spreadsheets that were larger than they should be. All the hideous merch he'd bought a couple of weeks back. "Did Ruth find out and plan to turn you in?"

If so, Max would be a suspect. He'd definitely have a motive.

Releasing a short laugh, he rubbed the bottle up and down the top of his thigh. "Hell, no. She helped orchestrate it."

I let that one sink in. No wonder he let her get away with so much. She had something on him.

Crap. One more motive for murder.

"Who are you laundering money for?"

He pushed out a sigh, then took another sip. "My mother."

His mother? Where was she getting the money?

"How long has this been going on?"

"Since I took over the bar. She told me it was part of the job."

"Max..."

He snorted. "Don't you dare feel sorry for me. I put my own damn self here."

"I take it you haven't told Marco."

"God, hell no. In the beginning he would have found a way to help me cover it up. But now..."

"It's like we were saying. Despite how he's feeling right now, Marco likes the rules," I said quietly. "He's broken a few for me, and it's killed him."

"Which is one of many reasons I haven't told him. I don't want to put him in a difficult position."

"Me either."

He swiveled his head to face me again. "So we agree to keep this between us?"

"For now. To be reevaluated when necessary."

He studied me for a moment before nodding. "Okay."

"So Ruth took home a folder with spreadsheets?" I asked. "Why?"

"Last night I printed off the monthly reports and put them on my desk right before we closed. I was going to take them to my mother this morning, but Ruth saw the folder and said she'd do it."

"Do you know if she gave them to your mother?"

"No."

"Can you ask your mother?"

"I don't want to involve her in this yet."

"Shouldn't she know if Ruth was murdered over papers she was supposed to get?" Then I smacked his arm. "Haven't you ever heard of secure emails? Password-protected online files? Why in God's name were you printing them?" A new thought hit me. "Max! You don't even protect the spreadsheets on your computer! I see them all the time when I sit at your desk."

"And you've never thought a thing about it, have you?" he asked. "It would have been so much more suspicious if I'd kept them password protected."

I didn't exactly agree with that but decided not to contradict him. We had bigger worries. "Did Franklin know about this?"

"Ruth swore he didn't."

"But what if he found out? What if he found out and told your father?"

His eyes widened. "That would mean my mother could be in danger. Especially if my father has hard proof of what she's been doin'."

"You have to warn her."

He nodded, then walked over to the kitchen and picked up the cordless receiver of his landline. Grimacing, he placed the call and held the receiver up to his ear. "Hey, Mom. There's a situation."

He was quiet for a moment, then closed his eyes. "Yeah. It's true. Ruth was murdered, and Franklin is missing." He paused, then said, "No. I don't think he killed her. I think someone else did. Maybe someone hired by Dad." He took a breath. "She had the monthly file, Mom. And now it's missing. She didn't by any chance give it to you this morning?" He made a face. "No? Okay."

I could hear her yelling through the connection.

"None of that helps right now," he said with a sigh. "I'll let you know if I find anything else. You do the same." He stabbed the end button on the cordless landline and set it on his kitchen counter.

"She doesn't have it?" I asked, even though the answer was obvious.

He stared out the windows over my head for a second. "No."

"What do you want to do?"

He shook his head. "I don't know."

I decided to ask a question burning in my brain. "Where did your mother get money to launder?"

Pushing out a sigh, he moved closer. "Some of it is my dad's. Some of it is from some side venture she has goin' on."

"What side venture?" I asked suspiciously.

"Beats me. She tells me not to worry about it. Just launder it and put it in the bank account she set up. She's got some fancy financial thing goin' on with an account in the Cayman Islands."

"Max," I said insistently. "If you're laundering money for your mother, you have a right to know where it's comin' from." I took a breath. "I changed my mind. I think you should tell Marco."

"No way," he said, his eyes slightly wild. "I'm not putting him in that position."

I leaned my head back and stared up at the ceiling for a few seconds, thinking, then met his gaze. "How much money are we talkin' about?"

"About a hundred thousand a month."

My jaw dropped. "And you've been doing this since you took over the bar?"

"After Wyatt left the bar, she came to see me in Knoxville and told me she needed help to escape my father. She wanted to save up several million dollars, and then she said she'd escape. But she got sick, and she couldn't leave."

"And what's stopping her now?"

"She says it's unfinished business." He gave me a grim look. "I'm worried that unfinished business involves you somehow."

"Bingham has something she wants. All things considered, it might not have anything to do with your father at all."

His mouth twisted to the side. "We need to have a chat with my mother."

The front door pushed open, and Wyatt walked in with a dark look in his eyes. "I think I'll be joining you in that chat."

I jumped, startled by his sudden appearance. How much had he heard?

"How the fuck did you get in?" Max asks, turning to face his brother.

"I have a key."

"I changed the locks."

"Fuck the locks," Wyatt snapped, walking past his brother to the middle of the room and staring hard at me. "Ruth is dead, and I want to know what you had to do with it."

Chapter Sixteen

"What the fuck, Wyatt?" Max demanded, furious.

"I heard she was the one who found her," Wyatt said, flinging a hand toward me as he glared at his brother. "That seems a little suspicious given everything Carly has her hands in."

"I was with her, you dumbass," Max snarled. "We went out there to check on Ruth together."

"She can't keep her nose out of other people's business," Wyatt snapped. "Carly finally pissed off the wrong person, and Ruth paid the price."

I gasped at his accusation. Was he right? Had I gotten Ruth killed?

Max must have seen the horror on my face. "You're not responsible for this, Carly," he said emphatically. "If anyone got her killed, it was me."

Wyatt turned to his brother. "What the hell are you talkin' about?"

"This doesn't concern you," Max said. "Now get the fuck out of my building or I'll call the sheriff and have you arrested for trespassin'."

"What does this have to do with *our mother?*" Wyatt asked, still fuming.

Max propped his hands on his hips. "Who said it does?"

"*You did.*" Wyatt shook his head in disgust. He took a deep breath, then turned to face his brother, concern overriding his anger. "Are you in trouble, Max?"

My stomach dropped. Max was in trouble—deep, deep trouble—but I wasn't so sure his brother could be trusted with his secrets.

Max looked Wyatt dead in the eye. "If I were, do you seriously think I would tell *you*? After all the shit you've pulled? You were workin' with Louise Baker and Derek Carpenter!"

Wyatt stared right back at him for a beat, then lowered his voice and moved closer. "You have to trust me on this, Max."

"Like hell I do! You owe me answers about what you're doing and who you've been associatin' with before I can even *begin* to trust you." He took a breath. "Why were you working with Derek Carpenter?"

Wyatt remained silent.

"Where's Jerry's phone, Wyatt?" I asked with a deadpan expression as I got to my feet.

He turned to me as his mouth parted in surprise.

"I know you took it."

His face hardened. "You *suspect* I took it. Unless you have proof, you don't know shit."

I shook my head in disgust. "That phone has evidence the sheriff can use."

"That phone didn't have anything useful." A sardonic grin lifted his lips. "At least I'm presuming it didn't."

Max's face reddened. "You stole Jerry's phone?"

Wyatt glared at his brother. "And if you really know something about the circumstances of Ruth's murder, then you're guilty of the same damn thing if you don't spill your guts to the sheriff's department."

The men continued their stand-off for several seconds before Max turned away.

"What exactly are you suggesting, Wyatt?" I asked, narrowing my eyes.

"I'm not suggesting anything other than Max needs to tell me what he knows."

"And let me guess," Max said, his tone bitter, "you'll still tell us nothing."

Anger flared through me. "You said you'd work with me, Wyatt Drummond. That was the condition for keeping your involvement with Carpenter from the sheriff's department." I lifted my chin and locked eyes with him. "So tell us what you're up to."

He stayed silent, and it looked like Max was about ready to jump him, but then Wyatt walked over to a chair and sat down, leaning over with his forearms on his thighs.

Max reluctantly sat down next to me and waited.

Finally, Wyatt turned to Max. "I'm pretty damn sure Louise has proof that our father murdered a kid fifteen years ago."

"That's what she supposedly had in the safe deposit box," I said.

Wyatt gave a single nod. "But Lula got the contents, and now Todd Bingham has 'em." He shot me a glare. "Then again, you likely know that since you're such good friends with the asshole."

He'd been accusing me of being in Bingham's pocket for months. If he expected me to deny it again, he'd be waiting for kingdom come. I wasn't wasting my breath.

His glare sharpened.

"Who was the kid?" Max asked.

"I don't know her name or anything about her. Just that he had her murdered. I heard him talkin' to Carson Purdy about it years ago, right before Dad sold that baseball that led to my arrest."

Wyatt's *drunk driving* led to his arrest, but it didn't seem helpful to point that out.

"Wait," Max said, holding up a hand. "You knew that monster murdered a kid, and you didn't report it?"

"What the fuck good would it do if I didn't have any evidence?" Wyatt asked in disgust. "Let me finish. He told Carson that Louise Baker showed up at the house the day before her husband's death claimin' she had proof of something that could put him away. So Dad went out to their property to get it."

I turned to Max, my eyes wide with shock. This wasn't the story Hank had told me, but then again, he'd said Bart was already out on the Bakers' land when he got there, arguing with Louise about Lula's parentage.

"Did he say what the proof was?" I asked.

"No," he said solemnly. "But between what I overheard and what was on that video Jerry shot, I'm guessing it was proof he'd murdered the kid."

I wanted to throw something at him. He'd obviously watched the video, which pissed me off anew. "I want that phone back."

He lifted his brow. "I want lots of things too, but that doesn't mean I get to have them."

"Jerry left that phone for me," I snapped. "If he'd wanted you to have it, he would have left it for *you*."

Guilt filled his eyes, and he glanced down at the coffee table.

"Arguing about a damn cell phone isn't gonna bring Ruth back," Max said, his voice tight.

"Whatever's on the cell phone isn't gonna bring her back either," Wyatt said.

"Well, how would I know since you've obviously stolen it and kept it for yourself?" Max said dryly.

"You're the one who just said arguing over it wouldn't help," Wyatt said in frustration. "I have one goal. Put our father away. That phone had the potential to help me do that."

I closed my eyes, already sick of Wyatt's games. "We need something that *can* help us find Ruth's killer. Are you holding on to anything other than the phone and the contents of the box?"

Wyatt's eyes narrowed. "No. Are *you*?"

"No."

He studied me, distrust oozing from his pores. "You know, this partnership only works if we're honest with each other."

I lifted my brows. "Funny, I was about to say the same thing." Bottom line: I didn't trust him, not one iota. Which meant this partnership was *never* going to work.

"We're gettin' off track here," Max said in frustration. "And you're just disrupting things, Wyatt. You need to go."

Wyatt's eyes flew wide. "You think you can do this alone?"

Max seemed to consider him for a moment before he said, "Do what? *I'm* not doin' anything. I'm leavin' the investigation of Ruth's murder to the professionals."

Wyatt's eyes filled with shock and disbelief. "You expect me to believe you're turning what you know over to the sheriff?" He shot me a look of disgust. "To *Marco*?"

"What do you have against Marco?" Max asked, jumping in to defend him before I could. "He's a damn good deputy

Shades of Truth

and detective, even if he doesn't hold that title yet. And he's been a far better brother than you ever considered bein'."

Wyatt drew in a sharp breath. "You really believe he's a better brother? Over your own blood?"

Max's back sank, vertebrae by vertebrae, as his eyes filled with tears. "You always made it clear that you thought you were better than me. You always sided with Dad over me."

Wyatt leaned forward with a pleading look on his face. "I was a fuckin' idiot, Max. I *did* think I was better than you. Then I went to prison and realized the truth—*you* were the better person. When I came back, I couldn't believe you'd stepped into the shoes that I'd left. That you'd been a hypocrite all along. You weren't better than me. We were just the same."

Max jerked upright. "Is this your way of sweet-talkin' me?" he asked sarcastically.

Wyatt sat up too, scrubbing a hand over his face. "I'm not sayin' this right."

"You think?" Max sneered.

Dropping his hand, Wyatt gave him another pleading look. "That's why I ignored you when I came back. I hated the person I'd been and, in my eyes, you'd become me." He leaned forward again. "But after the whole mess with Seth and then Lula, I realized I'd been wrong. You hadn't stepped into my shoes. You were trying to forge your own path while walking a delicate tightrope between our parents."

Max remained silent.

"Look, Max." Wyatt scooted forward on his chair. "I'm tryin' to make our father pay for what he's done to this town. To innocent people. To *us*." He reached over and put his hand on Max's knee. "We want the same thing, and our best chance of success is workin' together." His eyes leveled with Max's. "You know something, Max. Let me help you."

Max held his gaze a few seconds, then pushed out a breath. "How do I know I can trust you."

Wyatt squeezed Max's knee. "I would never hurt you, Max. I only want to help."

I could see Max caving, and I nearly snorted, but then I realized I had no right to judge. For all Max's talk about his employees being his family, in that moment, I knew that what he really craved was his brother's love, support, and respect. He was going to fall for Wyatt's pleas, and while Wyatt seemed genuine and I did believe he wanted a relationship with his brother, I also suspected him of having selfish motives.

Which still made him untrustworthy.

"Why all the secrets?" I asked in a clipped voice.

He turned to me, his expression blank. "What?"

"You said after Seth and Lula you knew he wasn't you. Why keep secrets from him after that? Why not tell him your plan?"

"Because I didn't trust *you*," he said, his eyes hardening. "You've been playin' into Bingham's hands. He may be our father's enemy, and we might be his wife's newly discovered brothers, but make no mistake: he bears no love for us."

Outrage filled Max's eyes, and he jumped to my defense. "If you think Carly—"

"No," I said calmly, holding a hand out to stop Max but keeping my eyes on Wyatt. "I know Wyatt's your brother, and you need to decide for yourself what you're going to do, but as for me..." I released a bitter laugh as I pierced Wyatt with a glare. "If you truly believe I'm that stupid, this will never work." I got to my feet. "And because I'm not stupid, I'm not falling for your pretty little story."

His face tightened with anger.

"You show up here with the tiniest bit of information, something that is no real revelation." I leaned over slightly.

Shades of Truth

"We both saw the damn video, Wyatt, meaning we both know what was supposedly in that safe deposit box. You didn't show up with anything new. You're just tryin' to find out what else I might have so you can use it for yourself."

He got to his feet too, towering over me. "You don't have shit."

"You have absolutely no idea what I do or don't have," I said in disgust. "You're trying to rile me up so I'll spill my guts. But *you* are the one who needs to prove you have information worth sharing." I put my hands on my hips. "What happened to Seth's videos?"

His face paled, and I saw panic in his eyes for a brief second before he covered it with a look of disgust. "You know what happened to them. They were erased. Stolen, I presume. We concluded that months ago."

"No," I said in disgust. "*You* concluded it and convinced me to believe you. Like an idiot, I did."

Max jumped to his feet. "What videos?"

I kept my gaze on Wyatt. "Seth had an online account with multiple videos. I don't know what was on the others, but in the last one, he'd set up an internet camera in your motel, hoping to get video proof of who'd supplied his mother with drugs. He had the code written on his arm, and with his dying breath he asked me to give it to his grandfather. I swore to him and then to Hank that justice would be done. But I trusted Wyatt and let him help me, while he was just scooping up what I found and using it for his own purposes. He offered up an email address Seth used, one only Wyatt knew about, and using that and the code, we managed to access the account on the computer in your office. There were multiple thumbnails for videos, and we watched the last one— the one where Carson Purdy's men found Seth in the room and dragged him out. Wyatt said he had cloud storage, and we set it up to download all the videos so we could take them to the state police, but he wanted to wait until after the funeral." I took a breath. I couldn't believe I'd been so stupid back then. "Then, lo and behold, the videos were magically gone, and the files we downloaded to Wyatt's account were inconveniently corrupted—not that I ever saw evidence of that for myself. I was too stupid to think he'd lie to me, so I believed him. But they weren't gone like Wyatt claimed. He took them."

"Is that true?" Max demanded.

Wyatt remained silent.

"You claim to have loved that boy," Max said, his voice breaking.

Wyatt's face was devoid of emotion. "Purdy had been killed, and Bingham took care of the rest. You didn't need those videos."

"But you *did?*" Max asked.

"What does it matter?" Wyatt asked, suddenly sounding exhausted.

"*Are you shittin' me?*" Max demanded. He stared at Wyatt in horror. "Jesus. You're worse than I imagined."

Wyatt's face hardened.

"Your brother also told me that he'd work with me to bring down your father," I said, "but he never followed through. He told me he was protecting me, but he was really protecting himself."

Wyatt didn't respond, keeping his gaze on his hands.

"Then Wyatt just happened to show up moments after Derek Carpenter ran me and Marco off the road, although he presumably didn't show himself until *after* he snatched Jerry's cell phone from the cab and set the truck on fire. That's when he said he'd work with me if we didn't tell the sheriff about his involvement with Carpenter." I shook my head in disgust. "He's lied to me from the beginning, and he's *still* doing it." I shot daggers of hate at Wyatt. "I don't trust a single fucking word that comes out of your mouth anymore, and I'm not telling you another damn thing."

Max's hands fisted at his sides. "Get out," he said in a tight voice.

"Max," Wyatt pleaded.

Max turned to him, regarding him with horror. "You did the exact same thing when we were protectin' Lula last December. You collected as much information as you could, sharin' just enough of your own to make it look like you were in it with us, when you were in it for yourself." Max cocked his head, staring up at his brother in confusion. "Why? What's your end game?"

Wyatt's face flushed with anger. "You both already know. I'm trying to bring down our father."

Max shook his head. "No. There's more to it than that."

"Why can't that be enough?" Wyatt asked. "Why can't destroyin' the man who destroyed me be enough?"

"No," Max said, his voice sad. "There's more, and you're just not tellin' us. Until you can tell me what your end goal is, we're done."

"You can't be serious," Wyatt snapped.

"Deadly," Max said, but there wasn't any heat in his voice. Only disappointment.

"You can't break this on your own," Wyatt said, obviously trying a new tactic.

"I'm not on my own," Max said. "The person I'm teaming up with has a much better track record than you."

Wyatt shot an ugly look at me and started to say something, but Max cut him off. "We're done here. You can show yourself out."

He lifted his chin. "Not until I find out why you need to talk to Mom."

"It's a question about Sunday dinner. I want to know if we're having steak or ham."

Wyatt looked pissed, but he took a step backward toward the door. "Don't do this, Max. Don't choose her over me."

Max let out a grunt of incredulity. "You're so far goddamned gone, you can't see that you're the one choosin'. Get out."

Wyatt looked like he wanted to protest, but he must have seen the futility of it because he turned around and left, slamming the door behind him.

Chapter Seventeen

"Is all that video shit true?" Max asked, his voice breaking.

"Yeah."

He collapsed onto the sofa, leaning his head back and staring up at the ceiling.

I sat carefully next to him. "What do you think he's up to, Max?"

His lips pursed. "I think he's goin' after Dad's position."

I stared at him in shock. I never saw that one coming.

Max sat up and grabbed the whiskey bottle off the table, taking another swig. "Think about it," he said after he swallowed. "He was born and bred for that position. Why wouldn't he want it? And what better revenge than to steal it?"

"Max…" I said in shock. "I don't know…"

"He knew Seth was goin' after the people who supplied his mother with drugs, and instead of discouraging him, he let it happen so he could make use of the information."

I shook my head. "No. I don't believe that. He genuinely cared for Seth. He seemed devastated by his death."

Max turned to face me, a hard look in his eyes. "That's because he never intended for Seth to get killed. He probably thought the boy's youth would protect him."

"He said he didn't know what Seth was up to," I protested. "He said he would have stopped him."

He gave me a withering look. "And we both know he doesn't lie."

The truth of his words burrowed into me. Hadn't he lied about those videos? Wyatt Drummond was a charming man when he wanted to be, and he knew how to make a lie sound true. Just like his father.

Max got to his feet. "I'm gonna make sure he left and deadbolt the door so he can't get back in."

"What if he bugged your apartment?" I asked, feeling like a conspiracy theorist, but the sense of foreboding was there, undeniable. "Or the tavern for that matter?"

"What?"

"Think about it," I said, sitting up. "How did a sixteen-year-old kid know how to bug a motel room to collect information? Especially in a town that doesn't have internet?"

Max cocked his head. "You think Wyatt's the one who put him up to it in the first place?"

It was hard to imagine him doing it intentionally. I'd seen good in him, or at least I thought I had, but maybe he'd given him the information inadvertently. Or he'd thought he would use it for a less dangerous stakeout. "I don't know, but he thinks you know something about your mother, and he wants to know what it is. I wouldn't put it past him to keep tabs on this place."

Max's eyes flew wide, and he spun around and bolted out the door and then down the stairs.

Shit.

I ran after him, reaching the bottom of the stairs just in time to see the back door bang shut. Max pushed it open an instant later as he raced out behind Wyatt.

I ran to the office and saw the computer tower missing, loose cords sprawled across the desk.

Double shit.

Wyatt had just stolen evidence of Max's money laundering.

I heard squealing tires out back and ran out the back door in time to see Max's truck tearing out of the parking lot. After Ruth's murder, it felt like a bad idea for the two of us to split up, so I ran out to my car to try to catch up to him, even if I had no idea which direction they'd gone.

Crap. We'd both been drinking, and even though I didn't have a buzz, Max had drunk a whole lot more than I had. He was also agitated enough that he shouldn't be driving, between what had happened to Ruth and our confrontation with Wyatt and those files...

I slid into the driver's seat and shut the door, trying to figure out what to do. I needed to find Max, but I had no idea where to look. Wyatt's? If that's where Max was going, was it safe to follow him there?

Should I call Marco?

I felt the rightness of the idea down to my bones, and I was about to get out of the car to call when the passenger door opened, and Louise slipped into the seat, bringing a stench of BO with her.

"Did you get it?" she asked gruffly.

I stared at her in shock. "Where have you been?"

"My whereabouts don't concern you, you stupid fool. Did you get what was in the box?"

"No. I did *not* get it."

"Why the fuck not? I heard you found the toolbox, and it held the key!"

I turned in my seat to face her, not in the mood to deal with her shit. "Are you kidding me? It was in Lula's name. She went to the bank, and Bingham took whatever was inside."

"Fuck," she said with a snarl. "I trusted you to get it."

I snorted. "Then that was your first mistake." I looked her up and down, not surprised to see she was looking more haggard than the last time I'd seen her. "Lula is trying to get ahold of you." Not exactly a total lie, but I needed to find a way to arrange a Louise and Bingham meetup.

"Then why didn't she return any of my calls?"

"Because Bingham deleted your number. If you give it to me, I'll slip it to her."

Her eyes narrowed. "So you can give it to just anyone? I'll pass."

"Wouldn't you like to see what she wants?"

"She had her chance. Too late now."

So why was Louise still in town? Did she think Bart was going to give in to her previous demands for one million dollars, or was she ready to hand over her information to the sheriff?

I decided to go a different direction. "How well did you know Ruth Bristol?"

Her eyes widened. "That bitch?"

"Well, that answers the question of whether you two were friends." Not that I'd thought it possible. I already knew Ruth couldn't stand her, although most of her dislike had been based on Louise's reputation, and that Louise thought Ruth had treated her daughter poorly at the tavern. Still, that didn't seem reason enough to kill her. After all, Louise herself treated Lula like dirt.

Still, while I had no reason to believe Louise was responsible for Ruth's death, I couldn't ignore that a lot had been happening in Drum since she'd come back to town a few weeks ago. It wasn't a stretch to think she might have been involved. Even if it was because of some kind of shitty ripple effect.

"What do you know about Franklin Tate?"

"Tater?" she asked with a laugh. "Not much."

"But you knew his nickname, so you know something." I paused. "Have you been watching Bart Drummond?"

She released a short laugh. "How would I be watchin' Drummond? I was barely allowed onto his property to pay him a visit after I got back from the pen."

"How'd you get Wyatt to work with you?"

Her body stilled, and a slow grin spread across her face. "You know about that, huh? How'd you get him to tell ya? You sleep with him? He's got it bad for you. Told Derek he could scare you, but he wasn't allowed to touch ya."

I'd already suspected Wyatt knew about Derek's visit to Marco's cabin, but this confirmed it. Of course, Louise might be lying—she seemed like the kind of person who would lie just for the sake of lying—but I didn't think so.

"Why would Wyatt want to work with you?" I asked.

"You mean why would he stoop into the gutter?" she asked with a bitter laugh. "He suspected I had something on his father. Started comin' to see me in prison. Said he wanted to help me once I got out. He said maybe we could work together to get revenge on the man who'd put us both behind bars. I told him we might be able to come to some arrangement. Of course, I had Derek waitin' for me, but I had room for two men in my life." A salacious grin lit up her eyes. "Of course, neither one of them really wanted to work with the other, but they settled down after a while. Until Derek bit the dust."

"Are you still workin' with Wyatt?"

She gave a sharp shake of her head. "Don't trust him. We may have the same goal, but I came to the realization that we had different ideas of how to achieve our ends."

"You mean he wasn't okay with committing murder?" I asked.

She laughed. "You got him on some kind of pedestal? He'd kill a man in a heartbeat if he thought it would serve his purposes." She made a face. "He just happens to have some hard limits I don't."

"What did you have in that box, Louise?"

Snorting, she said, "You really think I'm gonna tell you and risk losing my payout?"

"You really think Bart's gonna pay you a million dollars?" I asked in disbelief.

"I might not get a million," she admitted. "But I might get half a million. Or even a quarter million." A smug grin lit up her eyes. "I'm open to negotiation."

"That's great," I said. "Good for you, but I'm not sure what it has to do with me."

"Funny you should mention that," she said, leaning a bit closer, and it was even more apparent her body hadn't come into contact with a bar of soap in a while. "I'm gonna need your help with the negotiations."

"You expect *me* to negotiate with Bart Drummond for *you*?" I shook my head. This woman was out of her mind. "First of all, even if I wanted to negotiate for you—and believe me when I say I don't, because I *really, really* don't—I have no idea what you have on him, which makes me an ineffective negotiator."

"I'd give you just enough information that he'd believe you," she said.

I knew I should kick her out of my car, yet I really wanted to know what was in that safe deposit box. "Then what's to stop him from killing me on the spot?"

She shrugged. "Nothin', I guess, and if you don't come back to your boy-toy, I'll know you got killed."

"Gee, thanks."

She shrugged again.

"Do you have evidence that Bart murdered a child?" No sense beating around the bush.

"Was it one of his illegitimate children?"

Her mouth twisted into an amused smirk.

"Look, I'm not stupid enough to be fooled by the little facial twitches you have going on," I said, motioning my hand in a circle in front of her face. "Presume I can't see a thing and verbally tell me."

"You wearin' a wire, Carly Moore?"

I snorted. "No, but I'm done playing guessing games. Answer my questions or get out."

She burst out laughing. "You're a trip, Carly Moore."

"While I've been called many things, I'm pretty sure that's one thing I haven't been accused of."

She settled down and looked at me with a new appreciation. "Yeah, he killed one of his bastards. A baby. I've got proof he did this one himself."

I couldn't stop my gasp, and a satisfied smile curled her lips. She loved that she'd shocked me. I needed to remember that she lived for other people's reactions. Still, her news was worthy of a gasp.

But she was also a known liar, and I'd do well to remember that too. "I've searched the records—death certificates and news reports—there's no record of a child being murdered around here fifteen years ago."

"Maybe it weren't around here," she said. "Bart was known to wander to other places."

Like Knoxville and Chattanooga.

She leaned closer and lowered her voice. "Then again, you're thinkin' like an outsider. Not all births are recorded around here."

I knew that kind of thing had happened decades ago, but it seemed pretty unlikely now...or even fifteen years ago. "You're telling me that this birth—and death—wasn't recorded?"

"Not if the mother was trying to hide it from the world." Her brow lifted. "Or its father."

I stared at her in shock. Had he really killed a newborn? Was he capable of it?

What wasn't he capable of?

She handed me a folded piece of paper smeared with dirt. "Take this to Bart Drummond. I'll be in contact to see what he says." She opened the car door and started to get out.

"And if I refuse?"

"Then you just might end up like Ruth Bristol and get shot to death." She grinned. "Not that I would know anything about that."

Then she got out and sauntered down one side of the tavern, heading toward Main Street and leaving me to wonder if she'd murdered Ruth after all.

Chapter Eighteen

Of course the first thing I did was open the paper. Three demands were written inside.
 1. *Now I want 1.5 million*
 2. *Bring it to the tavern tomorrow at noon*
 3. *Leave Bingham out of it.*
    Louise Baker

Had she lost her mind? She expected to do the transfer in the tavern during the lunch rush? As far as I knew, Max wasn't even planning to open the tavern.

But what if she'd killed Ruth precisely because she knew Max would close the tavern?

The blood rushed from my head. Surely Louise wasn't that cold and calculating? I took a breath, waiting for the lightheaded feeling to fade. No, this couldn't have been done by Louise, because if she'd killed Ruth for that purpose, where was Franklin? And if she took him, for what purpose? Even though I was fairly sure he'd met with Bart the other night, I couldn't believe he'd work with Louise *or* hurt Ruth.

Was I really going to meet with Bart?

She'd indicated she'd give me information to help with my negotiations. Did she consider her highly vague insinuation about him killing a newborn information? I sure didn't.

Besides, if I showed up on his property on her behalf, he was likely to kill me before I uttered a word. And dealing with Louise so I could achieve my own ends would make me no better than Wyatt.

No, there was no way I was doing this. Sure, she'd threatened to kill me, but she didn't scare me as much as Bart Drummond did. Besides, she was setting me up. She'd admitted she didn't expect to get one million, and in her note, she'd asked for more.

I needed to wait for Max or Marco to return.

I glanced at the back door of the tavern, debating whether I really wanted to go back in there and wait alone. I needed to be with someone who would have my back if the killer came for me next.

Hank.

***

Belatedly, I wondered if I should have called Marco from the tavern to let him know where I was going—and left a note for Max—but by then I was already couple of miles from the tavern, and I wasn't turning back.

Hank was on his front porch when I pulled onto his property, his shotgun propped up against the house.

He regarded me with a grim expression as I got out of the car, and I already knew he'd heard the news about Ruth.

I climbed the stairs and leaned my shoulder into a support post once I reached the top. "I take it you heard?"

Squinting up at me, he frowned. "I did. How're you holdin' up?"

I shook my head, unsure how to answer.

"Do they know what happened or who did it?"

I ran a hand over my hair and stared up the road. "No. Louise claims she was shot. Max and I were the ones who found her. I couldn't tell for sure, but there was lots of blood."

He did a double take. "*Louise?*"

"She paid me a visit right before I came to see you."

Once he processed my comment, he waved it away. "You can tell me about that part later. Let's go back to the other thing you said. You and Max found her?" he asked in surprise.

"You hadn't heard that part, huh?"

"No. Only heard she was dead, and Tater was gone." Then he added, "Nosy neighbors."

I pushed away from the post and headed for the front door. "I need to let Marco know I'm here instead of with Max at the tavern."

"Why aren't you at the tavern?"

"Long story."

I knew Marco wouldn't get a text or a voicemail, so I called the sheriff's station and asked them to let him know I was at Hank's. I figured it was official business since someone needed to take my statement, but hopefully I'd get to talk everything over with Max first. They told me they'd let him know. Next I called both the tavern and Max's personal phone and left messages telling him that I was at Hank's place, and he should join us.

After I hung up, I grabbed a glass of ice water and headed back out to the porch, my kitten, Letty, shooting out the door with me.

I sat in the chair next to Hank's, and Letty jumped up into my lap. I stroked the back of her soft head as I stared up the road in the direction of Ruth's house.

"Wanna talk about it?" Hank finally asked.

"Talk about what?" I took a sip of my water and set it on the table.

"You just found one of your best friends murdered. Doesn't seem like a good idea to keep that bottled up."

"I'm not sure what there is to say." But that was a lie. There was plenty to say. I just wasn't sure if I should be saying it to him. Wyatt and Hank had been close—what if Hank had known Wyatt was after his father's power? But I was sure Hank hadn't known Wyatt's plan to use Seth. But then again, apparently, Wyatt wasn't one to share his playbook with his accomplices, only what he wanted them to know. I forced a grin. "You're not a touchy-feely kind of guy, Hank."

His smile was full of worry. "Maybe not, but *you* are, girlie."

His concern brought tears to my eyes. "I *want* to trust you, Hank."

I worried he'd be offended, but he looked resigned. "Carly, I know it's hard to trust that an old dog has changed, but I'm not in a power grab for this county. I'm too old and tired to run it. I just want to make sure the people are left in good hands." He held my gaze. "You can trust me."

I really needed to believe that. "What if I told you that Max thinks someone else entirely is after Bart's power? Someone we never considered?"

His brow furrowed. "Who?"

I took a deep breath. "Wyatt."

His eyes flew wide. "*Wyatt?*"

His reaction was genuine enough I believed he hadn't had a clue. "He's known for years about the kid his father supposedly killed fifteen years ago. He visited Louise in prison hoping to get information about it. That's why he worked with her after she got out."

He shook his head. "No. He'd never do that."

"He did, Hank. He admitted it."

His face paled. "Seth."

I set Letty on the floor, then got out of the chair and dropped to my knees at his feet. "The videos, Hank. Wyatt and I looked at the last of Seth's videos together. Then the videos were deleted from the storage website, and he let me think Max's cook Bitty deleted them." My voice broke. "It was Wyatt, Hank. And he said the files he downloaded to his storage cloud were corrupted, but he still has them."

"What?" he gasped.

"I think that's why he paid for Seth's funeral. He used Seth to get information, but he never expected him to get killed. He felt guilty."

Hank's body began to shake. "Are you sure of this, girlie? You have proof?"

"Max and I interrogated him about it. He said it didn't matter. That Carson Purdy is in jail and Bingham killed the other men who were involved. He looked pretty upset when Max realized the truth."

"You sure he's after his daddy's seat?"

"He wants his father to pay for what he's done."

"Those two things are very different."

"Agreed," I said. "It's speculation, but Max is certain of it."

"Where's Max now? He should be stickin' with you."

"He kicked Wyatt out. We started discussing everything we'd learned, and Max realized Wyatt might be searching for information in his office downstairs. And he was." I squeezed Hank's hand. "Wyatt stole Max's computer, and Max ran off after him."

His eyes narrowed. "What's on Max's computer?"

I was trusting Hank with my own secrets, but could I risk trusting him with someone else's? It wasn't my secret to share, but it was likely tied to Ruth's death, and I needed Hank's help now more than ever since I couldn't discuss this with Marco. "Proof that Max was laundering money."

"Sweet Jesus." He wiped his mouth as he glanced up the road. "I take it Ruth knew."

It wasn't a stretch for him to figure it out. He knew that Ruth ran things at the tavern. "Yeah."

He nodded, still not saying anything, just processing. "Who was he launderin' for? Bingham?"

"No, his mother."

He turned his surprised gaze to me.

"Max says some of it is siphoned from his father and the rest is from a side venture." I held up a hand. "And before you ask, Max claims he doesn't know what it is. He's been laundering money for her since he came back and started running the tavern. That's how she got him to come back. She guilted him into it, saying she needed the money to leave his father."

"How much money are we talkin' about?"

"About a hundred thousand a month."

His mouth dropped. "Where in the hell is Emily Drummond gettin' that kind of money?"

I shook my head. "I have no idea, and apparently neither does Max." I grimaced. "There's something else you should know: Ruth had a file with a bunch of spreadsheets in it, proving what they were up to. She was supposed to give it to Emily, but when Max and I got to the house, the file was nowhere to be found. And Emily says she never got it."

"So you and Max think Ruth was murdered for the file?"

"Possibly."

"And who would have stolen it and killed her?" he asked.

"Bart? Maybe he somehow found out that Emily was stealing his money. Todd Bingham's a possibility too, for who knows what reasons. And Franklin's a suspect too, since he's missing, but that one seems more unlikely to me. He loved her."

"Men kill the woman they love every damn day of the week," Hank said. "And we know he's been meetin' with Bart in secret." He pushed out a breath. "So whatcha wanna do?"

"What do you mean?"

"I know you, girlie. You're not gonna let this go. Are you wantin' to look for Ruth's killer?"

I started to answer him, but I cut myself off at the sound of a truck engine approaching us. I whirled around and saw Max pull into the driveway and park crooked in front of the house.

"Is he drunk?" Hank asked with a frown when Max nearly fell out of the cab.

I got to my feet. "Probably. He had several shots of whiskey before he took off after Wyatt."

Hank made a sound of disgust, then grabbed his crutch and pushed out of the chair.

"I didn't get it, Carly," Max cried out as he walked toward the porch steps. "He got away." His voice broke, and he released a soft sob.

Frowning, Hank mumbled, "I'm gonna make a pot of strong coffee. We gotta get him sobered up before the police show up to question him and realize he's been driving drunk. Or they take his statement and he blurts out the wrong thing." Shaking his head a little, he went into the house.

I walked down the stairs, intercepting Max, and he engulfed me in a hug and leaned his weight into me. "I'm fucked, Carly."

"No," I said, squeezing him tight. "Wyatt won't screw you over. You're his brother."

"But he might not care about protecting Mom."

"Well..." I paused, unsure of how to answer. "He loves your mother too. Last November he led me to believe he'd come back to Drum to protect her. Now, he could have been lying, but I think he'll want to protect her too." Whether she deserved to be protected or not. "Come on. Let's sit down and get you sober before Detective White tracks us down and asks for our statement."

I helped him up the steps and decided he was more grief-stricken and terrified than drunk, although the alcohol definitely wasn't helping any.

Hank appeared in the open doorway, leaning a shoulder into the doorjamb. "You two need to get your story straight. But your statements can't be too identical, or it will look suspicious. You gotta use different terminology." He nodded to me. "Carly, girl. You go first. Tell me what you're gonna say in your statement."

I still wasn't one hundred percent sure covering this up was the right thing, but I also knew if Bart hadn't been the one to kill Ruth, he'd find out about the laundering scheme and once he did, his wife would soon be dead, not to mention Max's safety would be in jeopardy. There was no refuge in the sheriff's department. If Bart *did* murder Ruth, there was a strong chance he'd have his corrupt people get him off.

I glanced down at Max who'd lowered into my chair. "Just that Trixie asked me to cover for her because she had some intestinal issues and couldn't get ahold of Ruth. So I worked the lunch shift, and Franklin's crew came in saying he hadn't shown up to work and hadn't called in."

"And then what?" Hank prodded.

"I went to check on her because I'd visited her the day before, and she seemed a bit distant. Like something was worrying her."

"And what do you think it was?" Hank asked.

Shades of Truth

I narrowed my gaze. "Do you want me to actually tell you, or are you asking about what I plan to say to the detective?"

"Was she truly worried?" he asked.

"Yeah. But I think it was about Franklin and his truck. She said he refused to sell it to Bingham, and he hadn't gotten any money from his insurance yet. And she was the one working extra shifts to help get a new one."

"That's good," Hank said, pointing a finger at me. "Be sure to tell 'em that."

I glanced down at Max again, suddenly feeling another stab of guilt that I wasn't planning to tell them everything. And that I *was* planning to tell Marco everything.

"You wipe that guilt away," Hank said. "You know we can investigate this a whole helluva lot better than the sheriff can. Especially since we all know there's still corruption in that sheriff's department."

"You're gonna help find who did this?" Max asked.

"Damn straight," Hank said, then turned around and went back inside. "Carly, this'll go a lot faster if you help me carry out the coffee."

"I'll be right back," I said before joining him. Max just gave a slight nod.

I walked into the kitchen as Hank was pouring strong, dark coffee into an insulated mug. "We gotta get everything we can out of him while he's drunk," he said.

"What are you talking about?" I asked, shaking my head.

"He knows things about the Drummonds he's probably keepin' to himself. But he'll be more willing to talk if he's half-drunk."

"I'm not taking advantage of him, Hank."

"We need to know what *he* knows," Hank said insistently. "That's the best way to help him." Then he shoved the mug at me. "Come on."

With a sigh, I took the mug and we headed outside.

Letty had curled up in Max's lap, and he was stroking her back while he stared out at his truck.

I handed him the mug and sat cross-legged on the porch in front of him, still not sure how to approach this. "We need to find out who killed Ruth. Which means Hank and I have to know everything, Max. Everything."

He looked up at me with unfocused eyes. "I told you what I know, Carly," he said, sounding like he was about to fall asleep.

"Do you remember Ruth having any run-ins with Todd Bingham?"

He shook his head. "She had a healthy fear of him, but I don't think there were ever any problems."

"What about your father?"

Tears filled his eyes. "Same."

"Do you think your father did this?" I asked quietly.

He slowly shook his head. "I don't know."

"Do you know anything that could be helpful in bringin' your father down?" Hank asked, standing by the porch steps.

Max lifted his gaze. "I wish to God I did. I only just found out I have brothers and sisters out there, and my father may be killing them off. I don't know how he does his favors or who for. I don't know shit." Bitterness drenched his words. "But I'll bet everything I own that Wyatt's not as clueless as he leads us to believe."

"We'll be dealin' with Wyatt later," Hank said, his voice tight. He turned to stare up the hill. "I suspect we're runnin' out of time before they show up to question you both. We still don't have your story straight."

We decided that my story could remain unchanged right up through breaking in the door and finding Ruth. Max went with me because he'd noticed that Franklin and Ruth had seemed at odds the night before and that, coupled with Franklin missing work, had made him anxious. We found Ruth, then went outside to collect ourselves before going back inside to call 911. Franklin's crew had shown up while we were on the phone, and while I'd left to talk to them, Max had stayed inside for a short bit to make sure the men didn't come in and disturb the crime scene.

Max had sobered up enough that he no longer looked like he was about to pass out, and by the time Detective White showed up, he'd stopped crying. She took us into the house separately to take our statements, and when we were finished, she had us all sit in the living room together to ask us more questions. Max and I sat next to each other on the sofa.

As far as I could tell, she didn't seem suspicious of our statements, and asked us both if we'd noticed Ruth having issues with anyone at work.

"Trixie," I said, glancing at Max. "She and Ruth had been butting heads."

The detective cocked her head. "Butting heads? How so?"

"Well," I said carefully, "when I dropped by to see Ruth yesterday, she said that Trixie was trying to get her into trouble. We both had the impression that she was after our jobs, and we even joked that we weren't sure what she was going to do with both of our positions." I glanced over at Max and started to cry.

He reached out and took my hand.

"Do you think Trixie is capable of murdering Ruth?" Detective White asked.

"No," I said. "Surely not."

"She *did* call in sick today," Max said.

I stared at him in disbelief. "Because she had...gastrointestinal issues."

"That's what she claimed," Max said. "For all we know, it was her alibi."

I couldn't believe he was throwing Trixie under the bus like this. Did he truly believe she was capable of murder, or was he trying to distract the detective from the missing file? Was that really a good idea?

"I'll be sure to interview Trixie," the detective said. "Along with everyone else who works at the tavern. Do you have their numbers?"

"Yeah." Max dug out his phone and gave her the numbers.

"Have you found Franklin yet?" I asked.

She made a face. "This is an active investigation, Ms. Moore. I'm afraid I can't tell you."

Which meant it was a big fat no.

"What do you know about Ruth's relationship to her boyfriend?" she asked.

"They were mostly happy," I said. "They had their ups and downs like most couples, but they seemed to really love each other. Ruth was upset that Franklin had totaled his truck last week. She was worried about money."

"So she's been acting differently lately?"

I shot a glance at Max. Had someone told her about Ruth being cranky over the last week?

"Mr. Drummond?" the detective prodded.

He ran his hand over his head. "Ruth hadn't been herself at work for the past few nights. She was distracted."

"Did she say why?"

"I didn't really ask her," he admitted, "but I did know she was anxious about replacing Franklin's truck. She was

Shades of Truth

worried the insurance wasn't gonna come through. Then Tater—that's Franklin—he showed up after the dinner rush last night and they talked. When he left, Ruth looked upset."

"Do you know what they talked about?"

Max shook his head. "No. I didn't ask, but in my defense, she probably would have told me to go fuck myself." A wry grin spread across his face. "She's not a touchy-feeling kind of gal." He sobered. "Past tense. She wasn't." Tears filled his eyes.

"I know this has been a shock," Detective White said. "But I promise you we'll do everything in our power to bring the person responsible to justice." She reached into her jacket pocket and pulled out two cards. "In the meantime, if either of you thinks of anything else that might help, anything at all, even if it feels inconsequential, please give me a call."

We both nodded and stood when she did, then saw her out.

As soon as her car pulled away, Hank said, "Get your shit together. It's time to get to work."

Chapter Nineteen

"What are you talking about?" I asked.

"We need to find out what Tater's crew knows," Hank said, grabbing a messenger bag from inside the door, along with his shotgun. "Let's take Carly's car." Then he headed for my sedan and opened the door to the backseat.

"Well, then. I guess we're going to talk to Franklin's guys," I said. "Got any idea where we're going, Max?"

"We should check out Tinker's house first. I suspect they're all together like you and me, trying to make sense of it all."

That sounded reasonable. We piled into the car and took off down the mountain.

Hank picked up a paper from the console and opened it. "What the fuck is this?"

I shot him a surprised glance. "It's from my surprise visit with Louise."

"What?" Max croaked. "When was that?"

"After you took off with Wyatt. She hopped into my car and informed me I was her negotiator with Bart."

"Excuse me?" Max said while Hank scowled.

"She's still claiming to have evidence your father wants, even though Bingham supposedly has it. She handed me this note and told me to take it to him."

Max snatched the paper from Hank's hand and quickly scanned it. "What the fuck?" He crumpled it with his fist. "You're not goin' to see him."

"I had no intentions of doing any such thing." But I couldn't help wondering if Bingham would be interested in the now-wadded paper. Then again, did I really want to get into the middle of that situation? Even if I had a chance to see the box contents? I was pretty sure I had enough on my plate right now. "Louise can go to your father herself."

Hank motioned to the side of the road and told me to turn onto a one-lane drive. "He lives down there."

I cast a glance at Max, who was in the front passenger seat.

He shrugged. "He's right."

Glancing in the rearview mirror, I asked, "How do you know where Tinker lives?"

"His daddy worked for me, back in the day. Delivery guy."

Max looked just as surprised to hear this as I was.

When I got to the end of the short lane, Tinker and his crew came into view, sitting in lawn chairs under a tree with beers in their hands. Tinker was resting his feet on top of a cooler.

I parked the car, and Max and I got out at the same time, with Hank a few seconds behind us.

"You come over to crucify Tater?" Tinker sneered.

"If you're asking if we think Franklin killed Ruth," I said, taking a few steps toward them, "I'm not convinced of that at all. He loved her."

"And the other two of you?" he asked, his gaze on Hank.

"I'm just here tryin' to get answers for my girl," Hank said. "One of her best friends is dead."

"And you?" Billy asked Max.

"I don't know what the fuck happened," Max said, his voice breaking. "All I know is Ruth is dead and Tater is missing. And if Tater didn't kill her, then we need to find him and save him before they kill him too."

None of the men said anything.

We walked closer, and Tinker swung his feet off the cooler. "Any of you want a beer?"

Max reached out his hand and started to reply, but I said, "No thanks. We already got our drinking in today." I nodded toward the short pile of empty cans. "We got a head start, but it looks like y'all are catching up."

"Tater was a good man," Billy said, pointing two fingers that held a cigarette at me. "He wouldn't have killed Ruth."

"I'm inclined to agree with you," I said, "but who did?"

None of them said anything.

"Did any of you tell Detective White that Franklin and Ruth had been fighting?" I asked.

Everyone but Pete shook their heads. They all turned to face him.

"Pete?" Tinker grunted. "What did you say?"

"I had to tell them the truth!" he protested.

"You just made Tater look guilty!" Billy said.

"But if he did it—" Pete started to say, but Billy silenced him by throwing a partially full beer can at his head. Although Pete easily dodged it, he looked a little shaken.

Tinker wordlessly handed a new can to Billy.

I propped my hands on my hips. "Like I said, I don't think Franklin did it, but I don't know who did. Maybe if we all put our heads together, we can come up with something."

Tinker frowned, then downed the rest of his beer before crumpling the can and tossing it to the ground. "What do you wanna know?" he asked as he leaned forward and pulled out another can.

"Franklin's accident last week," I said. "What do you know about it?"

"Not much," Tinker said. "He said a black truck ran him off the road, but I checked out his truck. I didn't see any black paint on it."

"So you think he was really run off the road?" I asked, surprised he'd told me as much as he had.

"I don't know what to think. I confronted him about it, and he told me he wasn't sure why there wasn't paint on his truck, but it happened. I asked him why someone would target him, and he said he didn't know."

"We already know what Tater *said*," Hank snapped from behind me. "We want to know if *you* believe he was run off the road."

Tinker swore under his breath. "Hell, no," Tinker said. "I know he was lyin'. He's a terrible liar. We beat the pants off him whenever we play poker, and I could see he was lying through his teeth. He said the accident report was gonna say he ran off the road on his own, and he wasn't sure how he was gonna tell Ruth."

"How did he lose control of the vehicle then?" Max asked.

"He didn't say, but maybe he fell asleep. I know he's been staying up late doin' God knows what while Ruth's at work. I dropped by a few nights over the past couple of weeks, and he wasn't there. When I asked him about it, he said he was at the tavern, but I know for a fact he wasn't. I checked the tavern parking lot."

"Do you think he had a part-time job?" I asked.

"Doin' what?" Tinker asked with a snort. "There's barely enough jobs around these parts for him to have one job, let alone two of 'em."

"So where the hell was he?" Max asked.

"Beats the shit out of me," Tinker said.

"I think he was sleepin' with someone else," Billy said. "Only they wasn't sleepin'."

My mouth dropped open.

Max's hands fisted at his sides. *Tater was cheatin' on Ruth?*" He took a step forward like he wanted to beat the shit out of someone and was looking for a substitute since Franklin wasn't there.

"Tater wouldn't cheat on Ruth," Tinker said authoritatively.

"So where was he going at night?" Hank barked.

"We don't know."

"Where is he now?" Hank asked.

"We don't know that either," Tinker repeated.

"There's either a whole lot of stupidity sittin' around here, or there's a whole lot of coverin' up goin' on," Hank said. "Which is it?"

Billy got out of his chair, looking like he was about to rush Hank. "Did you just call us stupid?"

"No," Hank said matter-of-factly. "I think you're all a bunch of mangy, lyin' sons-of-bitches."

Tinker slowly got up from his seat. "You dare to come onto my property and insult me?"

Max grabbed my arm and dragged me to the side, out of the direct line of fire between Tinker and Hank.

Hank's face hardened. "We're tryin' to find Ruth's murderer, and you assholes are lyin' through your teeth."

"You expect us to tell you what we know so you can run off and snitch to Marco Roland?" Tinker asked.

The men turned to look at me and Max.

"This is our own investigation," I said. "Marco's not involved."

Tinker narrowed his eyes. "Why not?"

"Because *I* can do things the sheriff can't," Hank said. "Max and Carly want to find whoever murdered Ruth, so they're in this with me."

"Since when did you give a shit about Ruth?" Billy demanded.

"I have my reasons," Hank said.

Tinker studied him for a moment, then pressed his lips together. "This have to do with you findin' your missin' gold?"

"What does it matter?" Hank asked.

"It matters if we think you're gonna hurt our boy."

"I won't hurt your boy," Hank said, "as long as he didn't kill Ruth. And if he did…" Hank paused. "If he did, he deserves everything he gets. Now I'm gonna ask you straight: do you think Tater killed Ruth?"

"No," Tinker said without hesitation. "I don't."

"*We* don't," Billy said.

"Then you need to be straight with us," Hank said. "What was Franklin up to at night?"

"We don't know," Tinker said. "That's the God's honest truth."

"But you have some idea," Hank pressed.

All three men remained quiet.

"He was gettin' money from somewhere," Pete said, confirming that he was the weak link.

The other men shot him glares.

"What?" Pete said. "He was. And the old guy's right. If some asshole kidnapped Tater, then someone needs to get him back. The police aren't goin' to do shit."

Tinker cursed under his breath. "I don't know for sure what the boy was up to, but he suddenly had a lot more twenties in his wallet."

"Do you think he was runnin' for Bingham?" Hank asked.

"No," Tinker said. "Tater hated Bingham. There's no way he would have worked for him."

"What about Daddy Drummond?" Hank asked.

Tinker snuck a glance at Max.

"I hate my father," Max said with a snarl. "I'm not part of what he does and would gladly put him away."

Hank held Tinker's gaze. "So let's have it. Is he workin' for Drummond?"

"We done told you we don't know who he's workin' for, but he didn't have nothin' against Drummond, so he could be."

"Do you know anyone who might have had it out for Franklin?" I asked. "Anyone he pissed off recently?"

"No. Do you know anyone who might have had it out for Ruth?" Tinker asked in a snotty tone. "She wasn't the easiest person to live with."

"No one pissed enough to kill her and kidnap Tater," Max said.

"You really gonna try to find her killer?" Tinker asked, studying each of us in turn.

"I said I was, didn't I?" Hank snapped. "If you think of anything else, contact one of us." Then he turned around and headed back to the car.

I shot a glance at Max, and he gave me a look that said *I guess we're done here.*

We started for the car, but then I turned around to face Tinker. "Last winter, Ruth said she and Franklin had been saving up to buy a house. Do you know anything about that?"

His brow lifted. "Why're you askin' me?"

"It's just that she made it seem like they had a down payment saved. If they did, where did that money go?"

He shoved his hands into the front pockets of his jeans. "Beats me."

"Did you know anything about them having any money to buy a house?"

"Nope, but she might have gotten some of it when her mother died. She sold all her mom's shit."

"There wasn't no money," Billy said.

I gave him my rapt attention. "Then why did she think there was?"

"Because Franklin told her he'd saved it up for her. He knew she wanted out of that trailer, and he told her he'd won a Powerball. One of them low payouts—twenty grand. But he was scramblin' to figure out how to get it, because she'd been pushin' him hard to buy a house. Last winter he said he'd found an extra source of income, but he wouldn't say what."

Was that when he started meeting with Bart?

I gave him a short nod. "Thanks."

When I got into the car, I turned on the engine. "Where to now?"

"Back home," Hank said. "Now that we've talked to the three amigos, we need to sort through what we know."

"We know Tater was workin' with my father," Max said bitterly. "And he probably had Ruth killed."

"Maybe so, but we can't prove it," Hank said. "We have to prove either one of 'em."

"Not if we take care of it on our own," Max said, his words clipped.

"Vigilante justice?" I asked in surprise. "Against your father? That's a terrible idea. For a multitude of reasons. The most important being that Marco only presumed he met Bart.

What if it was Bingham? The resort property *is* close to Bingham land."

He was silent for a few moments as I headed back toward Hank's.

"Even if it wasn't Bingham meeting Franklin, I can't help thinking that Bingham is part of this somehow," I said.

Hank turned to face me. "What makes you think that?"

"Nothing concrete," I said. "He's just been so cagey lately. He's up to something, and we know Franklin has been doing something at night."

"With my father," Max said.

"We saw him meet someone we thought was your father once, but that doesn't necessarily mean that's what he was doing every night. We know he was headed out toward Louise's cabin when he had his wreck."

"You're right," he said darkly. "I have no idea what he was up to."

"So let's look at Bingham too. We know he's been researching the history of Drum, but I've never been able to figure out why. I don't believe he's truly interested in history. So what's he up to?"

Both men were silent as they considered it.

"His family has always been in dispute with my family over that portion of land where the resort is going in," Max said.

"But a judge already ruled on that," Hank said.

"Still. Maybe he's trying to find proof that it belongs to his family in those records from the past?" I asked.

"Maybe," Hank said. "But I don't think so. It's obvious he knows something about Bart. We just need to find out what it is."

"As unlikely as it seems, it might be about Rodney," Max said, shooting me a glance. "Carly's the one who put that together."

"Rodney?" Hank asked in confusion.

"Bingham's little brother," I said. "His death doesn't fit the twenty-year or fifteen-year timelines," I said, casting a glance at Hank. "Still…"

"Why would Drummond kill Floyd Bingham's son? And what does it have to do with the younger Bingham diggin' into the past?" Hank shook his head. "Seems too far-fetched to me."

I glanced over my shoulder at Max, and his expression told me that he wasn't ready to let it go either. The problem was, I wasn't sure where to search. Bingham wasn't about to offer up information for free—he'd made that clear.

Marco's deputy SUV was parked in front of Hank's house when I pulled onto the driveway. The driver door was open, and he was pacing next to the door with a corded radio microphone in his hand. As soon as he saw my car pull up, he said something into the microphone, then tossed it onto the passenger seat.

"Where the hell have you been?" he shouted as I got out of the car.

I stared at him in shock. I couldn't remember him ever shouting at me like that. But I saw the fear in his eyes, so I went to him and wrapped my arms around his back.

"I told you to stay at the tavern," he said in a harsh tone, but he wrapped his arms around me too, holding me so tightly I could hardly breathe.

"I left a message for you at the sheriff's station. Didn't you get it?"

"They told me you were at Hank's but nothing else."

"Max took off after Wyatt, leaving me alone at the tavern, which seemed like a terrible idea for several reasons, so I came to Hank's and then called the station right away."

He pulled back to study my face, worry lines covering his forehead. "What happened with Max and Wyatt?"

I offer him a tired smile. "I'll tell you later. Or Max can. He's getting out of the car. Are you off work?"

He nodded to Max who was walking toward us. Then he said, "No," shooting a glance at Hank as he emerged from the backseat. "But I wanted to check on you and see if Hank would be okay with you hanging out here. With Ruth's killer on the loose, I don't want you alone out at the house. We don't know who killed her or why. I know you think it's a stretch, but we haven't ruled out that they're targeting Max's employees."

I doubted it…unless Ruth really was killed because she knew about Max's money laundering. What if they thought I knew about it too? "How late will you be working?"

"Probably pretty late. Detective White has asked me to help her with the investigation." He searched my face for my reaction. "And since it's Ruth…"

I gave him another tight hug, then released him. "Of course, Marco, but you're supposed to be on desk duty."

"Walkin' around's good for me."

I knew he was going to do this, one way or the other, and I didn't really want to stop him. If we couldn't figure this out, there was no one I trusted more with it than Marco. Still, I couldn't help worrying. "Just be careful."

"I don't think I'm the one in danger, Care." Something in his tone caught my attention.

"Wait," I said, my breath hitching. "Do you think my father's actually involved? Why would he have Ruth killed?"

Even though I'd told Ruth a little about my past, it seemed unlikely. Other people knew much more than she had.

No, it made more sense that this was tied up with Max's money laundering, and it killed me that I was keeping the truth from the man I loved. The man who trusted me. But Max was hurting over Ruth's murder, and I knew he needed his best friend to help him through this. And Marco was going through his own issues—his leg and the death of the boy he'd been trying to help. Telling Marco about Max's crime had the potential to put a rift between them. Still, I'd tell Marco. It was just a matter of when.

"I don't know," Marco said, glancing over at Hank. "But I'm not taking any chances."

"I'll keep an eye on her," Hank said. "Don't you worry." Then he added, "But I think we should go to your house. Sure, someone might come lookin' for her there, but we need to look up some things on the internet."

Marco's mouth dropped open in surprise, and I was just as shocked.

"You want to look up something on the internet?" I asked.

"Not me," he said. "*You.*"

I nodded. I wondered what he had in mind but knew better than to ask in front of Marco. Guilt followed that thought like a steam engine.

"I'll go with them," Max said, finally speaking. "I don't feel like hangin' out at my apartment alone."

"I'd feel better with you there," Marco said.

I wondered how he'd feel if he knew we were keeping a huge secret from him.

My eyes teared up, and Marco pulled me into a comforting hug, my cheek pressed to his chest. "I know you're upset, but we'll find who did this. I promise."

But how could he if he didn't know everything?

I caught Max glancing at me, and from the look of desperation on his face, he knew I was wavering. So I forced out, "The sooner you get back to it, the sooner you'll get the bastard who did this."

Marco gave me a tender kiss. "Be safe, okay?"

"You too."

Then he walked over to Max and pulled him into a bear hug, holding him tight. "We'll find who did this, Max. I promise."

Max broke down into tears again, and I walked over to stand next to him, wrapping my arm around his back to keep him close.

Marco waved to Hank, got in his SUV, then turned it around to pull out onto the county road.

"What are you wantin' to look up, Hank?" Max asked as soon as Marco's vehicle was out of sight.

"Ruth."

"What do you hope to find?"

"I don't know, but I think y'all need to do a deep dive. Does she have any kin around?" Hank asked. "We can talk to them as well as her close friends."

"Her family's all gone," Max said. "And her closest friend used to be Trixie, but she and Ruth haven't been seein' eye-to-eye lately."

A curious look crossed Hank's face. "Why?"

"I don't know," Max said.

"I don't either," I admitted. "And I confess, I was so tied up with everything else going on that I didn't ask. But Trixie really did seem to be after my job or Ruth's. But surely she wouldn't kill Ruth to get her hours."

"She's been at the tavern for a few months. Do you think she figured out about the money laundering?" Hank asked.

Max shook his head. "I don't see how."

"You leave those spreadsheets open, Max," I reminded him. "She might have seen them."

"You saw them and didn't think a thing about 'em."

"That's not entirely true," I said. "I was surprised the tavern seemed to be taking in and spending so much money, but I never stopped to think about it. Maybe Trixie did."

"But she hardly ever went into my office," Max said. "And why would she need the folder when she could have easily copied the information onto a flash drive?"

"I don't know, but you're right. It is a weird coincidence that she called in sick today," I said, still finding it hard to believe Trixie would hurt Ruth.

Hank cocked his head to the side. "Y'all should go see her. Her friend was just murdered. Shouldn't she hear it from you instead of Detective White?"

I glanced over at Max, who shrugged. "The man has a point."

"I'll be goin' with you, of course," Hank said. "I promised Marco I'd keep you safe."

Would Marco be upset with me for going? I doubted it. Hank did have a point. Trixie and Ruth were friends for years, even if they weren't getting along at the end. She probably needed to see us for moral support. If we learned something that helped us find Ruth justice, all the better.

Chapter Twenty

Forty minutes later, we pulled up to Trixie's mobile home after we stopped at the tavern so Max could get her address from her employment paperwork. There was no sign of any sheriff deputies, so I wasn't sure whether anyone had stopped by to talk to her yet. But her car was parked in the gravel and hard-packed dirt driveway. Then again, if she was really having gastrointestinal issues like she claimed, I doubted she was going anywhere.

We got out of the car, and I took the lead as we silently walked up to the rickety-looking front porch. I knocked on the door. Several seconds later, I knocked again and we waited.

"Maybe she's not here," Max said, glancing around the mostly dirt front yard.

The door opened and Trixie appeared, her face splotchy and covered in tears. "Carly," she said, releasing a sob. "I can't believe it."

I pulled her into a hug. "How did you find out?"

"A sheriff detective was here about a half hour ago," she said into my shoulder, then lifted her head. "Detective White.

She wanted to know where I was this morning since I called in sick."

"I'm so sorry, Trixie," Max said from the bottom of the porch steps. "We would have come to you, but Carly and I were the ones who found her, and we had to hang around and give our statements."

Not entirely true, but hopefully she wouldn't find out we'd talked to Tiny and Ginger over an hour earlier.

She shook her head. "It doesn't matter who told me. All that matters is that she's gone." Her eyes bugged out. "Wait. Y'all found her?" Then she shook her head. "What am I thinkin'? Come on in." She took a step backward and opened the door wider.

Max and Hank came up the steps, and once we were all inside, Hank shut the door behind him.

"Yeah, we found her," I said. "Franklin's crew came in for lunch and said Franklin hadn't shown up to work or even called in, so I knew something was wrong. Especially after they said they'd called the house, and no one was answering. So Max and I went out to check…" My voice trailed off as another vision of Ruth slammed into me. I figured I'd let her figure out the rest.

"What happened to her?" she asked, fresh tears coming to her eyes.

Either Trixie was truly shocked by this, or she was an excellent actress. I was going with the former.

"Honestly," I said, "I'm not really sure. There was a lot of blood, but we couldn't see how she was murdered."

Trixie flinched. "Do they know who did it?"

I shot a quick glance at Hank, who was still standing by the front door. His slight nod confirmed he'd noticed it too.

Trixie gasped. "Where are my manners? Y'all have a seat." She moved over to an armchair and grabbed a tissue from a box on her coffee table, dabbing her cheeks then blowing her nose as Max and I sat on the sofa. Hank stayed by the door.

"You don't want a seat?" Trixie asked Hank around her tissue. "I can bring in a dining room chair."

"Don't mind me," Hank said. "My leg's cramped from sittin' in the car."

Trixie nodded, looking unsure, then turned to face Max. "Do they know who murdered her?" she pressed.

"We don't think so," Max said gravely. "They're still investigating, not that they're telling us anything. But Tater is missing."

Trixie's eyes widened. "What? Was he kidnapped?"

"Nobody knows," Max said. "That's the million-dollar question."

We sat in silence for several seconds before Trixie said, "I can't believe she's gone."

"How long were you two friends?" I asked gently.

Reaching over, she grabbed another tissue. "Since we were kids. We were like two peas in a pod when we were younger, but we drifted apart in high school."

"Why?" I asked.

"Things weren't goin' well at home with her mom, and she started hangin' out with some other people. But those other people didn't give a shit about her." Trixie sniffed and wiped her face with the tissue. "They dumped her soon after we graduated. Ruth and I became friends again, but it wasn't the same as before."

"She got you a job at the tavern," Max said.

"Yeah, like I said, we were friends, and she knew I needed work."

"Did you hang out with Ruth outside of the tavern?" I asked.

"With her schedule?" she asked with a laugh. "That was pretty damn hard."

I could feel Max's body stiffen, and I reached over to place my hand over his on the seat cushion between us.

Trixie's eyes widened. "I didn't mean anything by that, Max."

He shook his head. "Facts are facts."

"Do you know if she and Franklin were having any problems?" I asked.

Her eyes narrowed. "You know, that detective already asked me this stuff." She studied me for a moment. "You're lookin' for Ruth's killer."

"We're just asking questions," I said.

"You don't trust the sheriff to solve this?" Trixie asked. "What about Marco?"

"Of course I trust them to solve it," I lied. "But Max and I found her." I paused to let the lump in my throat ease. "We just want to know why. Why would someone do this? And who killed her? The fact that Franklin is missing is *very* suspicious, but none of us think he'd be capable of something like that. Of killing her."

"They always say that, you know," Trixie said, leaning back in her chair. "People—usually men—brutally murder their wife or girlfriend and their kids if they have them, and the people they ask about it afterward say things like 'he was the nicest guy.' Franklin's just like a long line of other men."

Max leaned forward, resting his forearms on his thighs. "So you think he killed her and took off?"

Her face turned splotchy, and tears fell down her cheeks. "It's the most logical conclusion."

"But why?" I pressed. "*Why* would he kill her?"

She released a bitter laugh, swiping at fresh tears with her crumpled tissue. "You really do fancy yourself a detective, don't you?"

"Did Ruth tell you anything about Franklin?" Max asked, a hint of impatience in his voice. "Were they fighting?"

Her eyes hardened. "Ruth didn't tell me shit." She flicked a glance at me. "Guess she didn't tell you either."

I caught Hank's subtle movement by the door and the wary look in his eyes.

"You got a restroom I can use?" he asked. "That damn diabetes medication makes me have to pee all the time."

That was a lie, which meant he was up to something.

Trixie turned to glance over her shoulder. "Yeah, down the hall." Then she turned back to face us.

Hank shot me a warning look before he made his way down the hall, his crutches making a squeaking sound in the silence.

"You havin' money troubles, Trix?" Max asked softly.

Her eyes widened. "What?"

"I know you were desperate for more hours."

She stared at him in disbelief. "Do you think I *murdered* Ruth to get more hours?"

"Of course not," Max said, and thankfully it sounded convincing. "I'm just sayin' you seem to be in a bad situation, is all, and I'm worried about you since the tavern's gonna be indefinitely closed."

Her face paled. "What do you mean it's gonna be indefinitely closed?"

"Carly and Tiny and me…" His voice faltered, and he took a second to recover. "We're too torn up about Ruth's murder. And it just seems wrong to open back up when her body's barely cold."

"You mean you're too busy tryin' to find her killer to run the place," she said in a cold tone.

Max stiffened again. "You don't want her killer found?"

"Tater murdered her and took off," Trixie snapped. "You plannin' on chasin' him down?"

"We don't know that he did it," I said, trying to cover my shock at her anger.

"Of course he did," she said. "When a woman is killed like that, the husband or boyfriend *always* did it."

I could see this conversation was about to plummet off a cliff, but Hank was still down the hall doing who knew what. I needed to find a way to keep Trixie talking.

"Do you know if Franklin was up to something?" I asked, deciding it was worth the risk to ask.

Her body froze. "What do you mean?"

I studied her face. "We've been talking about Ruth, but what if this is about Franklin?"

"What do you mean?" she asked again, looking caught off guard and also scared.

Damn it. She knew *something*, and we were obviously making her nervous. I didn't want to tip my hand, but maybe I could poke her into telling us something.

I leaned forward and lowered my voice. "Not long after I got to Drum, Ruth told me that she and Franklin were looking for a house. That they had saved some money. But they never bought one, and when I asked her about it later, she always blew me off. Do you know anything about that?"

Trixie shook her head. "She never mentioned it."

Based on the shock on her face, I believed her. "I know she was stressed about Franklin's truck and working extra shifts to help pay for a new one." I paused. "I just can't help wondering what happened to the money for the house." Of course I knew the truth, but she knew more than she was admitting to. Maybe this would poke something loose.

"Maybe she made it up," Trixie said, her eyes looking slightly unfocused. "If you were new to town, she might have said it to impress you."

Why was Trixie so quick to dismiss Ruth's story about her savings? She was becoming more agitated by the minute, but Hank was still down the hall, so we needed to keep her talking.

"Do you know how Ruth and Tater met?" Max asked.

She blinked. "What?"

"Do you know how they met?"

She stared at Max in disbelief before shifting her gaze to me. "You're tellin' me that *you* don't know?"

"I don't," I said.

A smug look filled her eyes, but they were slightly unfocused. "You know Tater was married to May McMurphy when they started hookin' up."

"I'd heard," I said carefully. Trixie had gone from devastated to haughty in a matter of minutes. There was something off about her, but I couldn't put my finger on it. She was starting to look pale and a little clammy. Maybe she really *had* been sick.

"They met at a bar in Ewing. Like Ruth didn't get enough of workin' at bars at your place, Max."

Max remained silent.

"I heard Franklin was a rebound for May," I said.

"You mean after Wyatt's girlfriend Heather disappeared." She reached for another tissue, her hand shaking. "Or should I say *was murdered*?"

"Except nobody knew it at the time," I said. Everyone had thought she'd left town after Wyatt's arrest, but it turned out she'd been accidentally killed by her friend. "May was one of her best friends. She was devastated, so she latched onto Franklin. They weren't even married for a year."

"Because Ruth stole her man."

"I don't think May necessarily sees it that way," I said. Actually, given the short conversation I'd had with May a few months prior, I was pretty sure she did, but I felt no need to tell Trixie that. "When I talked to her while investigating Heather's death, she seemed happily married with kids. All water under the bridge."

"Ruth isn't to be trusted," Trixie said, her words slurring.

"Ruth is dead," Max said more harshly than I'd heard him speak to someone who wasn't a threat at the tavern.

Trixie stared at him with unfocused eyes that turned watery. "Oh. That's right."

I shot Max *a what the hell is going on?* look.

"Trixie," he said, his voice calmer. "Have you been drinkin'?"

I knew why he was asking, but she hadn't smelled like alcohol when I'd hugged her.

She shook her head. "I took a couple of extra Ativan after the deputy left."

"What?" I gasped.

"How many, Trixie?" Max asked, getting out of his seat and kneeling in front of her.

"Two."

I turned to Max. "Should we be worried?"

"How the hell should I know?" he asked grumpily. "I don't know shit about drugs."

"Ativan's for anxiety," Hank called out from the back. "She has a bottle in her bathroom, and the dose is low enough she'll be fine."

Max stared up at me with raised brows. I knew we were both thinking the same thing. Hank Chalmers, the pot king, knew about controlled substances. But then determination filled his eyes, and he turned back to Trixie, who was now slumped back against the chair. "Why'd you take Ativan, Trixie?" he asked in a gentle tone. "Did the detective make you nervous?"

"Yeah," she said while slightly nodding her head. "I was scared."

"Why were you scared?" Max asked, shooting a nervous glance to me.

"I thought she was here because of Bingham."

My breath hitched. "What about Bingham?"

She closed her eyes. "He said Ruth and Franklin have something of his. He wants it back, and he offered me five hundred dollars if I could get it."

"What was it, Trixie?" I asked in the sweetest voice I could muster. "We know you need extra cash, so Max and I can help you find it."

"It's a tin box with a lock on it," she said. "I thought Ruth had an appointment today, so I went over there this morning to see if I could find it."

A tin box? So she wasn't looking for the file.

"Wait. You went over to Ruth's place *today*?" Max asked in disbelief.

She nodded with her eyes still closed. "But Ruth wouldn't answer her door, and it was locked. Even the back door."

"What time was that?" Max asked.

"Just before noon. After I got Carly to cover for me."

"Did you see Ruth, Trixie?" I asked.

She stirred, lifting her head a bit. "I done told you she didn't answer."

"But you didn't try to get in?" I asked.

"I tried," she admitted sheepishly. "But I didn't want to bust a window, and my debit card broke tryin' to undo the lock."

A cold chill went through me. "Wait. You broke your debit card there?"

"Yeah, but I already called the bank, and they're sending me a new one."

"Trixie," Max said, placing a hand on her upper arm. "Did you get all the pieces?"

She looked up at him with unfocused eyes. "I think so?"

My gaze met Max's, and I knew we were both thinking the same thing. Guilty or not, Trixie was probably now a person of interest.

Trixie closed her eyes again. "I'm gonna take a little nap."

"Yeah," Max said absently as he got to his feet. "That's a good idea." He motioned for me to join him in the kitchen. I followed him, but shot a glance down the hall, wondering if Hank was searching through her belongings.

Max turned on the kitchen faucet and lowered his voice. "Do you think she did it?"

I wrapped my arms over my chest. "No. She's a shitty friend, but she's not a murderer."

His lips were pressed in a thin white line as he watched her. "Agreed. But I'll bet she didn't think to wipe her fingerprints off anything, and the deputies are gonna be all over the doorknobs."

"But not inside," I said in a hopeful tone. "But she's still going to look guilty for not telling the detective she was there."

"Agreed." He took a deep breath. "What do you think about the box?"

"What could be in it?" I asked. "And when did he ask? Bingham might have been referring to the tool box Louise used to store the safe deposit key. The one Jerry took from her cabin."

"Maybe," he said again, worry filling his eyes. "Let's ask her."

"She's about to pass out," I said, "if she hasn't already. I'm more worried about her dying from an overdose."

"She ain't gonna die from an overdose," Hank said as he rounded the hall corner. "The pills aren't even the strongest available. The question is why she has a full bottle with someone else's name on the label."

"Who?" I asked.

He looked grim as he said, "Ruth. And on top of that, the date on the prescription is from yesterday."

My eyes flew wide, and I spun to look at Max. "Maybe she stole them from Ruth's purse last night."

"Ruth didn't have her purse last night. She made a big fuss about it, saying she accidently left it at home."

"Why did Ruth have a recent anxiety prescription?" I asked.

Max pushed out a breath. "She told me she'd been under a lot of stress."

"So if Ruth didn't bring her purse, then how did Trixie get a bottle of her newly prescribed pills?" I asked in a whisper.

We all turned to study the apparently passed out woman. Maybe there was more to her story than we'd thought.

Chapter Twenty-One

Max walked over to Trixie and squatted next to her chair. "Trix, how did you get Ruth's pills?"

"Huh?" she asked, sounding groggy.

"Ask about the box," Hank said. "That's more important."

I wasn't so sure he was right about the level of importance, but Max asked, "When did Bingham ask you to get the box?"

She mumbled something unintelligible.

Max looked up at us with a hopeless expression, then asked again. This time Trixie ignored him.

Max stood and propped his hands on his hips in frustration. "Now what?"

Hank's jaw tightened as he pondered Max's question. Finally, he said, "We need to talk to Franklin's brother."

I swiveled to face him in surprise. "How do you know Franklin has a brother?"

"He owns a fish and tackle shop outside Ewing, close to the entrance to the state park over there. I've met him before when I took Seth fishin'." His voice was tight when he finished, then he swallowed and lifted his chin. "Ain't too many Tates around these parts. When I brought it up one time, he mentioned he had a brother named Franklin, but his friends called him Tater."

"Okay," Max said with a sharp nod. "Let's go talk to him."

Hank held up his free hand. "You hold up. Someone needs to stick with sleepin' beauty."

My back stiffened. "I thought you said she wasn't in any danger of overdosing."

"And I stand by that," Hank said gruffly, "but she obviously knows more than she told y'all before she passed out. Someone needs to stay here and grill her after she wakes up, and I told Marco I'd protect you. Which means you're stickin' with me."

Max didn't look too thrilled with this idea, but he pushed out a heavy breath and said, "Okay. Fine. I'll stay with Trixie. But how am I supposed to tell you when she's woken up?"

Hank swung his crutch toward a stack of envelopes on the kitchen table. He sat in a chair and ripped the flap off one, then picked up a pen and wrote down a phone number. "This here's my satellite phone number."

Max gaped at him. "You've got a *satellite phone*?"

"Gotta spend all that money on *something*," Hank grumped as he got to his foot, holding the torn strip in his free hand. He hobbled over to Max and held it out. "Call me after you talk to her, and we'll pick you up."

"If you're over in the far corners of Ewing when that happens, things could get pretty uncomfortable here," Max groused.

"Man up, Drummond," Hank said, already heading for the door. "Get that information."

I shot Max an apologetic glance as I followed Hank down the steps.

We both got into the car, Hank in the passenger side. I started the car and said, "Just take the highway to Ewing?"

"Not yet," Hank said, buckling his belt. "If the detective left Trixie less than an hour ago, it stands to reason she might go see Franklin's brother soon after. Let's give her a chance to conduct her interview. With any luck, we'll slip in right behind her like we did with Ruth's friend."

"So where are we going now?" I asked as I backed up onto the country road.

He paused. "Wyatt's house."

"*What?*"

"I need some damn answers," he grunted through his teeth.

"I doubt he's gonna give them to you, Hank," I said defeatedly. "He definitely wasn't telling his brother anything worth knowing."

He pulled out his phone. "We'll see." He punched in a number and waited a few seconds before he said, "Junior. Is your boss there?" There was a brief pause. "Okay. Thanks." He ended the call and looked up at me. "He went home for the day. Even better. Head there."

"Are you sure this is a good idea?" I asked, reluctantly heading in that direction.

"Don't you want answers?"

"Of course I do, but you have to know this is an exercise in futility. He's made it clear he's not going to talk."

His fingers dug into the door panel. "We'll just see about that."

We drove in silence for a few moments before I asked, "When did you get a satellite phone?"

He kept his gaze out the windshield. "Last week when I was out of town. Got one for you too."

I turned my head and stared at him in shock before quickly turning back to face the road. "What?"

"You keep traipsin' off, investigatin' shit. You need to be able to reach me or someone else if you need help. I'll show you how to use it later. I left it back at the house."

Bingham had a satellite phone too, and I'd looked into acquiring one. The price had nearly made me choke.

"I'll find a way to pay you back, Hank."

"The hell you will," he snorted. "It's my gift to you."

"It's too expensive."

"I've got more money than I know what to do with. Let me give you a damn phone," he snapped.

I reached over and placed my hand over his on the seat between us. "Thank you, Hank."

"Not a problem," he said, then crossed his arms over his chest.

We were both silent until we started up the long private drive to Wyatt's house.

"Do you want to sneak up on him?" I asked. "Or are we going right on up to the house?"

"I ain't sneakin' up on the bastard," he ground out through gritted teeth. "I intend to let him know I'm there."

That sounded ominous, but I didn't attempt to dissuade him as I continued driving the quarter mile to his house. I wasn't sure whether to feel relieved or disappointed that Wyatt's truck wasn't parked in the driveway.

"Do you think his truck's in the garage?" I asked.

"Don't matter," he said, opening his car door and getting out.

I got out too and called out over the top of the car, "Seems like it matters if you want to talk to him."

Ignoring me, he swung his crutch and hopped at a fast clip up to the front porch, his shotgun strap slung over his shoulder.

Shit.

I ran after him, but he was moving surprisingly fast. By the time I reached him, he was already pounding on the door. "Wyatt, you fuckin' coward! Open this goddamn door!" Then he gave it another few hard pounds for good measure.

Part of me wanted to stop him, but it seemed to me that Wyatt deserved to face Hank's wrath.

As long as it didn't involve that shotgun.

Hank pounded again, shouting more insults before he stepped back several feet, standing next to me.

"We can try again later." I gave him a sympathetic glance, then turned back toward the car—when a succession of loud booms made me jolt. I spun around in time to see the heavy wooden door bounce open, Hank still pointing his smoking gun at it.

"Hank!" I shouted. "You can't do that!"

"Looks like I just did." He swung his crutch and was through the front door within two seconds.

I glanced at my car, then back at Wyatt's shot-open door. There was no way I was going to let Hank poke around without me.

"Are we looking for something specific?" I asked as I walked in.

"Whatever we can find." Hank was in the kitchen, rummaging through drawers, dumping things onto the counter, and leaving the drawers gaping open.

"So I take it we're not hiding that we're here snooping around?" I asked.

He kept his gaze on his task. "Seems pretty pointless when there's no hidin' the gapin' hole in the front door where the doorknob used to be."

He had a point.

"See if he has an office somewhere." He glanced up at me. "And look for Max's computer."

"Surely he's not stupid enough to steal it, leave it here, then head out again," I said.

A sardonic look filled his eyes. "The man has balls bigger than wagon wheels. After all the other smug shit he's pulled, I wouldn't put it past him."

I didn't answer because he wasn't wrong. Still, I felt guilty searching Wyatt's house. For some reason, even after everything he'd admitted to, I wanted to believe he wouldn't betray me. Betray his brother. Betray Hank and poor Seth. I wanted to believe he really was trying to bring down evil, not steal his father's position for personal gain. But I couldn't ignore all the red flags, and this was our chance to finally learn what he refused to tell us.

Hank stayed in the kitchen while I went into Wyatt's bedroom. I was surprised by how nice it looked—his bed was made with a comforter designed with alternating sand and brown colored stripes, and he had an upholstered leather headboard. Floor-to-ceiling windows overlooked the valley below, and none of them had blinds or curtains. I guessed he didn't have to worry about people looking in.

The bed…the furnishings…the view. Those things cost money. More money than most people around here had. More money than the garage would likely earn him. Where the hell had he gotten it?

I rummaged through his dresser drawers, finding neatly folded stacks of shirts, sweatpants, underwear and socks, but nothing of interest. His closet was filled with wooden shelves for his shoes and folded jeans. Button-down shirts I'd rarely seen him wear were hanging from rods.

It all looked very impersonal.

His en suite bathroom was just as neat and clean. With tumbled stone floors, a matching shower, and a deep tub in front of a window with a view of the valley. No papers. Nothing personal.

I walked back out into the living room and found Hank now searching it.

"Anything?" he grunted, glancing up at me.

"No, but there's something off about it."

"What do you mean?"

"It's too neat. Too organized. Too nicely *furnished*." I shook my head. "It took some serious money to build and decorate this house. Where did it come from? And why does it look like Wyatt doesn't even live here?"

He stood upright and stared at me.

"But he must," I said, trying to work through the feeling. "He made me pancakes over there in the kitchen." I pointed to the island. "And I've dropped him off here." I ran a hand over the top of my head. "What's going on?"

"I don't know, but the kitchen was the same way. Same with the completely empty garage. Nothing personal."

"Who lives like that?" I asked.

His eyes narrowed. "No one normal."

"I haven't found an office yet."

There were doors on the other side of the house, so I headed over and found two guest rooms, the beds made, nothing in the dressers, the closets empty. The second bath was the same way.

When I came back, Hank was sitting on the arm of a chair, waiting with a scowl as he looked out the back of the house. "More of the same?"

"Yep."

He took a breath, then blew it out. "He's hidden something big."

"Obviously."

"He expects someone to come lookin' for it, which means it's either someplace else entirely, or he has a hidey hole here. I'm goin' with the hidey hole."

"Like a safe?" I asked. "We can look behind the pictures on the wall."

"Nope. Too obvious." He stood and moved behind the sofa. "We gotta move the rugs. We're looking for a trapdoor."

"You can't be serious," I protested.

"As a heart attack. This house ain't built on a slab. There's a raised foundation, which means there's a decent chance he has some sort of basement, only I never found a set of steps. Did you?"

"No."

"Start movin' furniture."

Hank was little help moving the sofa and chairs. He mostly stood back and watched as I dragged everything off and rolled up the rug.

"Nothin'," I said, breathless and working up a sweat.

"We'll try the bedroom next."

Which was easier said than done.

We headed into the bedroom, and he stood in the doorway as I moved the king-sized bed a few inches at a time, until I'd moved it far enough to lift the rug and check out the hardwood floor.

I gasped. "Oh my God."

"You found something," he said.

"Yeah."

It was a trapdoor about two and a half feet square, but I hadn't moved the bed and rug far enough to reveal the whole thing, so I wrangled them a bit more before stopping.

"I need a flashlight." Wyatt had put one in the drawer of his nightstand—probably for this very purpose—so I grabbed it now and flicked it on.

I looked into Hank's determined gaze. "If I find dead bodies down there, you're payin' for my therapy bills."

He snorted. "He ain't got no dead bodies down there. We'd be smellin' 'em." Snatching the flashlight from me, he leaned over and shined it into the hole. But the room was too bright and the hole too deep for me to see much.

"I'm gonna have to go down there, aren't I?" I asked with a sigh.

"We gotta know what's in his hidey hole."

True enough. I got down on my knees next to the hole, then leaned over and shined the light into the space. It was a small concrete room that looked to be about eight feet deep and eight feet wide. A ladder had been propped up against the wall below the opening, and a table stood against the far wall, covered with multiple items.

What the hell did Wyatt have down there?

"How did he get a table through that small opening?" I asked as I turned around to climb down the ladder, holding the flashlight in one hand.

"Probably put it in when he was buildin' the place."

"That's not creepy at all."

"Maybe he meant for it to be a storm cellar," Hank said as I started to descend into the hole.

"Yeah, right." I was pretty sure neither one of us believed that.

When my feet touched the ground, I slowly spun around the room, taking it in. It was mostly empty except for the table and some papers taped to the wall over it.

I took a step closer and gasped.

"What is it?" Hank barked.

"Um…he has a map of the area with multiple pinpoints on a wall next to the table. But on the wall next to that there are photos."

"Photos of what?"

"Us."

Chapter Twenty-Two

"He has photos of all of us on the wall?" Hank asked in disbelief. When I glanced up at him, he was sitting on the floor next to the opening to get a better view.

"Not just us," I said breathlessly, still trying to take it in. "Lots of people. His parents. Bingham. Lula." My voice broke. "Jerry." I took a breath. "Heather. People I don't recognize." Small 2 x 3 and 4 x 6 images of us, most of them candid shots, although some looked like they'd been cut from newspapers, attached to a large board made of one-foot cork squares. They were pinned in a haphazard manner and they all had colored lines connecting them to Hank, Bingham, Bart, or a question mark. I wasn't sure what the colors represented, but I had lines running to all three men. Light blue ones to Hank and Bingham, a red one to Wyatt's father. "It's some kind of pattern. Like he's plotting the town's allegiances or something."

Hank grunted. "What the fuck?"

"I need a camera," I said, glancing up. "I have to take pictures of all this."

"Fuck that. Just grab it all. I'll get a pillowcase."

I shook my head. "Not this. We wouldn't be able to make heads or tails of it if we did that. I need photos."

"Fine," he said with an unhappy sigh. "You start lookin' at the other stuff, and I'll look around for a camera."

"I have a small one in my glove box."

He muttered something under his breath as got to his feet, presumably with the help of the dresser, but about ten seconds later, he stood over the opening and tossed something down next to me.

"Start stuffin' the other shit into those pillowcases. We'll look at it later. We need to be gone before he comes back."

"Okay," I said, squatting to pick them up from the floor as I studied the board. Ruth and Franklin were on there too. While there were no lines connecting Ruth to Bart, she had a yellow line connecting her to Bingham. Nothing to Hank. Franklin had blue lines connecting him to both Bart and Bingham.

"If this is about loyalties, then who's working for who?" I asked the silence.

It took me a second to spot Seth's photo in the middle, with lines running to Bingham and a photo of Carson Purdy. This was an eight-foot-wide spider web of this town, and I realized that photos could never fully capture the complexity of what Wyatt had created here.

There was a photo of Max at the bottom. He had multiple colored lines running to other photos, including a blue one to me. Blue ran to Ruth as well. Dark blue to his mother. Carson Purdy had a dark blue one to Bart, but Jerry's line to Bart was white.

What did *that* mean?

There weren't many red lines, but I realized my red line connection to Bart didn't mean anything good. Louise had red lines to Bart, Bingham, *and* Hank. Louise's husband—who I recognized from newspaper articles I'd seen—didn't have a red line connecting him to anyone, confirming Walter Baker had been collateral damage. His death had meant nothing to Bart, but neither had his life.

How did Wyatt know all of this?

"Here's the camera. Hand up one of the bags and we'll exchange 'em," Hank said as he leaned over the opening.

Oh shit. "I didn't grab anything yet."

"Why the hell not?"

"I was looking at the board," I said, hurrying over to the table. It was covered with manila file folders, some thick, others thin. I narrowed my eyes. What was all of this? Then I noticed the names on the folder tabs. It looked like every photo on the wall had a folder.

Including me. Right on top.

I opened the flap and started going through it. There were handwritten notes about me with dates and information from that day. It was obvious this had been an ongoing project because the entries were written in differently colored ink. And it had started the very day I'd come to town.

I glanced up at Hank, who looked worried.

"I got a bad feelin', girlie. We ain't got time to be readin' that shit. Just stuff 'em into those pillowcases and let's go."

"We need to be more careful than that," I said, grabbing a couple of files and placing them carefully into a pillowcase. "We'll mix up the files."

"So why don't you hand a couple of 'em up to me, and I'll hand you the camera to get images of that photo wall?"

"Okay."

I closed the file and stuffed it into the case along with a handful of others, then climbed the ladder, doing my best to keep from jostling the bag. Hank and I made the exchange, then I went back down to grab more files.

I'd only gotten a few more when Hank called down. "Girlie. Get up here. *Now*."

Panic raced through my blood. "But I haven't gotten photos of the wall."

"We ain't got time. Five minutes tops. Wyatt's on his way up the mountain."

I didn't ask him how he knew. He could tell me later. Instead, I grabbed more files, making sure I got the ones on Wyatt's parents, Bingham, Hank. Marco. Max.

The bag was heavy, and I dropped it onto the floor as I started for the ladder. When I bent to retrieve it, my flashlight shone under the table. I froze in my tracks.

"We've gotta go, Carly!" Hank shouted.

"He has shackles," I said, barely above a whisper.

"What?"

"He has shackles. They're attached to the floor." Then, as though I'd been jolted by a zap of electricity, I slung the bag over my shoulder and rushed up the stairs.

"All the more reason to get the fuck out of here," Hank said, reaching for the bag when I got close to the top. "We gotta close up this hole. Buy us more time."

"He's going to know we were here," I said. "There's only one way up and one way down." And after seeing those metal rings embedded into the concrete, I really, really didn't want to be here when he showed up.

"I know a place to hide, but we gotta cover our tracks."

"There's no covering our tracks, Hank!" I shouted in panic. "We left the place a mess. You shot a damn hole in the front door! How are you gonna hide that?"

"Put the door back. Straighten the rug, and we'll get the bed back in place," he said, his voice threaded with tension.

I got the rug pushed down, and we both shoved the bed back in its original location, making sure the dents in the rug from the bed posts were covered.

"That boy's too damn smart for his own good," Hank said, as he headed for the living room. "Shut the front door behind you. Might buy us ten more seconds."

I did as he said, but it was too damaged to stay shut. He was in the front passenger seat when I jumped behind the steering wheel, and I started the car and said, "Now what?"

"Head back down but go as fast as you can. There's a turn-off. We'll pull in there and pray he doesn't see us."

I did as he said, trying to go fast, but the curves and switchbacks slowed me down. Finally, Hank pointed to a small dirt lane to the right, about fifty feet ahead. "There!" But as I started to pull in, he said, "Try to kick up as little dust as possible."

I drove with agonizing slowness, edging in as far as I could go before the road ended and I hit wilderness, about twenty feet in. Then we waited.

And as we waited, it occurred to me that if Wyatt pulled in behind us, we would be trapped. I leaned over Hank to grab the handgun out of the glove compartment, but he was one step ahead of me. After retrieving the gun, he checked the chamber to make sure it was loaded before handing it to me.

We were both utterly silent, as though speaking would clue Wyatt in to our location. My heart pounded so loudly in my ears I was sure he'd be able to hear that too.

The whine of an engine sounded a short way down the hill, and I held my breath, looking over my shoulder to see Wyatt's truck pass. Hank had his shotgun raised and pointed out the back window.

Finally, Wyatt's truck drove past our lane, not pausing as it continued up the hill. But Wyatt looked anxious from the short glimpse I got of his profile. As soon as he realized what had happened, he'd be coming back down.

Hank must have been reading my mind. "Not yet." He placed a hand over mine on the steering wheel. "Listen."

We could hear the truck move farther up the hill. A few seconds later, Hank said, "Now, but go slow. We don't want to alert him to our presence."

"Yeah, not a problem. I suck at backing up," I said as I went in reverse, wishing my car had one of those fancy rearview cameras so I didn't have to rely on the side mirrors and glances out the back window to find my way. But I made it, somehow, and I put the car in drive and started down the hill, hoping we had enough of a head start.

"How did you know Wyatt was coming?" I asked, gripping the steering wheel.

"He made a clearing in the trees, giving him a perfect view of the highway. He can see who's comin' and goin'."

"But only if he's there watching."

He barked a laugh. "That boy's got cameras."

My blood went cold. "What?"

"He has an alarm system. And cameras. I'm sure he came back because it alerted him. He's gonna know we were the ones who broke in and disturbed his hidey hole. That boy's gonna be lookin' for us."

I turned to Hank in terror. "What are we going to do?"

He gave me a wry smile. "Run."

Chapter Twenty-Three

I shook my head. "I can't run. I'm already running."

"Well, now you're running from two men. Only we ain't gonna run for long. Just long enough to regroup and look over all that shit in those bags back there." He thumbed to the pillowcases in the back.

Wyatt was going to be furious, and we *did* need time to figure out exactly what we had. "Where do you want to go?"

"Nowhere around here," he said as we approached the turnoff to the highway. "Go left. Don't head back into town."

"So where are we going?"

He grinned, but it didn't quite reach his eyes. "How about we kill two birds with one stone? Chattanooga."

I didn't question him, just drove for the next few minutes, trying to process everything. I realized I hadn't told Hank about my phone call with Tammy Franken and the Chattanooga bar with an animal name, but my terror was messing with my brain. The farther we got from Drum, the more I began to worry. "I can't leave town, Hank. What about Marco?" I gasped. "What about *Max*? We left him at Trixie's. We have to warn him about Wyatt."

"We can tell Marco and Max we're layin' low, but we can't tell 'em where we're goin'," Hank countered as he dug into his bag. "Just tell him the bare minimum about what we found."

Considering we still didn't know what was in those files, that wouldn't be too difficult. But our discovery was starting to slam into me hard, and my breath came in short bursts.

"Carly," Hank said, putting a hand on my arm. "I know you're scared, but it's gonna be okay."

"I'm not just scared for me," I said, daring to cast him a glance through my tears. "I'm more scared for Marco. And Max. What's Wyatt going to do when he realizes what we did? What if he hurts them to get to us? *To me?*"

"He's not gonna hurt his brother," he said in an acrid tone. "If there's one thing I've learned in all my years, it's that Drummonds never turn on their own. Not really. Wyatt's hated his father for years, but despite collectin' information on him, he hasn't done a damn thing. If he's plannin' on takin' over his father's kingdom, then he's waitin' for someone else to take the man out before he claims his throne."

"Bingham."

"Exactly. And Bingham's clearly up to something. He had Trixie snoopin' on Tater and Ruth. We know he's been diggin' into Drum's past. Wyatt must know what's goin' on and he's just waitin' for it to happen."

"But what are we gonna solve by going off to Chattanooga?" I asked in dismay. "We're running away, Hank! And what about Marco? If Wyatt is as evil as we think he is, he's going to be twisting in the wind." Marco and I were supposed to be doing this together, not separate. I didn't want to do this without him.

I turned to look at him. "I think we should go back. I'm sick to death of running from trouble. I want to face it and be done with it."

"And get your damn self killed," he grunted. "Don't be stupid. Stayin' right now would be a fool's errand. Just like if you'd stuck around after you overheard your father plannin' to have you killed. You like to berate yourself for takin' off, but it's one of the smartest things you've ever done. Besides, you only say someone ran when they don't intend to go back. You always planned to make him pay. Just like we're gonna go back and bust Drum wide open. But first we need to see what Wyatt has."

"I didn't get all the files," I said past the lump in my throat. "And I didn't get photos of the board." I drew in a sharp breath. "Shit. I left my camera down there!"

"What photos are on the memory card?" Hank asked.

I shook my head. "Some photos of me and Marco. And some of the birds on your birdfeeder." I smiled even though I felt like I was about to throw up. "Some I snuck of you."

Hank frowned. "I knew you took those damn photos."

"He'll know I was down there, Hank. The camera's going to give me away."

"He'll *already* know you were down there," he countered. "I done told you he had cameras of his own. He'll play back the footage. He'll know it was us."

"He had a place to shackle someone, Hank," I said, my fear rising again. "Do you think he's used it?"

He was quiet for a long moment. "I don't know. I guess I don't know the boy at all."

"I'm sorry."

He released a sharp breath. "Not half as sorry as that bastard's gonna be when I get done with him."

"I have to call Marco. I have to tell him what's going on and warn him that Wyatt might be coming for him."

He nodded. "We'll use my phone." After he pressed some buttons on his satellite phone, he set it on the dashboard as he placed the call. It rang once before Marco answered. "Deputy Roland."

Just hearing his voice settled some of the wildness in me. "Marco," I said. "It's me."

"What number are you callin' me from?" he asked, sounding concerned. "Why aren't you callin' me from the home phone?"

"I'm not at home," I said carefully. "I'm with Hank. This is his new satellite phone."

"Hank's got a satellite phone? Wait. Never mind. Where are you?"

"We can't tell you," Hank said. "But I had to get Carly out of town."

"Why?" Marco asked in a panic. "What happened?"

"We found some things at Wyatt's house," Hank said. "He's got thick files on everyone of importance in town. Including you. And a big spider web board with people's photos and their connections to one another. The man's up to something devious."

"What the fuck? What's he doin' with them?"

"We don't know," Hank said. "But it looks like he's been spyin' on people for years, makin' notes and plottin' out alliances. He had it all hidden in a pit under his bed."

"Is he workin' with Bart? Or Bingham?" he asked in confusion.

"We don't think he's working for anyone," I said. "We think he's working for himself. But we haven't had a chance to look at what we got. And we left a whole lot behind before he showed up."

"Did he catch you snoopin' around?"

"No," Hank said. "I was watchin' out and when I saw his truck on the highway through the clearing, we wrapped it all up and got the hell out of there."

"Is there any way you can get the other files?" I asked.

"I don't see how," Marco said. "I can't just go check it out. There's no way I'd be able to get a search warrant. And without a search warrant whatever I found wouldn't hold up in court."

"I doubt there'd be anything there by the time you showed up," Hank said. "If he's smart, he'll clear it all out. And he's smart. Wicked smart."

"Okay," Marco said in the voice he used when he was trying to work through a puzzle. "How did *you* find it?"

"We went lookin'," Hank said.

"*You broke into Wyatt's house?*"

"Yeah, and he's gonna know it was us," Hank said. "He had cameras."

"What am I supposed to do if he reports you?" Marco asked, his voice rising. "Was the front door open? You can argue that you thought he was home and went in."

"Nope," Hank said. "I blasted it with my shotgun. No room for doubt I broke in, but he's never gonna report it. If he does, then be sure to investigate the hidey hole under his bed."

"The *what?*"

"I told you there was a pit under his bed," I said.

"I thought you meant a big pile. Not an actual *pit.*"

I quickly filled Marco in on the files and corkboard.

"But Wyatt was comin' home while we were there," Hank said. "We got away, but it won't take long for him to come lookin' for us. And when he can't find us, he'll come lookin' for you and Max."

Marco was silent for a long moment. "What's in the files?"

"We haven't had a chance to go through them yet other than the quick glance I got at mine. He had notes on me. He started taking them the first night I got to town," I said.

"And you're drivin' now?" Marco asked.

"Yeah," I said. "We just escaped. This was the first chance we got to call and warn you."

"You know there's a good chance we won't be able to use any of it as evidence," Marco said. "You took it from his residence. He can claim you fabricated it."

"We won't be usin' it as evidence," Hank said. "At least not in any county or state court."

"I don't think I should be hearin' this," Marco said in a flat voice.

"And that's why I won't be tellin' you anything else," Hank said. "But I know for a fact you don't have all the information you need to solve Ruth's murder."

"But *you* know what we're missin'?" Marco asked carefully.

"Just might," Hank said, staring out the windshield.

"You realize you're hamperin' our investigation," Marco said in an authoritative tone.

"No worries," Hank said. "We'll be conductin' an investigation of our own."

"Vigilante justice has done nothin' but tear this place apart," Marco said. "Carly? Are you on board with this?"

"I know a key piece of information I can't tell you," I said, my voice breaking. "I'd do anything to tell you, but I'm protecting someone we both care about."

He was silent for a moment. "It could get this person in trouble?"

"A lot of trouble, and there's no way to tell you without putting you in a difficult position."

"I see." And I knew he understood exactly who I was talking about, which was why he wouldn't press the issue. "Sometimes I hate this fuckin' job."

"No, you don't," I said with a wobbly smile, wishing he could see me and vice versa. "You're damn good at it, Deputy Roland. You love it."

"I love you more," he said wistfully. "I expect I'll have to choose one over the other sooner than we expected, but then again, it's not really a choice at all. It's just a matter of when to pull the trigger."

I sucked in a breath and straightened my back. "That day's not today." When he didn't respond, I added, "We left Max at Trixie's, and he has no way to leave. Trixie took a couple of Ativan after Detective White talked to her, and she's passed out in her living room."

"And what were you doin' at Trixie's?" Marco asked.

"We were checking on her, of course," I said. "Max had already talked to Ginger and Tiny. He needed to do the same with Trixie. He knows she's worried about money, and he wanted to let her know the tavern's going to be shut down for a few days."

"Huh." It was obvious he didn't quite believe me, but he wasn't going to press the matter.

"In any case," I said. "I'm worried about him. We just left him there, and with Wyatt on the warpath..." I took a breath. "Marco, Wyatt has shackles anchored into the concrete pit under his bed."

"He has *what?*"

"I saw them under the table stacked with all those files. I don't know if he's used them, but they're there."

"Shit," Marco groaned.

"He's dangerous," Hank said, his voice tinged with anger. "I'm sure he's been workin' on those files since he got back to town, and we took most of the important ones. He's gonna want 'em back, and he's gonna want to make sure we don't hand them over to anyone who can do something with them."

"Like Bart Drummond and Todd Bingham," Marco said.

"And you, Marco," I said, panic rising in my chest. "He's probably going to wonder if I'll hand them over to you."

"She's right," Hank said. "You either need to make sure you always have backup or get the hell out of Drum."

"I can't leave," Marco said. "Not right now. It'll look suspicious as hell." He paused, then added, "Just like it's gonna look suspicious if word gets out that you left town, Carly. You were one of the people who found Ruth." Then he added. "She was shot, by the way. Once in the chest and once in the abdomen."

I flinched. I still couldn't believe someone had ended her life like that. Possibly someone I actually knew. How had Louise known? Had *she* been the one to kill her?

"There's nothing to be done about lookin' suspicious," Hank said. "The tavern's closed, so for all people know she's holed up at my place. As for you, stick close to Max when you're not on shift. Wyatt's gonna do anything and everything to get his files back, and I wouldn't it put it past him to use you two as bait."

"So Wyatt might eliminate me to keep me from usin' the information, or he might kidnap me to convince Carly to give it back."

"That's about right. Before…" Hank's voice tightened, and he paused before saying, "Before, I wouldn't have thought him capable of either option, but now…I just don't know what to think."

Shades of Truth

Marco was silent for a moment, then heaved a sigh. "Okay. I'll drop by Trixie's to check on Max, and I'll make sure we each have a buddy for the next few days."

"One more thing," I said, shooting a glance at Hank. "Trixie was at Ruth's house around noon. She said she broke her debit card trying to get in. And the Ativan she took? Ruth's name is on the bottle in her bathroom. The prescription was just filled yesterday."

Hank's eyes narrowed in aggravation at me for telling Marco. I suspected in his opinion, the less the sheriff's department knew, the better.

"What the hell?" Marco said.

"Max said Ruth didn't have her purse last night," I said. "So how did Trixie get the pills? You might go to the bathroom when you drop by to pick up Max. Maybe see them on the counter and ask Trixie how she got them."

"Tryin' to tell me how to do my job now, huh?" Marco asked with a hint of humor in his voice. "Thanks for the tip. Be careful, okay?"

"I will," I said. "You too."

"I'll take good care of her," Hank said. "You be worryin' about yourself."

Hank hung up, then dialed Trixie's number, barely giving me a chance to regroup after our call with Marco. When no one answered, Hank started to leave a message on the machine. "Max, if you're there, pick up. This is important."

Max answered seconds later. "Did you find out anything from Franklin's brother?"

"We never made it there," Hank said. "We went to Wyatt's house to look for clues and get your computer back."

"What?" Max said. "Did you find it?"

I'd been distracted by the dungeon in the basement, but not so much so that I could have missed his computer tower.

It hadn't been there. Actually, there hadn't been *any* computers.

"No," Hank said. "But we found a whole lot we hadn't bargained on. How often have you been out at Wyatt's house?"

"Not many times," he said. "Why?"

"It barely looks lived in," Hank said, "other than the concrete pit under his bed where he keeps all the information he's collected on everyone in Drum over the past six years."

"*What?*"

Hank and I quickly filled him in on everything, including our escape.

"We've left town, and we didn't have time to get you," I said. "Wyatt's probably already trying to hunt us down. He's going to come looking for you and possibly Marco. We warned Marco first, and he's on his way to pick you up."

Max was quiet for a moment. "So you never made it out to talk to Franklin's brother?"

"No."

"Then I think I need to head out that way."

"You can't be involvin' Marco in that," Hank said. "We told him about Trixie havin' Ruth's pills. That should throw the police off your scent for a bit."

"You sure that was a good idea?" Max asked.

"Just tell 'em you found 'em," Hank said. "You were invited into her house. It wouldn't be unreasonable for you to find pills on the counter."

"Did you find them on the counter?" Max asked.

"No," Hank said. "They were in a drawer, but that's beside the point. If the police question Trixie about her story, it'll fold like wet cardboard, but there's not a snowball's chance in hell she'll mention she went over there for Bingham…and if she did, the sheriff's department will have a real lead. Hell, for all we know, Bingham actually had Ruth killed, so we'd be helpin' 'em out."

It seemed just as likely to get Trixie killed.

Max must have been thinking the same thing, because he said, "It seems wrong to throw Trixie under the bus like this."

"Do you think she murdered Ruth?" Hank asked.

"No."

"Neither do I, and neither will that detective. But she just might give 'em something to help them find the killer." He shrugged. "And if she tells 'em about Bingham, they'll protect her. They know how dangerous he is."

"Okay," Max said, "But we still need to talk to Franklin's brother. I'm gonna borrow Trixie's car and head out to Ewing to have that chat." Then he added with a hint of amusement, "And don't you worry, Carly. I'll leave a note so I can't be charged with stealing her car. It will be clear I borrowed it."

"I'm not sure it's a good idea for you to be out on your own," I said. "And you need to be there when Marco drops by to get you and see the pills." Fear threaded through me. "But Wyatt's gonna know you're working with us. Your truck's still at Hank's house."

"He already knows, Carly," Max said impatiently. "And I'm not hiding out in Trixie's trailer, watchin' daytime talk shows." He hastily added, "No offense, Hank."

"None taken," Hank said. "And agreed. The time for observin' is done. It's time to act. Do you think Trixie will give you any trouble about using her car?"

"If she keeps poppin' pills like this, she won't be usin' it anyway."

"No," I said firmly. "Stay there. Wait for Marco. There's no need to rush after Franklin's brother. Wait for Marco."

Max grunted that he would, although he didn't sound happy about it.

"Keep us updated," Hank said. "Call this number. It's my new phone, and we'll call you back at Trixie's."

"Okay."

"Be careful," I said, my anxiety rising. "He might not kill you, Max, but he could lock you up in his dungeon."

He released a bitter laugh. "Then I guess you'll know where to look for me."

Chapter Twenty-Four

By the time we got to Chattanooga, we still didn't know anything about what was in the files. Hank had tried to read them, but he'd forgotten his reading glasses, and trying to read Wyatt's handwritten notes had made him carsick. I'd suggested we pull over somewhere so I could give it a go, but Hank had insisted on putting distance between us and Wyatt. I relented, starting to wish we'd brought Hank's car, which would have given me the opportunity to read while he drove. But a couple of hours wasn't going to make much of a difference in the long run.

When we got to the city, we headed straight to a Target. Hank said we needed fresh clothes and toiletries, but he also wanted to get hoodies and sunglasses to help disguise us from any security cameras we might encounter.

"You really think Wyatt's going to be checking security cameras in Chattanooga?"

"No," he barked, "but your father might."

A sharp reminder I couldn't let my guard down on that front either.

After we made our purchases, we picked up fast food for dinner and headed to a Days Inn. Hank made sure my face and head were covered but didn't put much effort into hiding himself. When I commented on it, he said, "It's pretty obvious it's me. There's no hidin' the fact I'm a one-legged man. Besides, I doubt your father would be lookin' for me. And if he is, you're in a whole lot more trouble than Wyatt chasin' our tails."

He had a point.

We dropped our stuff on the dresser and set the pillowcases on one of the beds. I pulled out the files and set them in unorganized piles on top of the bedspread.

Hank took it all in with a frown. "Bingham. Daddy Drummond. Me. He's got the big three. I say we start with those."

I agreed, but my gaze was firmly fixed on the one with my name.

His tone softened. "On second thought, why don't we start off by taking a look at what he has on each of us? You read yours, and I'll check out mine, and then we'll go from there." He added, "It'll help us determine the accuracy of his information."

"Yeah," I said absently as I picked up my folder and set it next to the pillows. Scooping up the other files, I stacked them on the dresser next to the bags. There weren't as many as I'd thought. A file each on Max, Marco, and Carson Purdy. I recognized the names of the guys who had been associated with Carson Purdy's drug scheme. I hadn't grabbed one on Emily Drummond, though. I wished I'd had the foresight to look for it. Then again, there hadn't been much time.

Hank sat in a chair by the window before he opened his file. I sat on the bed closest to the bathroom, resting my back on some pillows propped against the headboard. I opened the cover and steeled my back, ready for anything.

Or so I thought.

Just as I'd gathered in his pit, he'd been keeping notes on me. He'd handwritten them in a spiral notebook and then ripped out the pages and put them into the folder. The first entry was dated the day I'd come to town.

The woman claims to be from Atlanta. Is she here for the drug drop? Her car breaking down would be a convenient excuse to place her here. Great alibi. I dropped her off at Max's so she can stay at the Alpine Inn. I plan to do some surveillance to see where she goes and who she meets.

He then listed details about my car, my bags, what I was wearing, and my physical appearance.

The next day's entry recounted that I'd been discovered with Seth and Wyatt had then found me with Hank in his hospital room. He noted that the sheriff didn't know anything about what Seth had been up to, and he didn't think they would find out. I was the unknown, and he planned to keep a close eye on me.

He made daily entries until after Carson's death, and my blood turned cold as I read his perspective about that time.

My plan is to gain Carly's trust and find out more about her father. Perhaps I can use that to my advantage.

Although I'd known he was suspicious of me in the beginning, our relationship had seemed to change after he discovered my secret. But he'd been working his own angle the whole time.

Another entry, from after Seth's funeral, read: *While I told Carly I'd help her find evidence to have my father arrested, I think I can hold her off. It's too soon to go after him, and she could put a wrench in the entire thing.*

My stomach churned, but I kept reading. The entries were sparse for the weeks after that, but then I got to one dated the day before he'd supposedly gone to an auction in West Virginia to buy a tow truck.

Taking a flight to Dallas tomorrow to investigate Randall Blakely. I'm still not sure what I'll do if I find out anything about him and his crime organization. Maybe I can dole out bits to Carly to steer her attention away from my father.

The thing is, I started this thing with her to get information and keep an eye on what she's doing, but I'm starting to really like her. I keep reminding myself there's a master plan. Every time I try to picture her being part of it, I can't see it. So why do I want her anyway?

Even then, he'd been using me. Manipulating me. Putting me at risk.

The next entry was the night he'd come back to Drum.

My plan to hold Carly off with my father has stalled, and she's claiming we're done until I share something. I could have talked sense into her—or used her attraction to me to distract her—but Hank intervened and sent me away.

I can't afford to lose her now. Not after what I found in Dallas. I'll need to figure out a way to reestablish her trust. I have to keep her close, now more than ever. Still, I feel guilty using her this way. She trusted the wrong man before, and it burned her, yet here I am trying to convince her that I'm different? It doesn't sit entirely right, until I remember the end goal. Eye on the prize.

I set the file down, sick to my stomach. The smell of the still untouched fast food wasn't helping. "I need some air."

Hank looked up at me, concern filling his eyes. "You don't have to read it. I can do it."

"No," I said, getting to my feet. "I just need a moment."

"Don't go far," he said, watching as I made my way to the door. "Stay outside the door so I can keep an eye on you."

I nodded. I needed some space from that file, but I wasn't stupid enough to put myself in danger, not that I begrudged Hank for issuing the warning.

Shades of Truth

I went outside and breathed in the hot, humid air.

I was such an idiot. I'd trusted that man. Even after ending things with him, I'd still trusted that he cared about me. He'd claimed to *love* me. He'd claimed he wanted me in his life, whatever way he could have me. He just wanted me close so I'd be available whenever he was ready to pull some trigger, whatever that meant.

But then I moved past my bruised ego and realized I'd skimmed over something far more important than my hurt feelings.

He'd found something in Dallas.

I spun around and went back inside, shutting the door behind me. "He investigated my father."

Hank narrowed his eyes in confusion. "What?"

"The last entry I read was from a couple of weeks after Carson Purdy's death. Wyatt told us he was going to an auction in West Virginia, but it was just a cover story. He *really* went to Dallas to investigate my father. I think he was hoping to feed me information about my father to keep me distracted from looking into his. The thing is, he said he found something." I took a deep breath. "He has information, Hank. He might have something I can use."

He studied me for a long moment. "And he was holding it for when he needed to control you." He shook his head. "Why hasn't he used it already? He's been tryin' to win you back since last December."

"I don't know."

His eyes widened. "He knew you were livin' with me. And he was always comin' around to help out." His hand gripped the chair arm so tightly, I was surprised it didn't break. "He bugged my house."

"No," I said with an exhale. "No. He wouldn't."

He pointed to the open file on his lap. "After what little I've read in here, he would. His entries are cold and calculated. Not the way a man would write about someone he cares about."

"Like a person he was watching and trying to figure out how to exploit," I said, barely above a whisper.

"Yeah."

We were both quiet for several seconds, before I asked, "So what's his end game?"

Hank ran a hand over his head, looking exhausted. "I think Max is right. Power."

"But to do this for so many years." My voice broke, and I wrapped my arms over my chest. "Do you think he was ever really your friend?"

He drew in a deep breath and pushed it out. "A half an hour ago, I would have said yes. I would have told you he was a good man once, and things just got out of hand. Now…" His gaze dropped to the file. "After Barb died, I think that man saw a weakness in my armor. So he befriended Seth, hoping to get to me. Everyone believed I had money buried somewhere. Maybe Wyatt hoped to get his hands on it and use it to gain more power. He'd become like a son to me." The last words sounded choked, but then his jaw tightened. "He used me. He used my grandson to gain information, and it got him killed. Then he stole those videos from you." His eyes turned murderous. "He is vile and evil. I will deal with Wyatt Drummond."

I slowly shook my head. "No. No talk of violence tonight. I already feel like I've been sliced open. I can't deal with the thought of anything happening to you if you go head-to-head with Wyatt."

Hank pinched his mouth shut, but he didn't look angry anymore. Just worried. "There's something else to consider," he said quietly. "One of the files we left in that dungeon is clearly about Randall Blakely. Wyatt might not just have some information. He might have exactly what you need to bring your father down."

I'd already come to that same conclusion. Now I just needed to figure out how to get it.

Chapter Twenty-Five

It took me another half hour to get through the rest of my file, mostly because I had to keep going back and re-reading parts of it. Wyatt made multiple references to other files—Max's, Marco's, Hank's...my father's. The trip to Dallas after Thanksgiving last year wasn't the only one he'd made in an effort to dig up information on my father. He mentioned the big bust of the crime organization he'd partnered in, the Hardshaw Group, but the entry was focused on his speculation about why I was still in Drum. He did acknowledge that I'd claimed his father had blackmailed me, and while he believed I'd been threatened, he didn't think it was reason enough for me to stay. He thought I was starting to dig too deep, and he was worried I was about to unearth things he wasn't ready to come to light, so he pushed me hard to leave. Then got frustrated when I wouldn't. So he'd concluded I must have made some type of deal with Bingham to take down his father. That, and I'd become involved with Marco. He wrote that he was convinced I was with Marco because I felt safer being with a sheriff deputy. He also reasoned that was why I'd stuck close to Hank.

"What the hell is wrong with him?" I said out loud in frustration.

Hank glanced up in surprise. "Wyatt?"

"He just can't conceive that I would want to be with someone because I love them. That part of the reason I've stayed in Drum is because I'm emotionally attached to the people around me." I shook my head in frustration. "He thinks I'm only with Marco because he makes me feel safe. He thinks I'm with you for the same reason."

Hank sniffed, then set his file on the bed in front of him. "Wyatt's messed up, but look how he was raised. There was no unconditional love in that house. He earned attention but not love. He doesn't understand the concept." He gave me a sad smile. "In his notes in my file, he claims I let you live with me because I'm trying to atone for my mistakes with Barb and Mary. But it's obvious he's never loved someone. I don't think he even loves his brother. He definitely doesn't love his parents."

"He's a sociopath."

Hank's mouth twisted to the side as he considered it. "Maybe. But based on things he's written in my file, I think he *does* care about you." Sadness filled his eyes. "But not in the way you deserve."

A ringing sound broke the silence, and Hank groaned. "That's the sat phone. Get it out of my bag, will ya?"

I got up and found his phone in his bag and handed it to him.

He answered with a gruff, "Yeah." He listened for a moment, then handed the phone to me. "Marco. You'll get better reception if you take it outside but stay by the door so I can keep an eye on you."

I nodded as I took the phone, my stomach flipflopping as I walked outside. "Hey, Marco."

"Did you make it to where you needed to go?"

"Yeah," I said. "We're safe."

"I don't like this, Care," he said, his voice sounding shaky. "It's not supposed to be this way. You're not supposed to be hiding without me there to protect you."

That was exactly how I felt, but Hank was right. We needed to leave Drum, but it still didn't ease my aching heart. "I think we're safe for now. Hank's being super careful. We're holed up somewhere going through our respective files." I drew in a shaky breath. "It's just like I said. Wyatt took notes about me since the night I came to town. He's used me every step of the way, Marco. He never really cared about me at all. He only wanted me back so he could keep an eye on me."

"Care, I'm so sorry."

"I don't know why I'm so surprised, and it's not like I wanted *him*. It's just…"

"It hurts. Of course it does." He sounded sympathetic, but I could hear a growing anger in his voice. I knew it wasn't directed at me.

"Have you seen him?"

"No, and not for lack of tryin'. Max and I went out to his house. His front door was busted open just like you said. I peered in the front door, and I could see the place had been tossed, but there was no sign of him. And before you ask, no, I didn't go inside." Then he added, "But Max did, since it was open, and he's his brother, which gives him the right to look. You were right. Everything was gone."

"Even the photos on the corkboard wall."

"Max told me the table and corkboard were all that was left down there."

"And the shackles," I said, shivering despite the warm temperature.

Shades of Truth

"And the shackles." He paused a beat. "I 'found' Trixie's pills. She admitted to goin' out to Ruth's, and when she couldn't get in, she searched Ruth's car and found the bottle. We booked her on possession, mostly to try to coerce her to talk. She won't admit to doin' Bingham's dirty work, and she didn't admit to what she was really lookin' for, not that I'm surprised. He's put the fear of God into her."

"So no breaks on the case?" I asked.

"No. And no sign of Franklin either. When Marta and I talked to his brother, he claimed he doesn't know what Franklin was up to, but I got the feeling his amnesia would disappear the moment the sheriff's department left his premises." Then he added, "Which is why Max is in there right now, tryin' to get more out of him."

"You're outside the bait shop?" I asked in surprise.

"I'm off for the night, and if my best friend wants to buy some bait and doesn't have transportation, then a good friend would take him. Especially since all four of Max's tires were slashed on his truck in front of Hank's house."

"Crap."

Marco released a chuckle. "Max had much stronger words."

"So if Max is at the bait shop, I take it he's going fishing?" I asked with a laugh.

"In a sense."

I could hear the grin in his voice, and my heart ached. "I miss you."

"I miss you too, but I think Hank's right. The best place for you is out of Drum right now. Wyatt's gonna want those files back, and if he's as cold as he sounds in his notes, then he'll do anything to get them."

"There's something else," I said. "Wyatt has a file on my father."

Marco was silent so long I thought we'd gotten disconnected. "Did you grab it?"

"No. But he keeps referencing it in his notes about me. He went to Dallas multiple times to get information on my father. Information I could likely use to bring him down. He's sat on it, waiting to use it to keep me in line."

Marco released a long string of curse words. "I'm gonna kill the bastard with my bare hands."

"No, you're not," I said.

"Okay, I'm not, but I want to make him suffer."

"I want to make him suffer too," I said. "But we'll find a way to do it without resorting to violence."

"There's something I don't understand," Marco said. "You said Wyatt's been gathering information on your father to get you to fall in line, so why hasn't he used it? He's been pretty pissed at you for the past few months. Why not dangle that information to get you to do what he wants?"

"I don't know, and neither does Hank," I admitted. "None of it makes sense."

"I'd ask you to make a copy of everything and email it to me, but I'm not sure that's a good idea. Still, you probably should make copies and stash them *somewhere*. Just in case."

"Yeah," I said. "Good idea. I'll tell Hank, and we can do it first thing tomorrow."

"There's one more thing, Care," he said gently. "And I hesitate to mention it with everything else goin' on, but I figure you have the right to know."

My heart skipped a beat. "What?"

"I got an email from Tiffany. She wants you to call her ASAP."

Tiffany had been my mother's best friend since childhood. She lived in Atlanta and owned a huge cosmetics company. Marco and I had met with her a week ago, but I didn't entirely trust her. She seemed terrified of my father, and I couldn't be sure she wouldn't sell me out. "Why?"

"She didn't say, but she *did* say it was time sensitive. She gave me her personal number for you to call her. What do you want to do?"

"I'm going to call her," I said. "She must think it's important if she wants to talk to me right away."

"It could be a setup."

"There's only one way to find out. Besides, I'm with Hank, and he's one of the most suspicious guys around. He's not going to let me walk into a trap."

"I agree, but the situation still worries me. Can you get cell phone service where you're at? I can text her number to you."

"Yeah," I said, realizing I hadn't checked my old phone since we'd left Drum. I wasn't in the habit of checking anymore, since it never worked in Drum, and besides, Marco and Max both had Hank's satellite phone number.

"Let me know what she says."

"I will. And let me know what Max finds out from Franklin's brother."

"If you hang on for a few seconds, we can find out together. I'll put you on speaker." I heard some noises, then Marco said, "Carly's on the line. Tell us how it went."

"Hey, Carly," Max said, "I didn't find out much, but it was definitely interestin'. Tater has been lookin' into something that went down with Ruth's mom. But I guess Ruth didn't know."

"Ruth's mom?" I said in surprise. "She died several years ago from a drug overdose."

"Tater's brother said he wasn't sure what it was all about. He only knew Tater took a trip to Chattanooga a week or so ago so he could talk to someone about her mother."

We were all silent for a moment before Marco asked, "Did his brother know if Tater found what he was lookin' for?"

"Yeah. He did. He said he'd found the proof he needed."

"Did he tell him what he was gonna do with it?" Marco asked.

"He was gonna give it to someone and get paid for it, but Tater refused to tell him who."

"Your dad?" I asked. "We know Franklin was meeting with him in secret."

"Could be," Max said. "But why would my dad be interested in what happened with Ruth's mother?"

"Could be something about drugs," I said. "We know she was a drug addict."

"But Chattanooga?" Marco said. "Why there?"

"Lula used to run drugs to Chattanooga," I said. "Maybe Ruth's mother used to meet with their connection. Like Lula was doing."

"But why would my father care?" Max asked. "That whole drug syndicate was wiped out."

"I don't know," Marco said, but he didn't sound convinced the drug angle fit. "We also can't forget that Bingham thought Franklin and Ruth had a box he was after."

"I think that box is old news," I said. "The toolbox Louise was after."

"Maybe," Marco said. "But one thing's for certain, if Franklin had hard copy proof of anything, it wasn't in their trailer. We turned that place upside down."

"So you don't have any idea where he might have gone in Chattanooga?" I asked. We were already here. Hank and I could check it out if we had some direction. Did it have anything to do with the bar Tammy mentioned? Surely not. Ruth's mother didn't fit Bart's type—young and naïve.

"No," Max said. "Nothin'."

"Well, if you find out, let me know. I might be able to help," I said, hoping they got my meaning.

"Be careful, Care," Marco warned, but I wasn't sure whether he was cautioning me not to say too much over the phone line or cautioning me to be careful if we investigated where Franklin might have gone. All I knew was that danger was closing in all around us.

Chapter Twenty-Six

Hank was watching me as I walked back inside. "Any news on Ruth's murder?"

"The sheriff's department hasn't made much progress." I told him what Marco had said about Trixie.

"She's never gonna cave," Hank said grimly. "She's more scared of Bingham than jail."

"The most interesting information came at the end of the call. Marco was waiting in the parking lot while Max went into the bait shop to talk to Franklin's brother. He came out at the end, though, and said Franklin was looking into something that had to do with Ruth's mother. I guess he came to Chattanooga to search for it."

"What was he lookin' for?"

"His brother didn't know. I guess Franklin told him he'd found something, but he wouldn't say what. Sounds like he was planning to give the information to someone, but his brother had no idea who. Marco said whatever it was probably wasn't in the trailer. They searched the place, and it didn't turn up."

"Maybe it was taken by the murderer, along with Max's spreadsheets."

"Yeah," I said. "I considered that."

He gestured to the file on his lap. "I started reading the file on Drummond instead of continuing with mine. It was too much like visitin' a drunk Ghost of Christmas Past. He got some stuff about me remarkably right but others were way off the mark."

"Mine too. He was positive I had some kind of partnership with Bingham."

He gave a sharp nod. "We need to keep that in mind as we read about the others. Some of it is accurate, the rest speculation he takes as truth."

"The key will be figuring out which is which." I walked over to my purse and dug out my phone. "My mother's best friend, the one in Atlanta, called Marco and told him she needed to talk to me right away. He was going to text me the number so I could call her."

He frowned. "What do you think she wants?"

"I have no idea, but I want to find out." I checked the screen and saw a notification with Marco's text. There were also two messages from Wyatt.

Carly, I know what you have, and I want it back.

Call me. The *or else* was implied.

I held up my phone. "Got a message from Wyatt. Surprise, surprise, he wants his files back. He wants me to call him."

His brow lifted. "You gonna do it?"

"At some point. I don't know if I'll do it tonight."

Mischievousness filled his eyes. "Let 'im stew."

"Agreed." I gestured toward the door. "I think I'm going to make this call outside."

He nodded. "I'll keep an eye on you."

I walked back outside and entered the number, my stomach twisting while I waited for her to answer. "Yes," she said hesitantly.

"Tiffany? It's Carly."

"Caroline," she said, sounding relieved. "You called."

I cringed at her use of my name. "Marco said it was important."

"It is." She paused. "Caroline, William wants to see you."

It took a moment for the significance of her statement to hit me. William Blakely. My father's younger brother. My mother's secret lover. My biological father. "How do you know that?"

"He knew you were missing, and he was deeply worried. So I told him I saw you. He wants to see you for himself."

I snorted in disgust. "It's a little late for him to be concerned about me now."

"He knows he screwed up. He feels terrible, and he'd like a chance to give you his side of the story."

"Fine. We can set up a Zoom call next week."

"He's here," she said quietly. "He's in Atlanta. He asked me to arrange a meeting."

My heart skipped a beat. "When?"

"Tomorrow."

I ran a hand over my head, feeling lightheaded. *"Tomorrow?"*

"I know it's short notice, but he's here on business. He has to leave tomorrow afternoon."

Anger burned in my chest. "So he didn't make the trip to see me. He's just shoehorning me in. No thanks."

"Caroline, wait. Don't hang up."

I didn't respond, trying to control my raging emotions. I had too much other shit going on in my life to deal with that self-centered asshole.

So why hadn't I ended the call?

"He combined this with a business trip," Tiffany said quietly. "He did it to protect you. We're both sure Randall's having him watched, especially now."

"All the more reason to make it a video call."

"He doesn't trust the internet. And he's worried he'll be recorded."

"How is that my problem?"

"Caroline," she said, sounding exasperated. "*You* came to *me* asking questions about your past. About William. Now's your chance to get the answers you're looking for."

When it was convenient for *him*. Still, there was no denying they had me by the nose. She knew how badly I wanted answers, and he'd issued the time constraint.

"Let's suppose I agree to meet. When and where?"

"My office. Ten a.m. William's flight is at two."

I cast a glance out the window of our room, knowing Hank was watching. "I'll meet at ten, but not at your office."

"Then where?"

"I don't know yet. I'll text you with a location."

"How are you going to find a location?" she asked, in an exasperated tone. "You're not even from here."

"I'm pretty resourceful. I'll figure it out. I'll let you know the location by nine a.m." Then, before she could try to dissuade me, I hung up.

I started to go inside and caught sight of the texts Wyatt had sent me. Even though Hank and I had agreed it was better to let Wyatt stew, I really wanted to call him. That man had done nothing but lie to me, and I wanted to confront him. I needed it.

So I called.

"Carly," he grunted when he answered, and I was so furious with him, it took me a couple of seconds before I could respond.

"You fucking liar."

It was his turn to be silent.

"You knew about my past. You knew how much Jake had hurt me. You fucking knew, and you used me anyway. You must have had a good laugh at stupid Carly."

"You mean Caroline," he said in a smug tone, but I could hear the anger simmering below the surface.

I took a deep breath to try to control my raging emotions. "You have information on my father."

"And you have information on mine."

Was he talking about my own research or the file Hank was currently scouring? "The key difference is my father wants me dead and yours is just annoyed." When he didn't respond, I said, "It's obvious from your file on me that you have absolutely no respect for me. Add in the fact that you have information that could help save my life, and you're not just a self-centered liar, you're *evil*."

"We can discuss my character flaws all you want, but it won't change the fact that you took my property and I want it back."

"Or what?" I chided. "You'll lock me up in your dungeon?"

"I don't have a dungeon," he said dismissively.

"You have a concrete room under your floor that can only be accessed by a removable ladder, and there's a metal ring embedded in the floor so you can chain someone up. Tell me how that doesn't qualify as a dungeon."

"Bring me back my files, and I can show you."

"You're disgusting," I spat.

"You're playing with things you can't understand and will get you into trouble."

"You mean like your buddy Derek running us off the road kind of trouble?" I challenged. "Or telling my father where I am kind of trouble?"

"The workings of Drum do not concern you," he said, conveniently changing the topic. "Right now we need to coordinate you giving me back my files. The fact that you're responding on your cell phone tells me you're not in Drum. I'd tell you not to come back, but I want those files."

"You mean, you *need* those files. The real question is what do you plan to do with them."

He pushed out a heavy breath. "That doesn't concern you. I want those files back. You have until six tomorrow night."

Chapter Twenty-Seven

I wasn't sure I felt any better about the Wyatt situation, but at least I'd done something. It was better than stewing in silence.

"What did she want?" Hank asked when I went back inside.

I sat on the edge of the bed next to him. "My birth father is in Atlanta."

He sat still, waiting for me to continue.

"He wants to meet with me tomorrow before he flies back to his yacht."

His mouth tipped up into the slightest grin before he turned serious. "What do you want to do?"

"Tell him to go rot in hell."

He released a short laugh. "So you *do* want to see him?"

I sucked in a deep breath to calm my nerves. "Yes. No. I don't know. The timing is terrible."

"Is it?" he asked, and when I gave him a questioning look, he said, "It seems to me all of this is coming to a head. Your father. Drum. Maybe Wyatt is connected to this Atlanta development."

"You think *he* contacted my biological father?"

"I don't know," Hank said, rubbing his chin. "But I feel like there's a possible connection." He lowered his hand. "I think you should meet with the man tomorrow."

My anxiety kicked up. "What if it's a trap?"

"Then we set the rules of the meetin'," Hank said. "Time and place."

"Tiffany wanted to meet in her office at ten. I told her we'd meet at ten, but we'd pick the place and let her know by nine."

He grinned. "Good girl. We can look into it." He set the file on the table. "But first we need to go out for a bit."

"Why? We already got food." I gestured to the fast food bag that still contained my dinner. I could see a food wrapper on the table next to Hank.

"Two reasons. First, I want to get a cheap laptop. We need to start savin' this information to the cloud in case we lose access to it."

"You mean in case Wyatt gets it back."

"Or someone else. We'll get a document scanner. Then I'd like to go to visit a local bar that's listed in Drummond's file. He was part owner a couple of decades ago, but he sold it to the other partial owner. I want to see if she's still around."

"She?" I asked in surprise. "Not that I'm against women owning bars. It's just that Bart seems too misogynistic to work with one."

"My thoughts exactly, which makes me even more curious to talk to her."

"I'm even more curious to speak with her after talking to Simon Franken's niece this morning." I told him about our call and her lead about a bar in Chattanooga where women who were impregnated by a powerful, dangerous man were sent to get their problem taken care of. "Is the bar we're going to have an animal in the name?"

His brow raised. "One Trick Pony."

I tried to tamp down my growing excitement. Even if it was the right place, there was no guarantee we'd find out anything of use.

"Okay," I said, glancing at the files. "What do we want to do with those?"

"Take 'em with us. The important ones, at least." He stuffed files into his bag—Bart's, Bingham's, and Max's.

"What about the others?" I asked.

"We need it, but we don't want to carry all of them around. These are the three most important. Besides, I don't expect anyone to take 'em. We're just being careful."

I nodded. "So where's this bar?"

"Pine Street, but we'll go to the electronics store first. We need to get there before they close."

***

An hour later, we had a laptop and document scanner, plus two new smartphones listed under an alias Hank had whipped out an ID for—Chester Field, who resided in Knoxville, Tennessee. Hank said the sat phones were best used in locations we couldn't get cell service, like most of Drum and the surrounding area. The fact he thought he needed a regular cell phone made me wonder what he was planning. But at the moment, I zeroed in on his new name.

"I guess a satellite phone wasn't the only thing you acquired while out of town," I said under my breath as the salesperson set up Chester's account.

He grinned. "I'm just full of surprises."

When we left the store, we both had working phones, with each other's numbers saved under contacts—Chester for him on my phone, and Girlie for me on his.

"You didn't have to get me a phone," I said once we were out in the car.

"I suspect this mess we're embroiled in will draw us into the world outside of Drum, which brings me to the next part of my surprise." He reached into his bag and pulled out a large manila envelope. "I hope you don't need this, but just in case…" His voice trailed off as he put it in my lap.

I opened the envelope and looked inside. It was filled with papers, and I could see two passport booklets. Pulling them out, I opened the first one and saw a photo of me—one of the extra passport photos I'd gotten for my new identity. "Anne Louise Clifton. Age 33. Nashville, Tennessee."

"There's a driver's license and a birth certificate," he said, his voice rough. "You'd be set. It'll pass any test."

"This must have cost you a fortune, Hank."

"It's insurance is all."

I opened the second passport, expecting to see his face, but saw Marco's instead. A lump filled my throat.

"I made sure you're married," he said. "There's a marriage certificate too."

"How?" I asked, not sure exactly what I was asking. "Marco's photo…"

"He had it taken in Ewing. He knew what I was doin'. He's prepared to run with you, if it comes to that."

I pressed my knuckles to my lips, emotion roiling in my chest. "I don't know what to say."

"There ain't nothin' to say. I told you that you're like family to me, and I take care of my own."

I reached over and hugged him, starting to cry.

He patted my back, murmuring, "There, there. It's all gonna be okay."

"Why me?" I asked, pulling away and searching his face in the light of the setting sun. "I have two fathers, and neither one of them cares about me even a sliver as much as you do. Why?"

He cupped my face. "Because both of those men are goddamn fools."

I laughed through my tears. "I love you, Hank."

"I love you too. I'll stand by you 'til the end."

Leaning forward, I kissed his cheek. "And I'll do the same."

"Enough of this blubbering," he said, sounding cross. "Time to use that new phone and get us directions to the bar."

I put the address into maps and then plugged the charger cord, thrilled when my phone connected.

It was a fifteen-minute drive to One Trick Pony, which turned out to be a country western bar—no surprise. A fiberglass horse on a pole over the neon sign rocked up on its back legs every twenty seconds or so. The parking lot was half full and country music blasted into the parking lot.

"I'm struggling to see Bart in here," I said. I was nervous. We had the potential to get real information to bring Bart down. But we were just as likely to crash and burn. I hoped I didn't blow it.

Hank didn't answer, just got out of the car with his messenger bag slung over one shoulder.

We headed inside, and I knew the blaring music would give me a headache in about two minutes. There were people on the dance floor, but most of the patrons were sitting at tables drinking. Hank moved to the bar like a man on a mission, angling for a space between two different groups. He leaned closer when the male bartender approached us. "We need to speak to Patricia."

The bartender's eyes narrowed. "What business do you have with Patricia?"

Hank leaned even closer. "Tell her we're here about a man from her past."

The bartender didn't look happy, but he walked over to a phone and picked it up.

I leaned into Hank's ear. "Do you think she's going to talk to us?"

"I say we have a fifty/fifty chance of seeing her or gettin' kicked out. The barkeep didn't seem too happy I was askin', so maybe the odds are closer to forty/sixty."

Seconds later, a big burly man emerged from the back and walked over to us. A bouncer from the looks of him. Just when I was sure he was about to toss us out, he said, "Come with me," then headed back down the hall from which he'd come.

I shot Hank a glance, and we followed, but I could see Hank shifting his bag to give himself easy access to the contents. I knew he had a handgun tucked in there.

The bouncer took us to a closed door and knocked.

"Come in," a woman called out, and the bouncer opened the door and gestured for us to go in.

I expected to walk into a small office like Max's, but it didn't look a thing like the cramped space in the back of the tavern. The walls were lined with bookshelves, and a sitting area was situated to one side of the wooden desk. A woman who looked to be in her late forties or early fifties sat in one of the armchairs, smoking a cigar. She wore jeans, a short-sleeved black T-shirt, and turquoise cowboy boots. Her dark blond hair was cut into a bob that brushed her shoulders.

"I hear you're here about a man from my past. I have quite a few men from my past." She smiled, but it was tight. "You'll have to be more specific."

"We're here to ask you a few questions," Hank said. "About a couple of people we might mutually know."

She waved her hand to the tufted red leather sofa. "It's straining my neck to look up at you. Have a seat."

We took a seat while she watched us with an amused expression. "There seem to be a lot of people askin' questions lately. Why don't you tell me where y'all are from?" She held up her hand. "Let me guess. Drum."

My heart started racing. She definitely knew something. We were so freaking close. I wasn't sure how I'd handle it if she sent us away with nothing.

"We think a man named Franklin came to see you last week," I said, deciding to jump right in. She seemed like a woman who appreciated someone not wasting her time. "Franklin Tate. He might have gone by Tater. Did he meet with you."

She shrugged, but it was a delicate motion. "Perhaps."

"Franklin is currently missing, and his girlfriend is dead," I said. "We can't help wondering if your conversation with him could cast some light on what happened."

If my announcement shocked her, she didn't let on.

"Ruth was my friend," I said, the breaking of my voice genuine. "The sheriff's department has practically nothing to go on. We'd be grateful for anything you can give us."

"Was he here about Drummond?" Hank asked in a short tone.

Her brow raised with a smug expression. "What makes you think I know anything about this Drummond?"

"I know for a fact he was a partial owner of this bar a couple of decades ago," Hank said calmly. "What I want to know is what you held over him to convince him to give it to you."

Hank had held that part back when he'd told me about this place.

She took a drag of her cigar and blew out a ring. "What makes you think he gave it to me? Why wouldn't he sell it?"

Hank held her gaze. "Because there's no record of the sale. What did you know? And more importantly, why didn't he kill you?"

She laughed. "We're obviously talkin' about the same Drummond."

"How did you meet him?" Hank asked.

"What makes you think I'm gonna tell you anything?" Patricia asked, then took a long puff of her cigar.

"You told Franklin something," I said. "Whatever you told him likely got him killed."

"And I should tell you so you can run off and get killed too?" she asked with a laugh, then turned her gaze to Hank. "But not you. You're too much of a grizzly to get killed without a fuss."

Who the hell was this woman?

Hank shifted his weight and leaned forward. "Look here, Patricia," he said conversationally. "You're gonna tell us what we want to know. You know why? Because I've got proof that you blackmailed Drummond to give you his half of the bar, and I'm sure the DA's office would love to take a look at that."

I tried to hide my surprise. Had Wyatt put the proof in Bart's file?

She laughed. "And we both know the statute of limitations is four years. I'm well outside of that." Then she added, "If you *had* proof, which I don't believe you do."

"If you resort to extortion," Hank said, "I'm sure there are plenty of other crimes the police might be interested in. Like murder."

Murder? There was obviously more in the file about this place and Patricia than Hank had let on.

A slow smile spread across her face, and if I hadn't been watching closely, I wouldn't have seen her flinch. "That's a big leap, Mr.…?"

"Chalmers. Hank Chalmers."

She flinched again, her reaction more noticeable this time.

So she'd heard of him. Had Bart told her or did Hank have a reputation outside of Drum?

"Franklin came to you to find out information about Delores Bristol. What did you tell him?"

Did Hank know Ruth's mother's name? And then it hit me, the significance of his question.

She stubbed out her cigar in a dirty ashtray, then leaned back and crossed her legs. "Now why do I think you already know what I told him?"

"Because you don't best Bart Drummond without being smart," he responded. "Which means you're extremely intelligent."

"Okay," she said with a forced smile. "I don't get many compliments around here, so why not?" She crossed her legs. "Bart used to send his women to me. The ones who got knocked up and needed to take care of things."

"You mean abortions?" I asked. "Why not go to a clinic?"

"It's a hassle," Patricia said with a shrug. "I streamlined the process for everyone, and Bart was assured it was taken care of discreetly."

"And you charged a handling fee," I said.

She held her hands out, palms up. "As Hank so charmingly pointed out, I *am* an intelligent businesswoman. And more importantly, it was all perfectly legal."

"Delores came to see you?" I asked.

"She did. About twenty years ago." Something flickered in her eyes.

Twenty years ago.

"She didn't go through with it," I said flatly. But the baby wasn't Ruth. Ruth had been in her mid-thirties. Ruth had told me she was an only child. Which meant...

Patricia pointed a finger at me. "You're a smart woman too. I didn't catch your name."

"You don't need to know her name," Hank said. "You just need to confirm what she said is true."

She pushed out a sound of irritation. "It is. Delores came to me, but she changed her mind. She begged me not to tell Bart." She shrugged again. "I was willing to keep it to myself for a small fee."

"How much was the small fee?" Hank asked.

"Five thousand. Not much."

"That was a whole lot for a woman like Delores," Hank said.

She made a face that suggested it was no concern of hers.

And also highly questionable in the legal area. "But Bart found out," I said.

"Not for a good seven or eight months," Patricia said. "Apparently, she hid her pregnancy well, and even the birth. She had the baby at home, I hear. Her daughter helped deliver her."

I gasped. "Ruth?"

"If I knew her name, I've long since forgotten. But I'll never forget Bart callin' and demandin' to know why Delores hadn't gone through with the procedure. I told him I didn't force anyone to do what they didn't want to do. If she wanted to keep her baby, then that was her business. Well, a week later, Bart barges in through the back door of my office. He's got an infant carrier with him, and it's covered in a mountain of blankets."

My skin turned clammy.

"He sets it down on my desk and makes me take the blankets off. The poor thing was dead. He told me it was my fault. That poor Delores was going to mourn her child because I refused to follow simple directions."

"Bart killed her?" I asked.

"Delores thought he was going to give her up for adoption, but in truth, he didn't want any bastards runnin' around. So he killed her, but no one other than Delores knew the baby was gone. She'd never filed a birth certificate because she was too scared Bart would find out."

It had been pointless. He'd found out anyway.

"What about her daughter?" I asked. "She knew." But did she know the full truth? Had she told Franklin about having a sister, and he'd put it together and investigated?

"I'm not sure. Delores probably told her the same thing Bart told her. That the baby was adopted."

"How did *Louise* find out?" I asked.

"Louise Baker?" Patricia asked, then rolled her eyes. "She came to me, claimin' to be Delores's friend and askin' about what really happened. I didn't tell her shit. *Any* of the multiple times she's dropped in." Shaking her head, she added, "She's one crazy ass bitch."

So they *had* met. "But fifteen years ago, she supposedly went to Bart, claiming to have proof of a child's murder," I said. "You didn't give it to her?"

"What can I tell you? Didn't come from me. Delores must have told her."

"What happened to the baby?" I asked.

"Bart left that poor thing on my desk," she said, trying to sound casual, but she looked haunted. "Then he took off.

What he *didn't* know was I'd installed new security cameras and recorded the whole thing. I sent him a copy of the tape, told him I had multiple other copies and if he even thought about killing me, he'd be arrested for not only my murder, but the baby's too. Then he agreed to sign over his share of the bar, graciously free of charge."

"I suspect it wasn't so congenial," Hank said. "But it *was* smart."

"You could have gone to the police," I said. "You could have turned him in."

She gave me a long, hard look. "That baby was already dead, and there was nothing I could do to bring her back. So I figured I might as well get something out of it."

"Do you have any idea how many lives he's destroyed since then?" I asked, incredulous that she could be so cold.

"Not my problem. I got him out of my hair, yet his issues keep popping up like a bad penny. His son even insisted on taking a copy of the tape."

"Did you give it to him?" Hank asked.

She snorted. "The gun he had trained on me was pretty convincing."

"And his son's name?" I asked, my stomach in knots.

"Wyatt."

My shoulders physically sagged with relief.

"You thought it might be Max?" she laughed. "Bart always suspected that boy wasn't his kin. Had a DNA test to prove it, only it came back a match. Still couldn't stand the boy. Said he's too much like his mother. Maybe he should have been more worried about the older one."

"You make it sound like you've talked to him recently," Hank said.

"Recent enough," Patricia said, leaning to the side. "He drops by from time to time, likely to check up on me and my copies of his murder confession. I always assure him I've kept his secret to myself." She grinned. "I'm not above lyin' to save my skin."

"How do we know you're not lyin' now?" Hank asked.

"Because I've got that video to prove it." She got out of her chair and walked behind her desk. She grabbed the bottom of a painting of a lake and swung it out on hinges I hadn't noticed, revealing a safe. Blocking our view, she entered the code, and the door popped open. After she took something out, she closed it up and walked over to Hank, handing over a flash drive. "I seem to be passin' these out like party favors. Make sure you actually do something with it. The others assured me they would, and I've yet to see anything come of it."

"You gave one to Franklin?" I asked.

"Yep. And Wyatt. But not Louise. I didn't trust her."

"You know you'll be implicated in this," Hank said.

She shook her head. "My back is to the camera the entire time. But even if they find out it's me, I'll cooperate."

"What happened to the baby?" I asked, still horrified by the whole thing.

"I buried her in my backyard," she said, showing a hint of emotion for the first time. "Her name was Milly. Couldn't have been more than a month old." Her voice broke. "She was wearing a footed sleeper. She looked like a little angel. I planted a rose bush by her grave." Her face hardened. "Y'all got what you came for. Now it's time for you to leave."

Chapter Twenty-Eight

Hank and I didn't say anything after we got back in the car. I didn't even turn on the engine, just sat there staring at the entrance to the bar.

"That man is pure evil," Hank finally said. "And it sounds like his son is followin' in his footsteps."

I swallowed the lump in my throat. "That was all in Bart's file, wasn't it? That's how you knew what to ask. Wyatt wrote it all in there."

"Yep."

"How long ago did Wyatt come see her?"

"Two years ago."

"For two years, he's had exactly what he needs to bring that man down, and he didn't do a damn thing with it."

Hank reached over and covered my hand gripping the steering wheel. "We'll take care of it."

I nodded but didn't trust myself to say anything.

"Let's go back to the motel, girlie. You need a good night's sleep before you see your biological father."

"His name is William," I said firmly as I turned on the car and shifted it into drive. "I will not be calling him *my father*.

Even Randall Blakely gave me a place to live and food to eat. William Blakely gave me absolutely nothing."

"Fair enough," Hank said. "I suppose we could just call him Dog Shit."

I laughed, then tears slid down my cheeks. "There's a murdered baby on that flash drive, Hank. Bart Drummond killed a one-month-old baby."

"I know," he said softly. "And it's hard for you to imagine such evil, even after everything you've faced." He took a second, then said, "Which is why I don't want you to read Bart's file. Not yet."

My back stiffened, and all my old fears and distrust returned. "Why?"

After another brief pause, he said, "I'm not gonna make that decision. I'm gonna leave it up to you. But Wyatt's got more incriminatin' evidence on his father than you could imagine. Some truly horrific things. I say we hand it over to Marco and let him decide what to do with it. We can send everything to him tonight, but I think you'll be truly haunted if you read it. At least wait until after your visit with Dog Shit."

I barked a laugh at William's nickname. "Okay," I said as I pulled up to a stop sign. I turned to face him, looking him square in the eye. "I'm trusting you to keep your word, Hank."

"And I appreciate how difficult that is for you to do. I swear that I will never knowingly hurt you, girlie. You're like a daughter to me. I'd rather cut off my other leg than betray you."

"Thank you," I choked out.

He answered with a sad smile.

***

We didn't waste any time getting back to our room. While I was setting up the new laptop, I video called Marco from my new phone. "It's good to see your face," he said. He looked exhausted, but I wasn't about to call him on it.

"It's good to see yours too, but there's another reason I'm calling." Then Hank and I told him everything that had happened with Patricia.

"Will it be enough to bring Bart down?" I asked.

"It depends," Marco said. "How clearly can we see his face? Hear his voice? I'll need to see the video to know for certain."

"Wyatt and Franklin got a copy of the footage too," I said. "And now Ruth is dead and Franklin's missing. You need to be careful, Marco. Max too."

"Max is passed out on the sofa." He lowered his voice. "He's scared to death of goin' to prison."

I gasped. "He told you what Ruth had?"

His mouth twisted into a grim smile. "We're best friends. He knows that trumps my job."

That wasn't how his job worked, and I worried he'd get into trouble, but part of me was glad Max had confided in him. I didn't like having secrets between us.

"Will he go to prison?"

"Not if we can keep it quiet." He paused. "We still don't know who killed Ruth and took Franklin. Did Bart find out and take care of things himself? Or did Bingham kill them lookin' for information?"

"Are you upset with me for not telling you?" I asked, scared to death he wouldn't trust me now.

A soft smile lit up his face. "I love that you wanted to protect Max, and I know you would have told me." He tilted his head. "Just like Max did."

"I love you."

"I love you too. Now tell me—did you talk to Tiffany?"

The computer setup was complete so I started creating a Dropbox account for Hank's alias. I was grateful for the distraction so I didn't have to look at Marco as I told him.

"My birth father is in Atlanta for business. He's leaving tomorrow afternoon but wants to see me in the morning."

I darted a glance at Marco's stunned face. "How do you feel about that?"

"I have very mixed emotions. I'm pissed that he's the one setting the timetable, but Tiffany pointed out that I'm desperate for information and this is my chance."

"Fuck Tiffany."

I couldn't help smiling.

"So what do you want to do, Care?"

"I have to go see him. Otherwise, I think I'll regret it."

Marco's eyes softened. "Do you want me to come with you?"

"Yes," I whispered, then amended, "But no. I have Hank, and he's going to make sure I don't walk into a trap. Besides, I think I need to do this on my own."

I was worried he'd be hurt, but understanding filled his eyes. "Well, I'm here, ready to talk after you're done."

"If you have internet or cell service," I teased.

"What time's your meetin'?"

"Ten."

"Then I'll make sure I'm somewhere with service by 10:10."

The Dropbox account was set up and ready to go, so I uploaded the flash drive contents, telling Marco what I was doing.

"I haven't watched it," I confessed.

"You don't need to," he said gravely. "That's why I'm here. To assess if we can use it as evidence." He paused. "I'm gonna watch it and call you back."

"No," I said. "Don't hang up."

"Then I'll put you on pause."

I nodded, feeling weak, but I told myself that watching a video of a dead baby wouldn't make me strong. Except...not watching it made me a coward. "Wait, Marco. I'm going to watch it too."

"You don't have to do that, Care."

"I know, but I need to." I needed to see this for myself. I needed to see the full extent of Bart Drummond's evil to steel myself for what came next.

Marco shifted the camera to focus on his computer screen, and we watched the video together. It played out pretty much how Patricia had said it would. Bart walked in with an infant seat covered in blankets and set it on her desk, although it was a different desk than the one she had now, the office around it not quite so nice.

Patricia uncovered the baby and recoiled in horror. The camera had a full-on view of the dead baby, so there could be no doubt. Bart admitted to killing the baby in a conversation that was nearly identical to the one she'd recounted to us, and I had to wonder how often she'd relived it in her head. The back of her head was to the cameras, I couldn't see her face. Bart ended the conversation and left. The screen went black, and then the same scene played again, just from a different angle, and this time the side of her face was visible. The screen went blank again, and then we could hear a phone ringing. It was the phone conversation Patricia had told us about, in which she extorted Bart for ownership of the bar if she promised to keep it quiet. He threatened her life if she didn't, then the call ended.

We were both silent for several long seconds. Hank sat on the bed, wearing a grave expression.

"Well?" I finally asked when Marco turned the camera around. "Is it enough?"

A hard look filled his eyes. "We're gonna nail him."

Hank and I spent the next several hours making copies of documents and compiling them together in files on the cloud. Marco was reading the pages as they uploaded. At midnight, he told us to stop and do the rest the next day.

"It's overkill at this point, and you need to sleep. These documents may not be enough on their own, but with the video? The audio might be admissible if we can get permission from the woman. In fact, I suspect it's enough to indict. I'll take it to the state police first thing in the morning." He glanced toward his bedroom door. "And I'll be takin' Max with me. I don't trust Wyatt or his father around him."

"I still have a hard time believing they'd hurt him, even when I know how bad they actually are."

"He's shown his loyalty," Marco said. "Or lack thereof. No one is safe."

Chapter Twenty-Nine

Hank and I arrived in Atlanta by nine. I'd woken up early, unable to sleep, and since Hank was an early riser, we packed everything up and headed for a Starbucks drive through before we left Chattanooga.

We were on the highway and almost out of Chattanooga traffic when Marco called to let me know that he and Max were headed to Knoxville. He'd sent backup copies of the video and documents to two different cloud storages he'd purchased after our talk last night, and he'd already forwarded the link to one of the folders—one without Hank's alias attached—to a contact he had with the state police. He'd also sent it to Detective White.

"Just coverin' all the bases," he said. "No chance for Wyatt to delete them this time."

So where were those videos Wyatt had stolen? I hadn't seen any flash drives in his secret room, and there hadn't been any computers. Or had he completely deleted them? It seemed unlikely since he'd kept such meticulous records. He had those videos stored somewhere, and I was guessing they were in some other storage cloud. And where was Jerry's phone? Did he have another hiding place?

"We've got him, Care," he said reassuringly. "Just focus on your meeting with—"

"With Dog Shit," Hank supplied. "We're callin' him Dog Shit."

Marco laughed. "Sounds fittin' to me."

"Me too," I said with a smile, but it quickly faded as the enormity of what we were both doing hit me. "Be careful, Marco. I love you too much to lose you."

"You too. As soon as I get this settled with the state police and we figure out who killed Ruth, we're leavin' Drum. For good."

I shot a glance at Hank, who was busy staring out the windshield like he couldn't hear Marco's voice booming through the car's speakers. "No need to put the cart before the horse," I said. "We've got other things to deal with before we start makin' any decisions."

But we both knew the time was coming for us to act against my father. Where would that leave Hank?

We hung up and I reached over and patted Hank's hand resting on the middle console. "You know I don't plan on just running off when this is all over."

"Of course you will," he said, sounding pissed. "The worst insult you could heap on me is if you stay in Drum."

"I have friends there," I protested. "I have you." Then I added matter-of-factly, "Okay then. I guess you'll just come with me."

"I can't leave Drum," he said, but most of his anger had faded. "It's in my blood." He shot me a dark look. "But it's not in yours. You need to be somewhere else. Besides, Ruth is dead, and Lula is happily under Bingham's thumb. Max might have to go on the run for his money laundering, if he doesn't get sent to prison first. Marco will follow you anywhere. There's no one left in Drum to stick around for."

"There's you, and you're not nothing."

He released a long sigh. "Girlie, children grow up and leave their parents all the time. It's the way of things. If I'd only encouraged Barb to fly away, things might have been different. She might still be alive." He gave me a wobbly smile. "You deserve the world, Carly Moore, and I intend to help give it to you. Even if it means you fly away from Drum. *Especially* if it means you leave Drum."

I pressed my lips together. "Well, just like I told Marco, it's too soon to be talking what ifs. We need to deal with what's right in front of us before we can think about what's beyond that."

"There's no harm in dreamin'," Hank said, stretching out his good leg and leaning his head against the backrest. "Speakin' of which, I think I'm gonna take a little snooze."

"Good idea."

But after a couple of seconds of silence, I said, "Hank, what's your dream?"

"I'm too old to have a dream, girlie."

"That's a load of bullshit."

A grin stretched his face even though his eyes remained closed.

"You just got your millions in gold back," I persisted. "What's *your* dream?"

"To learn to be content." He cracked an eye open and turned his head to face me. "I was never content, not once…" He paused and opened the other eye. "And the rest of my dream is for you to be happy and safe. Everything after that is gravy. What about you? You said you don't want to think that far ahead, but I don't believe you haven't looked toward the future and seen yourself there. What do *you* want, girlie?"

I took a second to think about it before I said, "To be safe and to *always* feel loved. I never felt worthy of love when I was a kid, and I realize it's affected just about every decision I've ever made. I want to stop acting so defensively, and just live."

"Good goals," he said softly. "Does Marco fit into that?"

I smiled. "Marco is the one who made me feel loveable, despite all my imperfections. I *only* see Marco at the end of this. I don't know what the rest looks like."

And that was what scared me. It wouldn't be hard for my father to figure out he could use Marco to hurt me. Shoot, Wyatt already knew that. By loving Marco, I'd put a target on his back. I wasn't sure I could ever forgive myself if something happened to him because of me.

"Trust that everything will work out," Hank said, patting my hand. "You've got people on your side to make sure it does."

He went to sleep after that, leaving me to stew in my thoughts while I dealt with morning traffic near Atlanta, which turned out to be a bigger mess than I'd expected. Good thing we'd left extra early.

Using Google, we'd found a meeting place the night before. It was a restaurant near Tiffany's office and had lots of windows overlooking the street. Based on the few images we'd found on the internet, Hank thought it would be relatively easy for him to keep an eye on things should William bring any friends or in case my father was tracking him. Hank woke up as we approached Atlanta and sent Tiffany a text from my phone, giving her the address. We arrived fifteen minutes early, and I selected a booth on the wall opposite the windows. Hank claimed a seat a couple of rows behind me, giving him a view of most of the restaurant and the street beyond it.

Still, he was only one man with one pair of eyes, he reminded me. I needed to do my own due diligence.

The waitress brought me a menu, so I ordered coffee and told her I needed some time to look over the menu while I waited for a friend. There were multiple empty tables around, so I heard Hank make his order for something called the Big Peach Platter and a carafe of coffee.

It was hard to sit still, so I pulled out my notebook, more out of force of habit than because I was trying to tie a murder to Bart. We had that one in the bag. We just needed to figure out who'd killed Ruth and what he or she had done with Max's spreadsheets.

I pulled out my new cell phone and called Marco.

"That was fast," he said in surprise. "Is it over already?"

"No, he hasn't shown up yet," I said, keeping an eye on the door. "Are you at the state police headquarters?"

"Yeah. Max and I are in a conference room waiting for an investigator to come in and talk to us."

"So I'm sitting in this restaurant waiting for Dog Shit to show up, and I got to thinking—has Max talked to his mother about Ruth's murder? Does she have any insight about who might be after those spreadsheets?"

"He's here next to me. I'm going to let you ask him that question."

A few seconds later, I heard Max's tired voice, "Hey, Carly. I hear you're meetin' your birth father this mornin'."

"Yeah, but he won't be here for another ten minutes or so, and I've got nothing to do but think."

"Yeah," he said dryly. "I know the feelin'."

"Have you talked to your mom since you told her about Ruth?"

"I've tried a couple of times, but her maid says she has a migraine and is restin' in her room."

"Do you think she *really* has a migraine?"

"Not a chance in hell."

"Then should you be worried? Do you think your dad has hurt her?"

"No. She does this. It's her classic move. When something comes up that she doesn't want to deal with, she hides in her room, claimin' she has a headache, and Annie covers for her. It's been like that for years."

"That's surprising," I said. "Your mother doesn't seem like a stick-her-head-in-the-sand type of woman."

"I'm sure she's schemin'," he said, sounding disinterested. "It's her way."

"And does your father disturb her when she's nursing a migraine-slash-scheming?"

"No."

I flipped my notebook to the last written page and took note of that. "I'm just looking at some of the loose pieces and trying to figure out where they fit. Like why is Bingham searching the history of the town? And what does he have on your father?"

"All good questions I don't have an answer to."

"Are you worried your mother will be implicated in all of this?" I asked.

"Marco showed me that video," he said, his voice dull. "I plan to make my father pay for that. And all the other people he's hurt along the way. My mother has her own sins, but she didn't play any part in that."

"If your father took the spreadsheets, that means you're safe from the authorities. He won't turn you and your mother in, but you won't be safe from *him*."

"I doubt he'd kill me," Max said in the same dull tone, and I realized he was in shock. It couldn't be easy to watch your father talking about the murder of a baby as though he were discussing swatting a fly with a newspaper. Even if your father was Bart Drummond.

"Be safe and presume he wants to kill you anyway." After everything we'd learned the night before, I wasn't so sure I believed anyone was safe from his father.

"Yeah. Sure."

"I know this is hard," I said, lowering my voice. "I know how earth-shattering it is to find out your father is capable of something so cold-blooded. Trust me, Max, I know better than anyone. My father killed my mother. He wants to kill *me*." I took a deep breath, then lowered my voice even more. "Which means Bart *can* and *will* kill you if it guarantees his own self-preservation."

"I knew he was bad, Carly. And I knew he used his favor system to have lots of innocent people hurt or killed, but this was a *baby*." His voice broke. "My baby sister. And he killed her. Smothered her like she was *nothing*." He broke down. "He's a fuckin' *monster*."

"I know. But stick with Marco. He's going to make sure your father doesn't get away with it."

"Yeah."

"And call your mother again. I have a bad feeling about all of this."

"I know what you mean," he said. "But Marco says the state police will send someone out to bring her in for questioning. They'll want to find out what she knows about the murder. I'll try to talk to her after they question her. Offer to take her home." He chuckled, but it sounded forced. "Those trips to the station are usually one-way deals."

"Good idea."

I saw movement by the front door, and my heart skipped a beat as an impeccably dressed woman in a white dress and blood-red heels walked in, followed by a man in an expensive gray suit. She looked like she was in her forties even though I knew she was in her fifties. He had graying hair and wrinkles around his eyes, the kind you got from squinting in the sun, and I knew immediately he was my father's brother. They shared the same eyes. And apparently the same taste in fine clothes. It was apparent William's exile wasn't one of poverty. But then I'd gathered as much from the photos Marco and I had found on the internet. "Grayson Matthews" owned a yacht in Kennebunkport, Maine.

"Max. I've got to go. They're here. Tell Marco I'll call him as soon as we're done."

"Be careful, Carly."

"Yeah. You too." I hung up and lowered my phone into my lap, starting the voice recorder before I set it on the seat beside me.

Tiffany scanned the room, her gaze landing on me. Instead of the relief and concern she'd emoted on my visit to her office, she looked almost annoyed. She leaned into William and murmured something in his ear before nodding in my direction. He observed me with a grim expression before a determined look filled his eyes. Then he strode toward me, looking very much like my father in more than just his physical appearance.

This suddenly felt like a huge mistake.

Chapter Thirty

I watched him, trying to look as detached as possible, but my heart was racing. I got out of the seat to greet Tiffany, who nudged my uncle aside and embraced me in a tight hug.

"Don't you know you'd be safer in my office?" she whispered in my ear. "At least I have security there. Here you're completely exposed. And vulnerable."

I had Hank at my back, but she didn't know that, and I preferred to keep it that way. "Then we'll make the best of it," I said with a tight smile as she released me, leaving me face to face with William Randall.

He eyed me up and down, his face expressionless. "Caroline." His voice was gruff and low. He wasn't giving me the impression he wanted to be here, and I was beginning to wonder if Tiffany had dragged him into this meeting.

"I prefer Carly."

Surprise filled his eyes, likely because he remembered it was my mother's nickname for me, but he didn't comment, just gestured to the booth. "Shall we?"

I slid onto my seat. Tiffany hesitated, giving me an apologetic look. "I think I should leave and let you two have a chat alone."

I nodded. "That's fine." It was actually the way I preferred it, but now that I saw William's hesitation, I wondered how long he'd stay. I considered taking the offensive and calling the whole thing off, but any information was better than the nothing I had. Not to mention we had driven over two hours to get here.

"Will you come by my office when you're done?" she asked wistfully. "I really do want the chance to spend more time with you."

Even if I was tempted—and I wasn't sure I was—it wasn't a good time. I had too many other issues to deal with first. But the less she knew, the better. "We'll see."

She glanced around the restaurant. "Where's your handsome young deputy/protector?"

"Marco's working on an important case," I said.

Her gaze jerked back to mine. "More important than *you?*"

"It is."

"All the more reason for you to stay," Tiffany said in alarm. "We'll move this meeting to my office, and then you'll come home with me."

"No. I think Uncle William and I would prefer to stay here," I said, looking up at him. "Isn't that right, Uncle Will?"

Caught off guard, he lifted a brow. "Yes. That's right."

Tiffany looked torn, so I got up and gave her another hug. "It's okay. I'll check in when we're done."

"All right," she said, pulling back and giving my uncle a long look. "William. It was good to see you."

"And you," he said stiffly.

I took my seat as Tiffany headed for the exit.

Shades of Truth

William unbuttoned his jacket before he took a seat opposite me in the booth, then glanced around the room, probably making sure Tiffany had really left. I got the impression he wasn't impressed with our surroundings, which pissed me off. It wasn't a five-star Michelin restaurant, but we weren't in a roadside diner either.

"I see exile has treated you well," I said dryly. Obviously not the best way to start our conversation since I was hoping for answers, but I was furious, and about way more than his reaction to the restaurant.

His head jutted back. "Well, I suppose that answers *that* question," he said in a snooty tone.

"Which was?"

"If you were like your mother."

It was an insult, and it took me by surprise. My biological father had abandoned me to the murderer of the woman he'd claimed to love, and he had disdain for *me*?

"Well, I guess you have a point there," I said with a hard edge in my voice. "Randall Blakely killed *her*, though, and he's only tried to kill me." I took a sip from my half-empty coffee cup and watched for his reaction.

Irritation filled his eyes, and he shot a dark look at the waitress who was headed toward us.

"Would you like some coffee?" she asked him. "Do you need more time to look at the menu?"

"Nothing for me," he said. "I won't be staying long."

The hostility in his voice made her take a step back.

"Nothing else for me," I said, feeling guilty that she had to endure his attitude. Then, reading her nametag, I added sweetly, "Thank you, Anna."

She flashed me a smile, cast a worried glance at my breakfast date, then scurried off.

I folded my hands on the table, looked my uncle in the eyes, and asked bluntly, "Why are you here?"

"What are you talking about? I was told you wanted to meet."

"And based on your hostile attitude, that alone wasn't enough to convince you. How did Tiffany force you to come?"

His lips pressed together into a thin line. "She can be persuasive. Especially when she knows certain secrets."

"Good old-fashioned blackmail," I said, setting my cup down in front of me. "Charming."

He held out his hands and glared. "I'm here. What more do you want?"

I sat back in my seat, eyeing him with disgust. "That's a great question. Maybe I'd created some fantasy in my head that my biological father loved me and only left me with his murderous brother because he had no choice. But now I see you were only too glad to leave me there." I shook my head. "Were you just pretending to like me when I was little?"

"No," he said gruffly as he looked toward the windows. "That was genuine."

"When did you start to hate me?"

He rolled his eyes. "Don't be dramatic, Caroline."

"How can you sit there and say with a straight face that you love me after the greeting you just gave me?" I leaned closer. "I haven't seen you in over *twenty years*, and *this* is how you greet me?"

He leaned closer too, his eyes narrowing. "Can you imagine what will happen to me if he finds out that I met you?" he hissed. "He told me to leave and *never* contact you again."

"I see," I said, because I *did*—all too clearly. Until recently, I'd painted a picture in my head of a grieving father who'd always wanted to save me but didn't have the resources. But this man, my "uncle," was a self-centered asshole only looking out for himself. "Then I guess we'd better hurry this meeting along."

His mouth stretched into what was probably supposed to be a grin of sorts, but it only made him look constipated. "Let's."

I pulled out my notebook and opened to the next empty page. "Did you suspect my mother's parents were murdered?"

He blinked. "What?" He glanced around, then lowered his voice as he faced me. "Have you lost your mind?"

"No, actually. I know exactly what I'm doing. You've made it perfectly clear you're not interested in chitchat or personal stuff, so I'll get right to the point. Did you ever suspect my mother's parents were killed?"

He looked insulted. "I'm not going to answer that."

"Fine. Next question, did you know I was your daughter before my mother told you that my father was sterile?"

"Jesus," he said in disgust, jerking away from the table. "Have you no tact?"

"I have plenty of tact," I said through gritted teeth. "But I save it for people who are worthy of it. And yes, you can leave and not answer my questions. That's your right, but then I'll just run to Aunt Tiffany and tell her how uncooperative you were and let her pull whatever string or lever she's threatening you with." I gave him a fake smile. "But I don't think a coward like you will want to risk it."

Outrage covered his face. A vein throbbed on his forehead. "You dare to call me a *coward?*"

"Yes," I said, my voice tight with fury. "Any man who abandons his child is a fucking coward."

He started to get out of his seat, then thought better of it and sat back down and pointed his finger at me. "You have *no right* to judge me. You don't know the first thing about me."

"And whose fault is that?"

His face reddened, but he didn't get up to leave. Small win.

"So, let me ask you again: did you know I was your biological daughter before my father discovered he was sterile?"

"No," he choked out. "But I suspected. No concrete reason. Just a gut feeling."

I nodded, surprised he'd bothered to expand upon his single word answer.

"How did you find out? From my mother or my father?"

"Mary Caroline." His tone softened as he glanced down at the table. "She was terrified. But she thought the worst that might happen was that he'd divorce her. Neither of us thought he'd murder her."

"Even after he murdered her parents?"

He looked up at me, and I was surprised to see the vulnerability in his eyes. "I never suspected he murdered them. Not until Tiffany suggested it at Mary Caroline's funeral."

"Tiffany said you left town before her accident."

Guilt filled his eyes but was quickly replaced by anger. "She *told* me to leave."

"I wasn't insinuating anything. Only stating what I was told."

He tapped a finger on the table. "I asked her to go with me. I *begged* her. She still loved me, and their 'perfect' marriage had fast become far from perfect. She told me she'd think about it."

I wasn't surprised she'd considered leaving with him, not if she'd thought my father was on the verge of divorcing her.

"She obviously told you no."

His face rose, and I wasn't prepared for the hatred in his eyes. "No. She said she couldn't take you from him."

"My father?"

"She said he'd never let you go, and there was no way she could leave you."

"But I wasn't biologically his child. She could have fought it."

He shook his head in disgust. "He had money and lawyers. She would have fought him for years, and we all know he would have won. No, he probably wouldn't have gotten the full custody he claimed to want, but Mary Caroline's life would have been miserable, shuttling you back and forth to him from the East Coast. Even if she could get permission to take you there."

I stared at him in disbelief. "That is such bullshit."

His mouth dropped open. "Are you naïve enough to believe he wouldn't have fought her?"

"Oh, I *know* he would have fought her for me. But you're missing one very key part of this picture, *Grayson Matthews*."

His face lost color.

"You ran and changed your name. Why not change hers too? And mine?" When I saw the pain in his eyes, I realized the truth. "She wouldn't do it. She wanted to keep her name."

"She wanted to keep *your* name," he said bitterly. "She wanted you to have the Blakely fortune. Once Randall discovered the truth and didn't denounce you, she realized you would be his only child and thus the sole beneficiary of his estate. She refused to take that from you."

"So she stayed."

"She signed her death sentence."

"And you blame *me*?" I asked, incredulous. "An eight-year-old child? Your own daughter?"

"You were never my daughter. You were always his."

I released a bitter laugh. "Are you serious? It's like you don't even know the man. Do you really think he treated me like his daughter after he found out?"

He shot me a glare. "He was going to fight for you."

"Are you really that stupid, or do you just need someone to blame? He was going to fight for me because she wanted me so much. He never wanted me. Not after he found out the truth."

He studied me.

"Poor little William," I said condescendingly. "Had to run off to the fancy East Coast with a shit ton of money and a yacht. You had it so fucking hard."

His jaw tightened. "Your mother would hate to hear you speaking that way."

"Maybe, maybe not. I guess we'll never know since she was murdered, but you two aren't the only victims in this saga. My life was hell. My mother was murdered, and I had no one to comfort me. My father acted like I didn't exist. After he dismissed my nanny when I was in middle school, I raised myself. I was utterly *alone*." When I could see he wasn't swayed, I sat back, warring with my desire for information and my need to get as far from this man as possible.

"Has he tried to kill you?" I asked matter-of-factly.

He did a double take. "What?"

"You changed your name to hide from him. Did he ever find you?"

He started to say something, then stopped.

"I take it you weren't invited to my wedding," I said with a bitter laugh.

"No." He shifted in his seat. "Tiffany says you claim you're hiding from him. That he wants to kill you."

"I take it you don't believe that's true considering you used the word *claim*."

"What reason would he possibly have for killing you the night before your wedding? That makes no sense, Caroline."

"How about the fact I overheard him discussing his involvement in a crime syndicate with my fiancé?"

He blinked, then laughed. "Randall? In a crime syndicate?"

"Not just *in* it. A founder. One of the three leaders."

He laughed again. "You're deluded."

"Happen to hear about the big bust of a group called Hardshaw in Arkansas? A group with strong ties to Texas and Oklahoma? That's his group."

"You're insane."

"He murdered my mother. You're terrified he'll murder you just for meeting with me, so why is it so hard to imagine that he not only wants me dead but is involved in organized crime? He seems to have the perfect temperament for it."

He sat back and crossed his arms, stewing.

This meeting wasn't going anything like I'd expected it would. I'd thought he would be apologetic, not hostile. Why did he find it so difficult to believe Randall Blakely wanted to kill me after he'd already killed at least three people…maybe more?

And then it hit me.

Guilt.

"I don't want anything from you," I said, softly. "I'm going after my father, and I wanted to see if you had any information that would help me. I'll tell Tiffany you were cooperative. You're free to go."

His mouth dropped open. "Are you insane?"

"For telling Tiffany that you were cooperative?" I asked, knowing full well that wasn't what he meant. "Probably."

"You can't take him on! He'll destroy you."

"How can he destroy me if he's not dangerous?" I asked innocently.

"I never said he wasn't dangerous. I said it was doubtful he was going to kill you the night before your wedding."

"Look," I said, "you believe whatever you need to believe to help you sleep at night. I'm not going to try to convince you otherwise. So unless you have something else to tell me, we're done."

He started to get out of his seat, then stopped. "I never…" He swallowed and took a breath. "I understand why you're angry with me."

"Well, good for you," I said, "because you've treated me like shit since the moment you showed up, and I'm struggling to justify it."

"If I'm honest, I'm surprised by it too." He tapped the table again. "I've tried to find out how you were doing."

Did he think that would win me over? I lifted my chin and shot him a glare. "You never *once* contacted me."

"I wasn't sure you knew the truth," he said. "And Uncle William was persona non grata. I figured it was better to let you live your life."

I didn't respond.

"I'm not proud of what I've done," he said. "And, truth be told, I think I was projecting my anger at myself onto you just now, but if I'm totally honest, I do partially blame you for her death." A sad smile. "She would have gone with me if it weren't for you. She would still be alive. With me. I know it's not reasonable, yet the resentment is there all the same."

"Thank you for being honest with me, I guess."

"Are you happy, Caroline?" He made a face. "I know you're hiding from Randall, but you know. In general."

I wanted to laugh in his face and ask him how he thought I could *possibly* be happy when I was running for my life. I wanted to ask him where his concern for my life had been for the past twenty odd years, but I didn't.

Instead, I simply said, "Yes." I was still angry, but I knew I needed to find forgiveness in my heart—more for myself than for him. While I wasn't there yet, raging at him would get me nowhere.

He studied me, waiting for me to elaborate. I didn't. He'd been lucky to get that much.

"Again," he said. "I wish things had been different."

But he wanted them to be different for him, not for me, which made me feel better about my one-word answer.

"Is there anything else you can tell me?" I asked. "Or can you point me in a direction of where to look for evidence to use against him?"

He studied me for several seconds. "I guess it depends on what you're looking for."

"I'd love to find proof that he killed my mother, but if something like that existed, I figured Aunt Tiffany would have found it by now, or at least her private investigator would have."

He looked surprised by that piece of information, but he quickly covered his reaction. "No, I don't think you'll find anything. He'll have covered his tracks by now. But if you're fool enough to try this, he had a man who worked for him. Duncan Morris."

"Wait. His name sounds familiar." A large, muscled man popped into my memory. And then I remembered him from the visits my mother and I paid to my father at his office. He would make faces and take me to get candy bars while my mother and father spent "alone time" in his office. I hadn't thought about Mr. Duncan, as I'd called him, in years.

"I'm sure it does. He was Randall's assistant, but he was more of a bodyguard, enforcer."

"He would have done my father's dirty work." Which I found disappointing after I'd recalled such warm memories.

"Or found someone to do it. But he's not going to talk to you, Caroline. If he tells you anything, he'll implicate himself."

"Let me worry about that. Do you know if he still works for my father?"

He shook his head. "No. He stopped about a year after your mother died, but last I heard he was still in Dallas."

"Do you have any contact information?"

"No. I'd say I'm sorry, but if I had it and gave it to you, I feel like I'd be assisting you in your suicide mission."

"I'm doing this, with or without your help. So if you think of anything else that might give me a nudge in the right direction, I'd appreciate it if you'd let me know." I pulled a piece of paper from my bag and set it on the table. "My email address and a phone number are on there."

He took the paper and examined it before tucking it into his pocket. "I didn't entirely tell the truth when I told you why I was angry." He started to reach across the table, then stopped. "You look so much like her. It just seems so unfair that she was taken from me so soon. I hate that you remind me of her."

The sad part was that he could have had her. According to Tiffany, my mother had fallen in love with him first, only he'd refused to defy his brother. Still, I saw no purpose in pointing that out. A grown man who could dislike his daughter for reasons out of her control wasn't worth my time.

I knew I should thank him for giving me something, but I couldn't bring myself to do it.

He got to his feet and peered down at me, looking like he wanted to say something else, but instead he turned to walk toward the exit, only to find Hank blocking his path.

I hadn't even noticed that he'd gotten up from his table. I quickly stuffed my notebook and phone into my purse and got out of my seat.

"Can I help you?" William said, looking down at Hank, literally and figuratively.

"No," Hank grunted. "I wouldn't take help from you if you were the last man on earth."

"Excuse me?"

Hank glared up at him. "You're a goddamned fool. You threw away the best thing to walk into your life."

William glanced over at me as if to ask if I knew the man verbally accosting him, and he must have gotten his answer, because he turned back to Hank in confusion. "You knew Caroline's mother?"

Hank snorted in disgust. Then, to my surprise, he pulled back his left arm and punched William in the nose. "I'm talkin' about Carly, you stupid jackass."

William stumbled back and covered his face. "I could have you arrested!"

"You try that," Hank said. "And we'll be sure to let Randall Blakely know you met with his daughter. I even have photos to prove it."

"You low-life scum," William said, pulling out a handkerchief.

I started to intervene, but Hank held up a hand to stop me. "You had your piece, now I get mine." Holding onto a chair with his left hand, he lifted his crutch and shoved it hard into William's stomach.

William crumpled over onto the carpet.

Hank stood over him, his face red with fury. "I may be low-life scum, but you are the slime at the bottom of a cave. You aren't worthy to lick her boots." Then he added, "And in case it's not clear who I'm referring to, it's the incredible woman you left at that table. You fucking stuck-up jackass." Then he spun on his heel and walked toward the entrance, stopping to hand some money to the waitress who'd served him. "Sorry for the trouble. This should also cover her coffee."

She gasped and glanced around the room at the handful of people who were watching open-mouthed and in shock. "He just gave me a hundred-dollar bill!"

I thought about saying some parting words, but Hank was right.

William Blakely wasn't worth any more of my time.

Chapter Thirty-One

Neither of us said anything until we got into my car. I started to put the car in reverse, but Hank covered my hand with his own.

"Just take a moment, girlie."

I shook my head. "If I do that, I'm giving him power over me."

"You just met the scum who provided half your DNA. You have a right to take a moment to wipe Dog Shit off your shoe."

I laughed, but it quickly gave way to tears.

He patted my arm. "There, there. You have a good cry, then leave him in your rearview mirror where he belongs."

"Thank you, Hank."

He didn't respond, just patted my arm. When I finally settled down, I turned to face him.

"You punched him in the face."

He made a face and shrugged. "He deserved it and much worse."

"How's your hand?" I picked it up to examine his knuckles, surprised they didn't look too bruised.

"That's not the first asshole I've punched, and I'm sure it won't be the last."

I suspected Wyatt was next in line.

"So what do you want to do?" he asked.

"We need to go back to Drum."

"What about Wyatt?"

"He's the reason we're going back. I want to make him a trade. The files we have for the one he has on my father."

"And you really think he's gonna hand it over?"

"I have to at least try."

"If he's caught wind that Marco's meetin' with the state police, he's never gonna go for it."

I raked my teeth over my bottom lip. "I know."

"It might be dangerous."

"I know.

"Do you want to call Marco and let him know how it went? I can take a walk around the block."

I shook my head and pulled my cell phone from my purse, then sent Marco a text.

I'm done and have a lead to follow in Dallas. I'm not sure how I feel about how things went, but we can talk about it when I see you. Hank and I are headed back to Drum.

Then I turned my phone off before he could try to call me.

"You know he's gonna be callin' *me*," Hank said. "Especially if you told him we're headed back to Drum."

"I *did* tell him, and you know he's probably going to try to talk me out of meeting with Wyatt."

"Hell, I'm not sure *I* shouldn't try to talk you out of it."

I gave him a pleading look. "I need that file, Hank. Sure, William gave me a lead, but if Wyatt has something solid…"

"You can't count on that asshole to make a fair trade. Even if he agrees, he's probably gonna find a way to screw you over, like taking out the important things. You can't trust that he'll give you the full file. What are you gonna do if you can't get it?"

I gripped the steering wheel, suddenly exhausted. "Then I guess we'll get our own evidence."

"Girlie, you've been tryin' to bring Bart Drummond down for six months. What if it takes you that long or longer?"

I gritted my teeth. "All the more reason to get whatever he'll gives us."

"We didn't scan everything," he said. "And you haven't even looked at Bingham's file yet. Maybe we should hole up somewhere for another night and finish our task before we go back."

He had a point, but my gut was telling me it was time.

He took my silence as encouragement. "Let's steer clear of Chattanooga. We'll go somewhere else, spend the night, and head back first thing in the morning."

I considered it for several seconds. It wasn't a half bad idea. "Where would you want to stay?"

"Somewhere on the way back." He pulled out his new smartphone and tapped on the screen. "We can stop in Greenville or Asheville. Both are on the way."

It made sense, yet everything in me screamed to get back. "I know it's the smart thing to do. But I have to go back, Hank." I turned to face him with a pleading look. "I need to be there when Bart goes down. I need to be there for Max." Then I added wistfully, "I need Marco."

I needed him to hold me and tell me everything would be okay. I needed his arms around me, holding me together when I told him how William Blakely treated me like I was gum on his shoe.

Hank studied my eyes, then a warm smile lit up his face as he patted my cheek. "Of course you do. Let's go home."

I backed the car out of the parking space just as Hank's phone rang.

He gave me a sidelong glance. "I have to take this. He's gonna be worried."

"That's fine. I want to reassure him. I'm just not ready to talk about what happened yet."

With a sharp nod, he answered, "Chalmers."

He was silent for a few seconds, before he said, "She's doin' fine. The fucker was an asshole, but we both took care of him and we're now in the car, headin' back." He winked at me with a mischievous grin. "Yeah, we discussed the pros and the cons of comin' back, and the pros win out. What's goin' on with Drummond?" Hank gave me a worried look as he listened. "Is that so? How's Max takin' it?" He made a face. "Okay, we'll keep that in mind, but we're still headed back. We'll hole up at your place. Should be there by supper." A tight grin stretched his lips. "Will do."

"What happened?" I asked as he hung up.

"Emily Drummond wasn't at her house when they went to pick her up."

"Was she out running an errand?" I asked, knowing in my gut she wasn't.

"A bunch of her clothes were gone, and her housekeeper refused to admit it, but it looks like she took off yesterday."

"Shit."

"Marco and Max think she found out that the spreadsheets were stolen from Ruth, realized she was in a world of shit, then took off for some non-extradition country."

"Leaving Max to take the fall should it come to that."

"Yep."

"But who killed Ruth? Bart or Bingham?"

"My money's on Drummond. Ruth and Tater needed money, and Tater had that flash drive. It stands to reason that Tater blackmailed Drummond, and Drummond offed him, dumped his body somewhere, and killed Ruth to clean up the mess. Maybe she tried to save herself by telling him about the money launderin,' and he took the folder. But he killed her anyway."

I pursed my lips as I considered it. "It works. But what about Emily?"

"She took off within an hour of discovering the spreadsheets had been stolen. But if she didn't leave fast enough, then maybe Drummond offed her too. Still, Emily Drummond's a cagey bitch. My money's on her gettin' out of town." He leaned back in his seat. "I bet she's lyin' on a beach somewhere sippin' Mai Tais with a cabana boy waitin' on 'er."

"Yeah, I could see her doing that. But would she *really* just leave Max?"

"If she thought he wouldn't go with her, yeah. I bet she would."

Unless he was covering for her too, but I just couldn't see it. He seemed so tired of the whole thing. So defeated. "But what about Patricia? Wouldn't Bart go after her if he thought she was passing out flash drives like candy?"

"She told him it would go public if something happened to her. Maybe he believes her."

"So he's playing whackamole in the hopes he gets them all?" I made a face. "Just because Patricia didn't tell us that he called or dropped by for a visit doesn't mean it didn't happen. Maybe that's the reason she was so eager to give us a copy. Maybe Bart confronted her, and this was his big fuck you."

He nodded. "Sounds logical to me."

"I don't want to stop anywhere," I said. "I want to finish scanning everything at Marco's house. We'll work on Bingham's file next. Have you looked at it?"

"I have, but there isn't much in there. Mostly stuff about his father Floyd, plus a few things Seth told him when he was dealin' with Bingham."

"His folder on me didn't just have notes. He talked about how he planned to manipulate me. Does he say anything like that about Lula and Bingham?"

"Some," he said. "He was convinced that you have some sort of relationship with Bingham, but just can't figure out the nature of it. He was hopin' to use Lula to find out." He grimaced. "He planned to tell her that you were sleepin' with Bingham, hopin' she'd break and tell him more about Bingham's operation."

"If Bingham found out, he would kill her." Last December, Lula had been terrified of Todd Bingham…even though she knew he might be the father of her baby. Surely she wouldn't fall for Wyatt's scheming. Then again, if Wyatt played the supportive big brother role…she might.

"Wyatt has one goal in mind. To take over the town. Sure, he has what it takes to get his father out of the way, but Bingham's in a better place to slip into those empty shoes than he is. Which means he has to eliminate Bingham. And with all of this goin' down with his daddy, he's acceleratin' the timetable."

The coffee in my stomach wasn't sitting well. While I'd figured out that Wyatt was shady, I was still struggling to accept this new version of him, who'd manipulated every last person around him.

Including Hank, who looked more beaten down than I'd ever seen him.

"We're going to make him pay, Hank. I promise."

He nodded. "Yeah. The question is how to handle it."

"Patricia seemed tired of keeping Bart's secret. Why else would she be passing out flash drives after all this time? Maybe she can cut a deal to testify against him. Lord knows the state police know how evil he is and will jump at the chance. All of that to say we'll turn him over to the authorities," I said firmly. "The state police. We'll let the justice system handle him."

"Sittin' in a prison cell is too good for 'im. Seems like he needs a gunshot to the chest just like my boy." His voice broke. "Let him see how it feels to bleed to death."

Maybe going back to Drum was a bad idea. I didn't want Hank to murder Wyatt and end up doing his own prison sentence. That wouldn't do anyone any good.

"Let Marco handle it. I trust him to do what's right. For now, let's scan the rest of these documents and see if we can get Wyatt in the jail cell next to his father."

Chapter Thirty-Two

Marco wasn't home when we got to his place, not that I'd expected him to be, but he arrived soon afterward, finding me and Hank working at the kitchen table, scanning the remaining files.

He gave me a questioning look, and I went to him, pressing myself into his chest and soaking in the feel of him, the smell of him. I loved every bit of him, and seeing William had made me realize how lucky I was to have him.

He held me tight, pressing a firm kiss to the top of my head, then whispered, "Are you okay?"

I leaned back to look at him, capturing his face in my hands and giving him a long, tender kiss. "I am now that I'm with you." Pulling free, I reached for his hand. "Let's take a walk. You can show me the spring you found a few days ago."

He kissed me back as if seeking reassurance, and I understood why. He'd sought to give me comfort, and I'd pretty much turned him away. It would have scared me if the circumstances were reversed.

I tugged on his hand, saying, "Hank, we'll be right back."

"I'll keep workin'."

We walked out the front door and headed toward a path in the trees Marco had recently discovered—a probable animal trail. We didn't say anything until we reached the tree line.

"So it was pretty awful, huh?" he asked.

"Worse than I imagined."

He squeezed my hand and held onto it until the path narrowed and we needed to walk in a line.

"Did you find Wyatt or Emily?" I asked.

"No. And now Max is wondering if Wyatt was working with his mother all along."

"He led me to believe he came back here for her. So maybe he was." But it seemed unlikely to me. Wyatt was in this for himself. Everyone else be damned. "Have the state police picked up Bart?"

"Yep. Holding him in a cell in Knoxville but they haven't filed any charges yet. Your source at the bar in Chattanooga is cuttin' a deal in exchange for showin' the state police where the baby is buried. We're all praying for a DNA match, and if nothing else, maybe some trace DNA on the baby to prove Bart had contact with the baby."

"Thank God."

"Max is pretty sure it's outside of Bart's range of influence, especially since he lost his shit when he figured out where he was goin'. Max figures he would have played it cool if he'd ended up in the county jail, knowing he just had to grease a few palms or call in a few favors to get out."

"Do they think the charges will stick?"

"Yep," he said smugly. "And I suspect he won't be gettin' out on bail. Seein' how his wife has already taken off, he'll definitely be considered a flight risk. They already got a search warrant to search the house and the property. Max is up at the Drummond house with the state police watchin' while they search the place."

The path opened to a clearing, revealing a small pool of water and a thin stream that headed toward the downward slope of the mountain.

I looked up at Marco and smiled. "It's beautiful here. Peaceful."

"I thought you'd like it." He took my hand again and led me to a boulder with a smooth top. We sat down, listening to the low ripple of the pool, the calls of the birds around us, and the soft rustle of the leaves. Marco wrapped an arm around my back, and I leaned into him.

"I want to ask about your visit," Marco said hesitantly. "But you…"

I looked up at him. "I'll tell you about that, I promise, but I'm not ready yet. First I need to hear if you've made any progress on Ruth's case."

"No big breaks yet, but I've given a statement that I saw Franklin meeting with Bart at the resort, Franklin's brother sayin' he was lookin' for something in Chattanooga related to Ruth's mother and Bart, and then the video. It wasn't an open and shut case, but now that the bar owner is coming forward and not only admitting she's the person in the video but that Franklin came to see her last week and got a flash drive, they now have motive. Which means he'll be in jail awaiting the charges for murderin' the baby, givin' them plenty of time to build a case for Ruth's murder."

"Thank God. But what about the Drummond estate and the resort?"

"I guess it depends on Bart. Will he turn it over to Wyatt or Max? If Wyatt's wantin' to take over, seems to me he has a plan for that too. Maybe he intends to blackmail his father to gain control."

Shades of Truth

I stared at the small pond, relishing the feel of Marco wrapped around me. "Wyatt had some master plan, and I don't think he was ready for his father to get arrested. He needed Bingham to fall first." I told him what Hank had said about Wyatt's intention to manipulate Lula. "We screwed things up by getting some of his most important files and handing them over to the state police."

Marco pushed out a long breath. "I only turned over Bart's file. The rest are in my cloud." His arms tightened around me. "But Wyatt's gonna be furious."

"He's gonna come after us, Marco."

"Which is why I asked for an extended medical leave."

I jerked backward so I could get a good view of his face. "What?"

"Who am I kiddin', Carly? My limp's gettin' worse, not better. I can't chase a suspect right now, and I hate workin' desk duty." He paused a beat. "They took me off Ruth's case."

"Marco..."

"Besides, if I ask for more medical leave now, it won't look suspicious when we leave town."

"What?"

A sad smile lit up his face. "It's time, don't you think? I'm sure Hank told you by now about the aliases he got for us. We can use those if we need to."

"But we'll have to leave Hank," I said, tears stinging my eyes. "And what about Max?"

"I'm tryin' to convince Max to come too. I know it's not very romantic, but three heads are better than one. And we can try to persuade Hank to change his mind."

I shook my head and glanced down at his chest. "He won't come. Not if you and Max are with me. He says he belongs in Drum."

"Maybe we can change his mind after we take care of your father. Or we can come back for lots of visits."

I pressed into his side and wrapped an arm across his stomach, hooking my fingers on his belt loop. "He defended me this morning."

"I wouldn't expect anything less from Hank Chalmers."

"He punched Dog Shit in the nose."

"I wish I'd been there to see it."

"Yeah," I said quietly. "Me too."

We sat for nearly a minute, me just soaking Marco in while he held me tight—not like he was afraid I was about to walk away but as if he sensed I needed to be cocooned.

Finally, I said, "He didn't want to see me. Tiffany coerced him somehow. I suspect blackmail is actually a more accurate term for what she did."

Marco didn't say anything.

"We found a restaurant close to Tiffany's office. Hank scoped it out. Lots of windows so we could see the street. We got there early, and he sat at a separate table close enough so he could watch and listen. Tiffany made the introductions then left."

Marco's thumb stroked my bare arm.

"He made it pretty clear he didn't want to be there, but he…" I took a breath as my chest tightened and my eyes stung. I was not going to cry. After I took another breath, I said, "He pretty much hates me. He resents me for being alive when my mother's dead. He hates that I look like her, and he blamed me for her death. Still does, if he's honest."

Marco's body stiffened, and he loosened his hold to stare down at my face. "How in God's name could he blame *you*? You were a child!"

"He said she wouldn't leave my father or Dallas without me. And she wouldn't consider changing our names and running. He said she wanted me to inherit Randall Blakely's fortune."

"Why in the hell did she think he'd give it to you?"

"Because he didn't denounce me as his daughter, and he had no hope of having a biological child." I paused. "I guess neither one of them thought he'd kill her. A long, messy divorce, yes. But murder? No."

"I don't get it, Care," Marco said. "She'd decided to stay and not divorce him, and Randall didn't want you anyway. Why kill just *her*?"

A memory popped into my head, a vague one of me begging my mother to take me with her. My father had been "in a mood" as she called it, and I didn't want to stay with him. But I'd been sick that day, sniffles and a slight fever, so she'd told me I had to stay home with the nanny.

I jerked free from Marco's hold. "Oh my God."

"What?"

"He *did* try to kill me. I was supposed to be with her." I glanced up at him. "I can't remember where she was going, but I was supposed to go. I had to stay home because I was sick."

He pulled me close and held me again as the truth hit home. My father had intended for me to die years ago. So why had he let me live for so long?

Maybe he figured out he needed me for the Hardshaw line of inheritance. But I intended to ask him when I finally saw him again.

"I asked William to give me a lead to follow," I said, feeling stronger.

Turned out revenge gave me backbone. Wasn't that how I'd become strong as Carly? Carly didn't lie down and accept her fate like I would have done as Caroline Blakely. Carly was out for justice.

My voice was strong as I said, "He told me it was a suicide mission, and I insisted that I wasn't running from it. After some prompting, he told me to look into a man who worked for my father until a year or so after my mother's murder. He was some kind of security guy, I think. William said he was like an enforcer. I barely remember him, but he was fond of me, so maybe we can use that to our advantage. William said he's still in Dallas. His name is Duncan Morris."

"That's good," Marco said. "Something to track down."

"We need the file Wyatt compiled on my father," I said. "I want to make a trade."

"What do you plan to trade?" he asked, incredulous. "The files you took? I suspect they're worthless to him now."

"When I talked to him last night, he still wanted them."

Marco stiffened. "He's never going to give you that file, not even a copy. And trying to get it is too big of a risk. If he found useful information, then we can too. In fact, I have a lead of my own. I think we should go to Arkansas."

I turned to look at him. "Why?" I was excited by the idea of seeing my friend Rose again, but she had a new baby. I didn't want to bring more trouble to her doorstep.

"A man was arrested in conjunction with the big Hardshaw bust. I want to see if he'll tell us something."

"Why would he?" I asked.

He hesitated. "Because he has ties to your friend Rose."

I stared at him in shock. "Skeeter Malcolm?"

James "Skeeter" Malcolm had been king of his own crime syndicate in Fenton County, Arkansas. He'd become an informant for the FBI or ATF or some government authority, but he'd reneged on the deal to save his ex-girlfriend's baby. Then promptly lost his deal. Last I heard, he was in a jail cell somewhere waiting for his trial.

He nodded once. "You'll have to ask Rose to convince him to talk to us. Do you think she'll do it?"

"I suspect she will, but…" Based on the last message I'd received from her, Rose seemed happy. She deserved to be happy, and I really didn't want to go digging up skeletons in her closet. Still, I knew she'd do it. I just hated to ask. "She will."

"I say we pack up and head out of Drum tonight. If Max won't come now, maybe he can meet us somewhere along the way."

Nodding, I said, "Yeah. I agree. The sooner we leave, the better."

So why did I still want to try to contact Wyatt?

But Marco was right. It was too dangerous. He would never agree to a trade, and he'd never even give me a snippet of that file. He could have at any point over the past six months. Why would he do so now?

"We'll go pack our things. I'll call Max, and you see if you can talk sense into Hank. Then we'll take off. Maybe we'll stop in Knoxville tonight and get to Arkansas tomorrow."

I tried to find a bit of good news in all of this. There was a good chance I'd see Rose and all my other friends in Henryetta in about twenty-four hours. Marco could meet the people who had saved me, and they'd see I'd ended up with a good man.

For the first time since Seth's death, leaving Drum felt right. "Okay. Let's do it."

Chapter Thirty-Three

Thank goodness I'd done laundry a couple of days ago so I had enough clean clothes to pack. But Hank couldn't be persuaded to come with us.

"Somebody's gotta stick around and feed the cats," he said. "Besides, you need eyes and ears in Drum. But don't let Max stay behind. The boy needs to get out of here."

"I plan to convince him," Marco said, then picked up his phone to call him. "Our cover story is that Carly is visiting friends in Arkansas—which is true—and we took Max with us to get him out of town for a few days."

Since Marco and I had both packed our bags, and being in the same room with Hank made me want to cry, I grabbed my suitcase and carried it out to Marco's Explorer.

But when I opened up the hatch, I was startled to find myself face to face with Wyatt, a handgun pointed at my face.

The blood fled from my head for two seconds before my senses returned. "You planning on killing me, Wyatt?"

His body was rigid with suppressed anger. "I'd rather not, but I will if I must. Your six o'clock deadline is up, and I want those files."

"Well, that's a little difficult considering we already turned them into the state police."

His focus narrowed. "You're lyin'."

Partially, but he didn't need to know that. "Why do you think your father's sitting in a jail cell right now? It was a combination of that and Franklin's flash drive." Also not entirely true, but I wasn't ready to let him know Hank and I had paid Patricia a visit.

He tilted his head, and the eyes I'd once thought soulful turned hard and cold. "Now I know you're lying, since *I* have Franklin's flash drive."

It took me several seconds to realize what he was saying. "*You* kidnapped Franklin?"

"Why would I kidnap him? I needed that video, and I had to keep it quiet." But he didn't look as confident as he had before. He looked a little haunted.

I gasped. "You *killed* him?"

"Do you think I wanted to?" he asked, rubbing the back of his neck with his free hand. "He was only supposed to watch you and report back to me. But then he caught wind that you were lookin' into my father's favors, and he suddenly recalled Ruth tellin' him about a baby sister who just disappeared one day. Only no one else but she and her mother knew because they'd hidden it."

"That's why she dumped Trixie and got new friends," I said, starting to cry. "She was trying to forget." Then it hit me full force, and I choked out, "You killed her. *You* killed Ruth. Not your father." I glared at him in horror. "You had the nerve to blame it on me!"

"You were diggin' up too much shit, Carly! And Tater was flat out greedy. He planned to blackmail my father with that video, but he was still trying to figure out how to make contact."

"He didn't have to try too hard," I said. "He was already meeting Bart out at the resort late at night."

He stared at me for a second then released a chuckle, but it sounded forced. "You knew about that?" He shook his head. "What am I sayin'. You know all kinds of things you shouldn't. But you got that one partially wrong. Tater was meetin' a Drummond, just not my father."

My jaw dropped. "You?"

"You wouldn't talk to me, and I needed to know what you were up to. Tater agreed to keep tabs on you, but then he got greedy."

"Greedy enough to justify murder?" I sneered.

"Tater brought that on himself. But Ruth..." He had the nerve to look sad.

"How could you?" I cried out. "You *monster*!"

"I couldn't risk it gettin' out," he said. "And if anyone's to blame, that was all you, Carly."

"Me?" I asked in disbelief. I was sick to death of men trying to blame their shit on me.

"I never would have had to kill her if you hadn't been stirring up shit!" he whisper-hissed.

"Oh my God. You're insane!"

His brow lifted. "I'd be careful and keep it down if I were you. I don't want to kill anyone else, but I will if they come out here."

"You'd kill Hank? The man who treated you like a son?"

"The man who fucked me over for you?" he demanded, his eyes burning with anger. "You caused this, Carly. You stir up shit everywhere you fucking go. I had a plan, and you blew it to fucking hell. So whatever happens from here on out was caused by *you*."

I stared up into his cold eyes and knew he meant every word of it.

"Carly?" Hank called out from the front porch. Marco's vehicle was blocking my view, so I knew he couldn't see Wyatt or me. "Everything okay?"

Wyatt shoved the gun tip into my chest and gave me a warning look.

"Just fine," I said, keeping my gaze on Wyatt's ice-cold face and trying to keep my voice from shaking. "I saw a lizard and it freaked me out. I'll be in in a moment."

"Okay. Marco's still workin' on Max." Then I heard the front door shut.

Wyatt slid out of the back and nodded toward my suitcase. "Goin' on a trip?"

"That's none of your fucking business," I snarled.

He grabbed my face and lifted it up so I had to look at him. His fingers dug into my flesh, making sure I knew he was in control. "If you plan on taking my files, then it *is* my fuckin' business."

"You're crazy, Wyatt!" I hissed.

"Maybe so. I've been plannin' this for years, and you're fuckin' everything up. But we're gonna make things right, and you and me are gonna go inside that house and get my files."

I tried to shake my head, but he was still holding onto my cheeks as tears streamed down my face. While I was scared for my life, I was utterly terrified for Hank and Marco. "No. Hank will never let you take them. He'll kill you."

"I'd like to think you were crying for me, but we both know your tears are for him." Then he added, his voice cold, "And Marco."

Ice ran through my veins. He'd already murdered two people who I knew of, simply because they'd gotten in his way. He hated Marco for taking me. He'd kill him for no reason at all.

Then again, he'd been using me from the beginning. So maybe he didn't hate Marco. At least that's what I tried to convince myself.

"Please don't do this. Please. I'm *begging* you, Wyatt."

He released a short laugh. "*Now* you're beggin' me?"

"I'll get the files, okay? I'll go in and scoop them up and bring them out to you, then no one gets hurt."

"Do you seriously think I'm stupid? We're goin' in together." Then he released my face, grabbed my arm, and marched me toward the front door.

I was so terrified my body shook, turning my legs into rubber. But I managed to get to the front porch and the door leading inside.

I took a shaky breath, trying to calm down as Wyatt kept his gun trained on my temple.

"Nice and slow," he murmured softly. "Let's try to keep everyone alive."

He opened the door, and we both walked in. To my surprise, Hank wasn't at the table.

Was he hiding, ready to pop out and surprise Wyatt? But I didn't see how that was possible with Hank's amputation and crutch. The fan in the hall bathroom was running, so it was more likely Hank would be a while in the bathroom, and based on the closed bedroom door, Marco was still talking to Max.

I didn't waste any time, just started gathering up the files. With any luck at all, I'd be able to hand them over to Wyatt before Marco or Hank came back out.

If Wyatt planned to let us live.

The way he was acting, I was guessing that was less and less likely.

Wyatt held the gun on me as he surveyed the table. "What the fuck is goin' on here?" he grunted.

Hank had been scanning Bingham's file. The folder was open, and two stacks of paper lay within it. The ones that had been scanned and the ones that were waiting.

"What is this?" he repeated in a whisper.

"We scanned the files and put them onto the laptop," I said. "This is the last one," I lied. We still had about twenty more pages to scan.

He walked over to the computer screen and studied it, his jaw tightening.

"Marco has them going straight to the state police," I said in a hushed tone. "So even if you get them back, the state police will have it all."

"Fuck." His face reddened, and he turned his rage in my direction. "Forget the files. Get the laptop."

I closed the lid and picked it up to hand it to him.

He grinned, but it wasn't friendly. "You're gonna carry it outside for me."

If I left this house with him, he was probably going to kill me outside, but if I let him shoot me in here, he might end up killing Marco and Hank too.

I heard water running in the hall bathroom, which mean Hank would be out any second.

I started for the front door.

"Good choice," Wyatt said, following behind me. Once we reached the front porch, I considered screaming or shouting a warning, but I doubted Hank would be carrying his shotgun, ready to shoot. Wyatt would get to him first.

We headed down the steps, then Wyatt grabbed my arm and started dragging me toward the back of the Explorer. When we got there, he didn't stop. He kept dragging me toward the road.

"What are you doing, Wyatt? You got your files, now let me go."

He didn't respond, just kept going. I figured I was far enough away from the house that I'd bought Marco and Hank time to get their guns and defend themselves, so I started dragging my feet and resisting.

He pointed the gun at my forehead. "I *will* shoot you, Carly. I shot Ruth and Franklin. Don't think I won't kill you too."

Except something wavered in his eyes, and I remembered his notes in my file. Even though he'd been using me—or attempting to—he still cared for me at least a little bit. Or at least he'd wanted to win me from Marco. I believed he would kill me if he was forced to, but I didn't think he'd do it now.

Was I willing to bet my life on it?

"You got what you wanted, Wyatt," I said softly. Apologetically. "You got the files. Now go."

He shook his head, but he looked torn. Dark circles underscored his eyes, and I wondered how much he'd slept over the past couple of days. Killing in cold blood had to haunt a person. "We both know it doesn't matter anymore. You fucked this up too." But he didn't sound as angry. He sounded resigned.

"I'm sorry."

His anger returned. "The fuck you are." His grip on my arm tightened, and for a few terrifying moments, he glanced back at the house, looking like he was trying to make a decision.

Dear God, please don't let him kill Hank and Marco.

"The deal was you'd get your files and let me go, Wyatt."

"First of all—" he said, picking up his pace. I struggled to keep up. "—we never had a deal. Second, even if we did, it would be null and void. The plan I've been working on for the last five years has just been shot to hell."

We reached the road, and I saw a black cargo van parked on the road.

What the hell was he up to?

I didn't want to find out. I'd rather him shoot me than get me in that van.

"So what's your new plan?" I asked.

He looked down at me, and I could see the indecision in his eyes.

I lifted my chin and tried to stare him down, but I was terrified, and my breath was coming in short pants, so I wasn't sure how effective it actually was. "If you're going to kill me, Wyatt, just do it now. Don't drag it out."

He lifted a hand to my cheek. "I'm not going to kill you, Caroline. I'm going to take you to your father."

About the Author

New York Times, Wall Street Journal, and USA Today bestselling author Denise Grover Swank was born in Kansas City, Missouri and lived in the area until she was nineteen. Then she became nomadic, living in five cities, four states and ten houses over the course of ten years before she moved back to her roots. She speaks English and smattering of Spanish and Chinese which she learned through an intensive Nick Jr. immersion period. Her hobbies include witty Facebook comments (in her own mind) and dancing in her kitchen with her children. (Quite badly if you believe her offspring.) Hidden talents include the gift of justification and the ability to drink massive amounts of caffeine and still fall asleep within two minutes. Her lack of the sense of smell allows her to perform many unspeakable tasks. She has six children and hasn't lost her sanity. Or so she leads you to believe.

You can find out more about Denise and her other books at www.denisegroverswank.com

Printed in Great Britain
by Amazon